PATHWAY TO LOVE

Acclaim for Radclyffe's Fiction

"Medical drama, gossipy lesbian romance, and angsty backstory all get equal time in [*Unrivaled*,] Radclyffe's fifth PMC Hospital Romance...[F]ans of small community dynamics and workplace romance without ethical complications will find this hits the spot."—*Publishers Weekly*

"*Dangerous Waters* is a bumpy ride through a devastating time with powerful events and resolute characters. Radclyffe gives us the strong, dedicated women we love to read in a story that keeps us turning pages until the end."—*Lambda Literary Review*

"Radclyffe's *Dangerous Waters* has the feel of a tense television drama, as the narrative interchanges between hurricane trackers and first responders. Sawyer and Dara butt heads in the beginning as each moves for some level of control during the storm's approach, and the interference of a lovely television reporter adds an engaging love triangle threat to the sexual tension brewing between them."—*RT Book Reviews*

"*Love After Hours*, the fourth in Radclyffe's Rivers Community series, evokes the sense of a continuing drama as Gina and Carrie's slow-burning romance intertwines with details of other Rivers residents. They become part of a greater picture where friends and family support each other in personal and recreational endeavors. Vivid settings and characters draw in the reader..." —*RT Book Reviews*

Secret Hearts "delivers exactly what it says on the tin: poignant story, sweet romance, great characters, chemistry and hot sex scenes. Radclyffe knows how to pen a good lesbian romance." —*LezReviewBooks Blog*

Wild Shores "will hook you early. Radclyffe weaves a chance encounter into all-out steamy romance. These strong, dynamic women have great conversations, and fantastic chemistry." —*The Romantic Reader Blog*

In **2016 RWA/OCC Book Buyers Best award winner for suspense and mystery with romantic elements** *Price of Honor* "Radclyffe is master of the action-thriller series...The old familiar characters are there, but enough new blood is introduced to give it a fresh feel and open new avenues for intrigue."—*Curve Magazine*

In *Prescription for Love* "Radclyffe populates her small town with colorful characters, among the most memorable being Flann's little sister, Margie, and Abby's 15-year-old trans son, Blake...This romantic drama has plenty of heart and soul." —*Publishers Weekly*

2013 RWA/New England Bean Pot award winner for contemporary romance *Crossroads* "will draw the reader in and make her heart ache, willing the two main characters to find love and a life together. It's a story that lingers long after coming to 'the end.'"—*Lambda Literary*

In **2012 RWA/FTHRW Lories and RWA HODRW Aspen Gold award winner** *Firestorm* "Radclyffe brings another hot lesbian romance for her readers."—*The Lesbrary*

Foreword Review Book of the Year finalist and IPPY silver medalist *Trauma Alert* "is hard to put down and it will sizzle in the reader's hands. The characters are hot, the sex scenes explicit and explosive, and the book is moved along by an interesting plot with well drawn secondary characters. The real star of this show is the attraction between the two characters, both of whom resist and then fall head over heels."—*Lambda Literary Reviews*

Lambda Literary Award Finalist *Best Lesbian Romance 2010* features "stories [that] are diverse in tone, style, and subject, making for more variety than in many, similar anthologies... well written, each containing a satisfying, surprising twist. Best Lesbian Romance series editor Radclyffe has assembled a respectable crop of 17 authors for this year's offering."—*Curve Magazine*

2010 Prism award winner and ForeWord Review Book of the Year Award finalist *Secrets in the Stone* is "so powerfully [written] that the worlds of these three women shimmer between reality and dreams…A strong, must read novel that will linger in the minds of readers long after the last page is turned."—*Just About Write*

In **Benjamin Franklin Award finalist** *Desire by Starlight* "Radclyffe writes romance with such heart and her down-to-earth characters not only come to life but leap off the page until you feel like you know them. What Jenna and Gard feel for each other is not only a spark but an inferno and, as a reader, you will be washed away in this tumultuous romance until you can do nothing but succumb to it."—*Queer Magazine Online*

Lambda Literary Award winner *Distant Shores, Silent Thunder* "weaves an intricate tapestry about passion and commitment between lovers. The story explores the fragile nature of trust and the sanctuary provided by loving relationships." —*Sapphic Reader*

Lambda Literary Award winner *Stolen Moments* "is a collection of steamy stories about women who just couldn't wait. It's sex when desire overrides reason, and it's incredibly hot!" —*On Our Backs*

Lambda Literary Award Finalist *Justice Served* delivers a "crisply written, fast-paced story with twists and turns and keeps us guessing until the final explosive ending."—*Independent Gay Writer*

Lambda Literary Award finalist *Turn Back Time* "is filled with wonderful love scenes, which are both tender and hot." —*MegaScene*

Applause for L.L. Raand's Midnight Hunters Series

The Midnight Hunt
RWA 2012 VCRW Laurel Wreath winner *Blood Hunt*
Night Hunt
The Lone Hunt

"Raand has built a complex world inhabited by werewolves, vampires, and other paranormal beings...Raand has given her readers a complex plot filled with wonderful characters as well as insight into the hierarchy of Sylvan's pack and vampire clans. There are many plot twists and turns, as well as erotic sex scenes in this riveting novel that keep the pages flying until its satisfying conclusion."—*Just About Write*

"Once again, I am amazed at the storytelling ability of L.L. Raand aka Radclyffe. In *Blood Hunt*, she mixes high levels of sheer eroticism that will leave you squirming in your seat with an impeccable multi-character storyline all streaming together to form one great read."—*Queer Magazine Online*

"Are you sick of the same old hetero vampire/werewolf story plastered in every bookstore and at every movie theater? Well, I've got the cure to your werewolf fever. *The Midnight Hunt* is first in, what I hope is, a long-running series of fantasy erotica for L.L. Raand (aka Radclyffe)."—*Queer Magazine Online*

By Radclyffe

The Provincetown Tales

Safe Harbor

Beyond the Breakwater

Distant Shores, Silent Thunder

Storms of Change

Winds of Fortune

Returning Tides

Sheltering Dunes

Treacherous Seas

PMC Hospitals Romances

Passion's Bright Fury (prequel)

Fated Love

Night Call

Crossroads

Passionate Rivals

Unrivaled

Rivers Community Romances

Against Doctor's Orders

Prescription for Love

Love on Call

Love After Hours

Love to the Rescue

Love on the Night Shift

Pathway to Love

Honor Series

Above All, Honor

Honor Bound

Love & Honor

Honor Guards

Honor Reclaimed

Honor Under Siege

Word of Honor

Oath of Honor
(First Responders)

Code of Honor

Price of Honor

Cost of Honor

Justice Series

A Matter of Trust (prequel)

Shield of Justice

In Pursuit of Justice

Justice in the Shadows

Justice Served

Justice for All

First Responders Novels

Trauma Alert	Wild Shores
Firestorm	Heart Stop
Taking Fire	Dangerous Waters

Romances

Innocent Hearts	When Dreams Tremble
Promising Hearts	The Lonely Hearts Club
Love's Melody Lost	Secrets in the Stone
Love's Tender Warriors	Desire by Starlight
Tomorrow's Promise	Homestead
Love's Masquerade	The Color of Love
shadowland	Secret Hearts
Turn Back Time	

Short Fiction

Collected Stories by Radclyffe
Erotic Interludes: *Change Of Pace*
Radical Encounters

Stacia Seaman and Radclyffe, eds.:
Erotic Interludes Vol. 2–5
Romantic Interludes Vol. 1–2
Breathless: *Tales of Celebration*
Women of the Dark Streets
Amor and More: Love Everafter
Myth & Magic: Queer Fairy Tales

Writing As L.L. Raand
Midnight Hunters

The Midnight Hunt	The Lone Hunt
Blood Hunt	The Magic Hunt
Night Hunt	Shadow Hunt

PATHWAY TO LOVE

by

RADCLYᖴFE

2021

PATHWAY TO LOVE

ISBN 13: 978-1-63679-110-4

THIS TRADE PAPERBACK ORIGINAL IS PUBLISHED BY
BOLD STROKES BOOKS, INC.
P.O. BOX 249
VALLEY FALLS, NY 12185

FIRST EDITION: NOVEMBER 2021

CREDITS
EDITORS: RUTH STERNGLANTZ AND STACIA SEAMAN
PRODUCTION DESIGN: STACIA SEAMAN
COVER DESIGN BY TAMMY SEIDICK

Acknowledgments

This was a tough one written during a year that was a hard struggle for the whole world. I am as always grateful to family, friends, readers, and the amazing team at BSB for their encouragement and skill. Special thanks to Sandy for irreplaceable support in the office and beyond, to Paula for her steadfast counsel personally and professionally, and to my editors Ruth Sternglantz and Stacia Seaman, who worked overtime on this one to keep me out of trouble.

And as ever, Lee, amo te.

Radclyffe, 2021

Chapter One

Court Valentine opened her eyes to a hazy dawn, the steady *tap tap tap* of a woodpecker in the trees outside her open windows, and soft warm breath against her shoulder. Ten minutes until the alarm went off. She didn't need to check the time to know. She'd always had an innate sense of time and never wore a watch. Funny thing to think about now—time—when she had none to spare, and memories of Jane and the night before rekindled an unmistakable pulse of pleasure she'd very much like to explore. Thoughts of Jane moving above her, hands gliding expertly over all the places that made her melt and tighten simultaneously, of Jane's fingers slipping so effortlessly and so damn precisely where she needed them. The only thing that came close to the satisfaction of good sex was conquering a tough surgical case, and in a little over an hour she had to be ready for the OR.

Court groaned and eased a few inches away, putting a little space between them before she let her priorities be clouded by her urges. Jane's arm slid from around Court's waist, and her fingers trailed lightly down over her hip and along the top of her thigh, coming dangerously close to exactly where Court imagined them just a moment before. Court clenched in a dozen different places, one in particular that was going to leave her very uncomfortable if she didn't get a grip very quickly. She grabbed Jane's hand before Jane put her fingers somewhere Court didn't have the will to say no to.

"Good morning," Court said.

"It could be." Jane boosted herself up on an elbow and leaned over, her hair, California blond and a little tangled from where

Court had run her hands through it the night before, teasing Court's cheeks. Her Pacific Ocean–blue eyes met Court's, sharp and bright and completely awake. Her full mouth spread into a grin. "We've got nine minutes. How fast do you feel?"

"Eight and a half," Court said, appreciating both the invitation and the option to say no. Jane never assumed and never made any demands, which was one of the reasons they were waking up together. Court already had too many demands and obligations in her life—she didn't need the complications of a relationship added to them. She smiled. "To tell you the truth, I feel pretty well taken care of after last night."

"Now that's a nice way to say no." The teasing note in Jane's voice said she wasn't offended. She kissed Court and slipped from bed, giving Court a view of her long, lean body that she was sure to remember for a very long time. "I've got to roll anyhow."

"You're flying first shift today, aren't you?"

"Yeah. And with leaf season right around the corner, traffic is heavy everywhere. We'll probably be busy."

"If you're busy, we'll be busy too. I'm on backup flight call if the second team goes out," Court said as she tapped off the alarm on her phone before it could go off. Jane flew for Air Star, the medevac flight team based out of the medical center that had grown up around the Rivers hospital. In the last few months, flight calls had skyrocketed, and the patient census and complexity of cases had tripled, not that Court minded. She wanted every bit of experience she could get. Another big reason to keep life outside the hospital simple. Speaking of which, there would probably never be a better time than now to take care of a potential complication. "So, team tryouts start this week."

"I know," Jane said absently, sorting through the pile of clothing they'd shed the night before onto the floor beside the bed. "I got my official notice of acceptance the other day and a tentative schedule of games."

"Congrats. We need more good refs." Court paused while Jane shimmied into her leathers. The sight deserved her full attention. Jane's pants fit the way motorcycle pants should, like a second skin. The beat of lust between her thighs started up again. She hurried on before the beat turned into a barrage she couldn't ignore. "There might be talk if one of the refs is sleeping with an assistant coach."

Jane laughed, righted her inside-out black T-shirt, and pulled it over her head. "In a place this small, somebody's always sleeping with or related to someone else associated with a team. Coaches have kids on teams, or lovers on an opposing one. You think anybody's going to care?"

"Probably not."

Jane went still and cocked her head, studying Court. "But *you* care."

"Some." Court rose and retrieved an oversized red-checked flannel shirt she used as a robe. It had been her father's, and silly as it seemed sometimes, she couldn't seem to throw it out. As if someday he'd walk through her door and ask for it back. "I have to think about the kids too. I wouldn't want anything I was doing to come back on their success."

"Fair point. Are you also trying to let me down easy again and saying this is good-bye?"

"If that was my objective, I would've just told you about it outright." Court circled Jane's shoulders and kissed her. They'd bonded over sports one night at the new brewpub in the center of the village, ended up closing the place, and woke up together the next morning. They'd repeated a few times when their schedules matched—more frequently than Court usually slept with the women she occasionally dated—but they'd never talked about what they were doing or where they were going. That had seemed fine until it felt like they'd gotten to a point where they ought to be talking about it. The point Court usually wished she didn't have to keep reliving, which probably explained why she hadn't been sleeping with anyone else all summer. "I can't think of a way to say this that doesn't sound completely clichéd."

"You don't have to do the just-friends routine." Jane pulled her hair back and caught it in a tie she'd left on the bedside table the night before. "If you hadn't, I would have pretty soon. I'm not looking for anything more than we've had going, and I never was. I love sleeping with you. You're easy to be with. Oh, and did I mention great in bed."

Court slapped her lightly on the chest and gave her a little shove away. "Once or twice…every minute or so last night."

Jane grinned. She was damn good-looking when she did that.

"I'll miss that," Jane went on, her gaze suddenly serious, "but as long as I don't miss *you*…"

"Hey, no way," Court said. "I'm not planning on going anywhere."

"Well, neither am I." Jane stepped into her chunky motorcycle boots and grabbed her leather jacket from the straight-backed chair by the door. "Burgers at the Bottom tonight around seven?"

"If I can make it," Court said, a surge of relief making the day seem a little brighter.

"I'll text you." Tucking her motorcycle helmet under her arm, Jane sent Court a blazing smile on her way to the door. "By the way, you have a hickey on your neck."

Court slapped a hand over the mildly stinging spot on her neck that she'd noticed earlier but ignored.

"God damn it, Jane," she yelled as Jane disappeared laughing down the hall.

"You said *bite me*," Jane called back.

Court stared at the empty hall outside her bedroom, heard the front door open and close, and stomped into the bathroom. All right, yes. She probably *had* said that. Sometimes, right when she was ready… With a sigh, she leaned toward the mirror over the sink and turned her head to view her neck. There it was. A faint pink splotch halfway between her jaw and her collarbone. Not so terrible, really. It probably wouldn't substantially bruise. She smiled, remembering the moment.

All things considered, totally worth it.

She jumped in and out of the shower in ninety seconds, a skill learned in medical school and honed in the first few weeks of her surgical residency. She pulled on scrubs, since that's what she'd be wearing all day, and refreshed the clothes in her backpack in case she actually got out of the hospital in time to pursue some human activity like going out to eat with Jane or meeting friends somewhere at the end of the day. By five fifteen she was ready.

Some mornings she'd leave a little earlier and run or bike five or ten miles before heading to the Rivers, but today she didn't have time. She locked up her little house—just big enough for her and a cat who sometimes deigned to visit, but it was hers and that's what mattered—walked to the end of the street, and angled toward the playing fields behind the high school to shave fifteen minutes off her time. She needed that fifteen minutes for a coffee run. And a doughnut. Two doughnuts.

As she walked along the side of the gymnasium, the familiar thud of a basketball bouncing on hardtop grew louder. Early for any of the kids to be practicing, but she detoured in the direction of the courts to see who was putting in extra time. She slowed and stopped by the corner of the bleachers on the gym side of the court.

Court had spent the most important years of her life in the village, and she knew or had at least a nodding acquaintance with everyone. The short-haired brunette playing alone on the court was a stranger. Court didn't need to watch her for more than a few seconds to be intrigued. Her good-looking-woman-on-the-horizon alert would have gone off no matter where they'd met, but what captivated her most was the way the woman moved. Quick, confident strides. Driving the ball with a fluid touch that made it look as if it was part of her, an extension of her arm, flowing from hand to hand, so fast Court could barely follow it. And then the pull-up, the nearly invisible set, the flow of arms up and out, the slightest flick of wrists, and the arc of the ball rising...falling...and whispering through the net with hardly a sound. From midcourt. Lucky shot?

The brunette caught the ball on the bounce, pivoted, drove the length of the court again, stopped, set, shot. Another flawless basket. Way beyond the arc. Her form was perfect, her timing immaculate. Hell, she wasn't even breathing hard. She was good. Way better than good.

And way better than good-looking. Now that Court had a chance to really look, gorgeous. Thick, straight black hair that she probably brushed back on the sides but that ruffled in the wind as she ran and stuck in very sexy, sweaty strands to her neck. Sharp strong features, well-muscled torso in a black tank top and tight black workout shorts that clung to powerful thighs, and a physical confidence that Court found very, very hot.

Court blinked, her brain finally kicking in. She'd been standing there for a good five minutes, basically staring like a Peeping Tom of some sort. A little embarrassed, she backed up and hurried away. When she reached the far side of the field, she looked back over her shoulder. The basketball court was empty, but the image of the solitary woman and the way she moved, all fluid power and finesse, stayed with her as she headed into the village.

❖

Bennett was used to people watching her, although not so frequently in the last few years and not usually when she was alone at five o'clock in the morning. She hadn't expected to run into anyone on the court when she'd left the motel—the town had seemed dead asleep at a quarter to five. The quiet might have been what awakened her, come to think of it. Nashville, like New York and every other big city she'd ever visited, really did never sleep. Even with the slowdown recently, sirens blared and trucks rumbled through the streets twenty-four-seven, and intrepid passengers rode the elevators in her high-rise apartment building at all hours. Not in this sleepy little village. When she'd driven in a bit before six the night before, she hadn't noted a whole lot of activity on the single main street and hadn't been inclined to investigate.

She'd spent a restless night in the musty motel room and had gotten up early to search for coffee. The manager who'd checked her in the night before had told her there'd be complimentary coffee in the office, and she was hoping that meant soon. She'd been right about country hours. He was there when she walked in before dawn, in a different version of the short-sleeved checked shirt he'd been wearing the night before, in the same place behind the little kiosk-like, cracked-Formica counter. Round faced, with thinning gray hair and a laconic, droopy-lidded expression, he nodded and said, "Hiya."

"Morning."

An urn of coffee with a little dish of individual creamers and sugar packets sat on a card table tucked into a corner underneath a map of…hiking trails in Vermont? Okay, well, she wouldn't be needing that. She filled one of the disposable cups, added a couple of Mini Moo's, and took a cautious sip. She'd been wrong about the coffee. It was excellent.

"Good coffee," she said. "Thanks."

"The wife makes me grind it from some beans she orders from the place in Saratoga. Death Wish Coffee." He didn't sound like he minded.

Bennett smiled. "Well, tell her thanks from a grateful guest."

As she sipped, looking out the plate glass window to a street that intersected Main, she tried not to second-guess her decision to come. She hadn't seen Flann and Harper in years. She was a city person down to her bones, and here she was in a place where people kept horses in their front yard and chickens in their driveway. She'd seen stars the night before and been surprised. You didn't see stars in in the city. But she couldn't stay there, and here she had a chance to set up a department, even if she wasn't going to stay. She'd be busy— that's what mattered. She finished her coffee, recycled the cup, and turned to the manager, who'd been studying her unapologetically.

"Passing through or staying?" he asked.

"Staying."

"You gonna rent the room by the week?"

"*For* a week," she said, trying not to shudder. If she hadn't found an inhabitable place to stay in a week, she'd pitch a tent. The motel room was clean enough, and there was the incentive of the very excellent coffee, but she'd been able to hear two people enthusiastically fucking in the room next door the night before.

"That's fine," he said. "You can pay by the day. Maid service is extra."

"I can take care of whatever I need done in the way of housekeeping," Bennett said, "if you can supply clean sheets midweek?"

He nodded. "Can do that."

"Thanks. There's one more thing."

He raised a brow.

"You wouldn't happen to have a basketball, would you?"

He didn't seem to find that an unusual request and pulled a key off a peg behind him. He tossed it to her and said, "There's a shed at the end of the row of units. Ought to be one there. Probably flat, but there's a bicycle pump if you can dig it out."

She pocketed the key. "Thanks."

She'd changed into something she could run in, rejuvenated

the basketball, locked up the storage unit, and left the key on the counter. The court she'd noticed at the high school across from the motel fronted the street near the big building she guessed was the gym. She'd been playing long enough to empty her mind and break a sweat when the sound of a motorcycle caught her attention. A woman, by the looks of the long blond hair streaming from beneath the smoke-black Yamaha helmet and the slender lines of her body, roared by in the direction of the village. Now and then a car passed on the street, close enough for her to hear, but other than that she was alone.

Until the woman appeared on the far side of the court. She'd been wearing scrubs, so likely on her way to the hospital. From the way Ben remembered Flann and Harper talking about the place, it sounded like half the people in the county worked there. Plenty of people in the village too, probably. Maybe she'd run into this woman again. She didn't think she'd forget her. Blond hair the color of the wheat fields she'd passed driving in the afternoon before, a strong profile with just short of delicate features, distinct even from a distance. Trim athletic body. Younger, but not by all that much, than her. The blonde had watched her for a while, and Ben had to wonder why. Or more accurately, had to wonder what she saw. If she recognized her, which still happened far more than she liked, she'd be seeing a faded image of the person Ben had been. Like those life-sized cutouts they stuck in the foyers at arenas before big games. There'd been a time she'd been happy to coast on image—especially when she was young enough to think that was an effortless way to meet women. Thankfully, she'd outgrown that, but by the time she had, she realized she'd never had the time to learn how to connect any other way.

Ben mentally shook her head as she headed back to the motel. She'd seen a woman—an attractive woman, true—watching her for a few minutes, and all of a sudden she was ruminating on past history. She couldn't go back and undo any of it. She'd likely never see the blonde again. A hospital was a big place, and she wasn't going to have much time to do much of anything except sit in meetings, get her fledgling department off the ground, and take care of patients. Still, the image lingered, and she didn't try to erase it.

CHAPTER TWO

A bby buried her face in Flann's neck, stifling her gasps or trying to, as her back arched, her arms tightened around Flann's shoulders, and her hips rose to meet Flann's final deep thrust. Pleasure whipped through her, leaving her weak and trembling, and she relaxed into the tangled sheets with a gratified sigh.

Flann chuckled and kissed her throat. "I'd ask you if it was good, but…"

"Like you have to," Abby murmured. "By now I think we've established you're good at it."

Flann nuzzled the soft skin beneath her ear and gently nipped her earlobe. "It's all you, babe."

"Whatever," Abby said with a rush of supreme satisfaction, "it's all working just fine."

"You ready for coffee?"

"I suppose we have to." Abby opened her eyes, their usually intense green hazy and sated. As she gazed at Flann, clarity returned and, along with it, the focus Flann recognized so well. She loved that about Abby—how she could go from sensual to intense in a heartbeat. "Is today the day you and Harper have that early meeting?"

"Yeah, Harp thought it would be a good idea to give Bennett a rundown of how things work before the department head meeting later, since she'll be straddling both medicine and surgery, really." Flann eased to her side, reluctant to break contact with her wife and switch into work gear for a few more precious minutes. Waking up together, and especially waking up to sex together, wasn't all that common given their schedules. When life and death—sometimes senseless, frivolous death—was her daily fare, she'd learned not to let any moment of pleasure pass unnoticed. Or unsavored. "I don't see why we need the special intro, but Harp's the boss."

Abby sat up, her forehead creasing. "Does that bother you?"

"What? Harp being the assistant chief of staff?" She snorted. "Hell no. Firstly, she's always been the heir apparent, and we all knew it—everybody at the Rivers knew it. She wasn't just born to it—she was born *for* it. I just meant I don't see that Bennett needs any coddling."

"Coddling?" Abby laughed. "Harper just likes to make sure new staff feel a part of the team right away. She did the same for me."

"Mm," Flann murmured, dipping in for another kiss. She'd only meant it as a quick *I love you* kiss, but Abby's mouth was so damn soft, and she smelled so inviting, and maybe they could afford just a few more minutes…

"Flann," Abby whispered, pulling away. "Coffee time."

"Okay." Shaking her head, Flann rolled out of bed, pulled on a pair of sweatpants, and shrugged into a T-shirt. "I'll grab you the coffee, and you can grab an extra five minutes."

"I was that good, was I?" Abby said with a look that almost made Flann climb back into bed. The only reason she didn't was they both had to be at the hospital in less than an hour.

"You always are." Flann took a second to take in the way the early morning light highlighted the curve of Abby's jaw and the finely etched arch of her cheek before leaning down to kiss her again. "You're an incredibly beautiful woman, and I'm very glad you're mine."

Abby's lips parted faintly. "You are just angling for more."

"Always."

Abby grabbed her hand before Flann could move away and said, "I love you."

Flann grinned. "I was that good, was I?"

"Just go get my coffee."

Flann padded barefoot into the kitchen of their brand-new house. They'd only been in a week, but every inch of it felt like home. All the renovations had been done exactly as they'd envisioned, and the extra space was welcome. She missed the coziness of the little schoolhouse, the place where they'd first lived as a family, but it was nice that Blake had his own room now, and much better to have a couple of extra guest rooms that always seem to be filled with his friends on weekend nights. For a new kid starting school in a new place, he'd made good friends right away. Of course, the fact that her little sister Margie—not so little anymore, as she had to remind herself at least once a week—was best friends with Blake didn't hurt. Margie tended to be the epicenter of everything, in and out of school. Of all her sibs, Margie was the light, the one who shone the brightest. But Blake could hold his own in any situation. He was naturally confident and intrinsically good-humored.

And there he was, standing by the open door to the rear deck in navy sweatpants that matched hers, although his were a few years newer, a faded gray sweatshirt with the sleeves cut off, and what looked like a cup of coffee in his hand. Coffee was a new addition to his food selection.

"You're up early," Flann said, pouring two more cups from the coffee maker on the counter. "New room hard to sleep in?"

"No," Blake said, turning to face her. His deep brown hair was tousled and still a bit damp, so he hadn't been up too much earlier than them, but still a good two hours before he needed to leave for school. If he was waiting for one of them to get up, that usually meant he had something to discuss.

Flann added cream to the coffees. "I need to bring this in to your mother. She might be a few minutes."

"Sure," Blake said.

"Be right back." Flann carried the coffee into Abby, who was checking her phone. "Blake's up."

Abby took the coffee and set her phone aside. "He's not usually up this early unless he's got something he wants to tell us."

"That's my guess."

"Give me a minute." Abby pulled on a tank top and shorts and scuffed into flip-flops.

Carrying their coffee, they both returned to the kitchen where Abby said, "Hi, honey. Something going on?"

"Not really." Blake set his cup on the counter and slid his hands into the pockets of his sweats. "I just wanted to get you both, and this is the best time to do it."

"Yeah, it sucks when your parents are doctors," Flann said

dryly. She could say that because she came from a family of doctors, and though her mother wasn't one, she was always up with her father—usually before her father—getting the family organized for the day. If Flann or any of the other kids wanted to talk to their parents together, they usually needed to be early risers or wait for Sunday dinner. Come to think of it, that was still pretty much true. "You can always come knock on our door."

"Yeah…no." Blake rolled his eyes. "Anyhow, it's not…it's no biggie."

Abby sipped her coffee and pulled a package of cinnamon rolls from the freezer. As she slid them into the toaster oven, she said, "If it got you up before seven on a day when you're not going to the clinic and you don't have a shift in the ER—neither of which is true today—it must be somewhat important."

"Tryouts for the school basketball team are coming up soon," he said in a rush. "I just wanted to let you know I was going to try out."

Flann looked at Abby. Thank God, he hadn't said football. Blake watched basketball on TV now and then, but she didn't know he wanted to play seriously. Then again, he tended to think things over until he was certain of a decision before he said anything. "Okay. When is it?"

"The next couple of Wednesday afternoons after school."

Abby leaned against the counter, her coffee cup cradled in her palms. "How do you think it's going to go?"

"The tryouts?" Blake lifted a shoulder. He'd put on a little weight the last couple months, and his shoulders had broadened a bit, but he was still lean and slender. "I've had some pickup games, no problems."

Bells sounded in Flann's head. "Problems?"

"I mostly played when Dave was there. Guys are used to us hanging out together, and"—he grimaced—"I don't think most people really want to start something with him."

"No one said anything?" Abby said.

"No."

"But you think they will now?" Flann said.

"I don't know for sure," Blake said. "But you know, it'll be new. A trans guy on the team. If I make it." He looked away. "Of course, I might not."

Flann blew out a breath. If she got pissed every time Blake had to face not just the challenges that every kid growing up faced, but double that because he was trans, she'd be pissed a lot. And that wouldn't change anything or help Blake. "Chuck Rossi coaches basketball. He's a good guy. I don't think he's going to make an issue out of it."

"*He* might not," Blake said, "but the guys on the team, or maybe their parents, might."

"You already said you were going to try out, and you've thought of all this," Abby said. "Are you asking how we feel about it?"

"I guess," Blake said carefully. "I just wanted to give you a heads-up. Because, you know, maybe it will get complicated."

Abby put her coffee cup down and laughed quietly. "Honey, life is complicated. And I'm not trying to make light of this or anything you have to face. Your life will probably be more complicated than some other people's. And it sucks if your being trans is an issue where it shouldn't be, but sometimes it might be. You know it, and so do we. And you know what? That's never stopped you yet, and I hope it never does." She hugged him, and after his first reflex I'm-too-old-to-hug reaction, he relaxed and squeezed her back.

Flann met his gaze and said, "Everything your mom just said. Just go and show them how it's done."

Blake laughed. "It's just tryouts."

Flann shrugged. "Never too soon to show them what you've got."

Blake grinned. "We're good then."

Flann reached for Abby's hand. "We're great. I'd come watch, but Wednesdays I have office hours, so—"

"Uh, no," Blake said quickly, "but thanks."

Abby laughed. "Just let us know how you do, okay?"

"Sure thing." Blake put his cup in the sink. "I'm going back to bed."

Flann waited until they heard him disappear upstairs. "What do you think?"

Abby sighed. "I don't know. It's new territory for everyone, for him, for the boys he'll be playing with, for the coaches. I suppose it's too much to hope that everyone will just accept him, but sometimes people surprise."

"Yeah, they do," Flann said, and she only wished that all the surprises were good ones.

❖

Blake hadn't really planned on going back to bed. He was still getting used to drinking coffee—he liked the taste and the way it kind of energized him, but today he was wired without it. He just hadn't felt like talking anymore. His parents were great, and he knew he was lucky. He never felt like they didn't get it, that him being trans was just *him.* He wasn't sure, though, that they really understood all the rest of it. What kinds of things might happen. He hadn't told them about the online trans group he'd joined. Some of the stories people shared there were pretty terrible. Some kids had gotten kicked out, or had to pretend they weren't trans—even with other family members—so they *didn't.* How was anyone supposed to live like that? He'd been doing fine since they moved here, but he wasn't dumb enough to think most people were going to understand him—or accept him.

He hadn't been all that happy when his mother'd said they were moving to the country. Like, really? He grew up in New York City. He didn't even know how to drive, except he wasn't old enough then, but still. And what was he going to do in some little village in the middle of no place he'd ever heard of? He lay on his back on his bed in his new room and tried to imagine living in New York City again.

Why would he want to? Without his friends, and the animal clinic, and the way the morning smelled through his open window? His mother'd been right about that. They did belong here. He only hoped that he could belong somewhere on his own.

Worrying about it wasn't helping, but he knew what would. *Who* would.

Blake texted Margie.

you up yet
is the sun shining

ha ha
want to go for a ride
yeah
be there in five

Five minutes later, dressed for school in black jeans, sneakers, and a Doors T-shirt, he walked out the front door just as Margie pulled up in her red pickup truck, the one Flann had given her. He was only a little jealous about *that*.

"How come you're up so early?" he said when he hopped in. Margie wore her usual low-slung jeans with a pale green tank top and sandals. She'd tied a short silk scarf around her mass of strawberry blond waves to keep them from blowing around in the wind streaming in the open window.

"I like to get up for breakfast when my father is home," she said. "He's still taking night call even though he keeps saying he's cutting back. My mother always cooks something special. Plus I get a chance to see him then."

"Did you bring me anything?"

"There might be an egg and biscuit sandwich in that bag behind the seat."

"Yes," he said, hoping what he'd smelled was meant for him. He reached around to find it and munched as Margie drove out of the village past the Rivers Homestead and into the countryside. They did this a lot—rode around. Not going anywhere special, just hanging around for a little while before they met up with the rest of their friends.

"So," Margie asked, "did you tell them?"

"Yeah." After demolishing the sandwich in three bites, he pulled a bottle of water out of the compartment on the door and swallowed some. "They were fine."

"Are you worried?" Margie asked.

Margie was never roundabout when she had something to say—or ask—about anything. She asked what she wanted to know and said what she thought. He liked that about her. He never had to guess, and he never had to worry that she expected something or wanted something from him that he was missing. And he always felt safe saying what he thought.

"Yeah, some."

"About making the cut? You're pretty good, Dave said."

Blake huffed. "Oh, well, if *Dave* said it, then it must be true."

Laughing, Margie lightly punched him on the thigh. "You know what I mean. I think you're pretty good too. Although your jump shot could use a little work."

"Oh, sure," Blake said. "Like yours is so great."

"Hey, who won the last one-on-one?"

"That was just a lucky shot, that last one you made."

Margie snorted. "How about all the other ones?"

"So when are *you* trying out?" Blake prodded. "The girls' team is supposed to be really good."

"I'm thinking about it," Margie said, "but I'm not sure I want to put that much time into it. And don't change the subject."

"I'm pretty sure I'm good enough to make the team," Blake said. "I'm fast, and I've got a good three-pointer. Not a lot of the guys have that."

"So what's really bugging you?" she said.

"Donnie Butler is a starter, and he hates my guts."

"He's just one guy. He's a butthead, for sure, but he's just one guy."

"With friends."

"And?"

Of course she would know there was more to it. He'd been putting up with Donnie Butler or a few guys like him practically since he'd gotten to town. He was used to it now, and after what happened with Billy Riley, most everybody left him alone except for the muttered insults that they made sure he could hear when no one else was around.

"The thing is," he said, "this makes it sort of public, you know? If I play on the team, and we play other teams, you think nobody is going to say anything?"

Margie sighed. "Yeah, you're right, and maybe someone will make an issue of it. Maybe there'll be an article in the newspaper or something."

Blake's stomach tightened. "Yeah, that's what I'm afraid of."

"Well, that will suck," Margie said. "And most people will think it sucks too. It won't be forever, though. People have the attention span of ants."

He rolled down his window to let the brisk air blow some of the sweat off his neck, telling himself it hadn't happened yet, and worrying about it before it did, if it did, wasn't going to help. And it wasn't going to change anything.

"It doesn't matter," he said. "I'm still going to do it."

Margie reached over and grabbed his hand. Hers was almost as large as his, warm and a little rough on her palms from the calluses she got from working around the farm. He gripped her hand, and somehow their fingers ended up interlaced on his thigh.

"It matters," she said, an edge in her voice that was hardly ever there.

When he glanced at her fierce expression, he knew she would fight for him. And that took away a lot of the twisty, sick feeling in his stomach.

"So," he said and heard his voice crack. Damn it. His voice had deepened a lot in just the last few months. He liked that a lot, but it hadn't settled yet. He swallowed and tried again. "*The Avengers* is playing at the Hathaway."

"Yeah, I saw that." Margie took the pickup down a feeder road and headed back toward town and school.

"You want to go?"

"Yeah, sure. Did you ask Dave and the rest?"

"I meant you, you and me," Blake said.

Margie's eyebrows rose but she kept her gaze forward on the road. "Just us."

"Yeah," he said, the pounding of his heart making the word come out softer than he meant.

Margie's thumb brushed over his. "Sure."

Blake grinned, and suddenly the specter of tryouts didn't feel quite so daunting. "Cool."

Chapter Three

B en stopped at the motel office to drop off the ball. The manager was still behind the counter, leaning forward with forearms spread on either side of some kind of trade newspaper. When she got close enough to see, she made out what looked like advertisements for tractor parts. Or what she assumed were probably tractors.

"Thanks for this," she said, spinning the basketball in one hand. "If you give me the key, I'll put it back."

"Why don't you just keep it in your room if you're going to want to use it again," he said.

She'd been planning to buy one when she had a chance, but on the drive in from the airport the day before, she'd gradually begun to realize that as she got closer to her destination, she not only saw less in the way of houses, but less in the way of much of anything. Gas stations here and there, usually associated with convenience stores, but nothing that resembled shopping centers or big box stores. There had to be someplace where people went for the essentials of life, right?

Somewhere that very obviously wasn't here. The entire business district—a term used loosely—couldn't span more than ten blocks, and all she'd noticed had been a hardware store, a pizza place, some kind of bakery which she prayed had coffee, a bar, several antique stores, an attorney's office, a four-story brick building with a sign proclaiming it was an honest-to-God playhouse, a storefront Chinese takeout place, and a railroad car diner. She'd figure out where to go to get what she couldn't get in the village in the next few days, but until then, she'd take him up on his offer to borrow the ball.

"Thanks, I'll do that."

"Don't forget to ask for the sheets," he said as she headed for the door.

"I'll remember. Appreciate it."

The door of her unit opened from the parking lot directly into the single room with a double bed, a bureau with a small flat-screen TV on it, a shallow closet, and an adjoining bathroom about the size of the closet. All she had flown out with had been what she could pack in a suitcase and her computer bag, and those pretty much filled up the floor space. She'd sold the condo furnished, so she didn't have to worry about storing anything or even finding a place to live all that soon. By the light of day the room didn't look all that bad, as long as the enthusiastic lovers of the night before weren't regulars. No matter. She had plenty of time to figure out her living arrangements. She wouldn't be spending much time away from the hospital anyhow.

She showered quickly in the perfectly serviceable but narrow stall shower and dressed in casual black pants, a gray open-collared shirt, and black loafers. She drove the rental car five blocks into the village and parked in front of the place that seemed to be the epicenter of activity. Pickup trucks and SUVs lined the street on both sides of the bakery she'd seen the night before. This had to be the place with the caffeine.

To her infinite relief, when she walked in, she instantly smelled coffee and a plethora of other things that reminded her she hadn't had any dinner. People queued up to a counter just inside the door with a hand-lettered menu behind it and two service people, a young woman and younger guy both in T-shirts and jeans, who were taking orders and passing them through an open window into the kitchen. Bennett was aware of the people milling about her and seated at tables openly surveying her. Just curious glances, and she ignored them. She'd been scrutinized enough in her life not to mind any longer. When she'd ordered and gotten the little flag with the number on it to put on her table so they could find her with her order, she grabbed a two-top by the window and took her own turn looking around. A few couples, mostly elderly, a group of teenagers, and mostly men in work clothes helped themselves to coffee or sat at tables in the single large, high-ceilinged room. She guessed the café had once been a bank, which, given the open vault in the back corner that now served as kind of a walk-in display area, and the full front wall of floor-to-ceiling glass windows that faced the street, was probably a pretty good guess.

Everyone except Ben seemed to know someone who walked in, unlike the coffee shops in the city where most people were so busy rushing to their next destination they couldn't have described the person standing in front of them a minute later. Conversations rose and fell above the general hum of activity, no one particularly worried that others might overhear. Relaxing in the congenial atmosphere, she alternately checked her phone and watched the swinging kitchen door through which her food, please God, would soon appear. The outside door opened and closed with regularity, and when a blonde in scrubs walked in, Ben sat up straighter.

The woman from the ball field.

Closer now, she was indeed as attractive as Bennett's first impression. While Ben had been running up and down the court, she hadn't been able to see her eyes, but she could now. Brown. Unusual for a blonde. She seemed to know everyone and everyone knew her, her laughter full-throated and warm as she chatted with people in line and at the nearby tables. A nearly visible aura of energy swirled around her that Bennett swore made her skin tingle from ten feet away. Which really couldn't be possible, any more than she routinely fell captive to the spell of strangers.

"Hey, Courtney," the guy behind the counter called, "here's your coffee."

"Thanks, Kai, you're a lifesaver," the blonde—Courtney—said as she took the coffee, and Kai blushed.

Courtney.

Ben smiled. Nice name. And time to stop staring. She wasn't beyond noticing an attractive woman, but noticing and being unable to *stop* noticing were two very different things. She shifted her gaze away just as the street door opened to admit a slim blonde in head-to-toe black leather, a smoke-black motorcycle helmet tucked under her arm. There couldn't be two of them in a place this size—had to be the same biker who'd ridden by the basketball court that morning.

"Hey," Courtney said, giving the biker a wide smile, "I thought you'd be at the hospital by now."

The motorcycle blonde grinned. "It was such a nice morning, I detoured."

As they talked, Courtney casually rested a hand on the woman's forearm. Familiar. Maybe more than just familiar. Given the comment, and considering Ben had seen the biker in the same neighborhood where Courtney had appeared a few minutes later, it was hard not to jump to conclusions. Something else she never did—personally or professionally. But they did look good together. Weirdly, Ben found that idea disturbing.

"I gotta run," the woman in leather said after collecting a paper take-out bag. "See you later, maybe."

Courtney put a hand on the center of her back, another familiar gesture. "Have a good one. Text me."

The blonde grinned. "Will do."

Courtney watched her go for a second, then turned, scanned the room, and her gaze met Ben's. Too late to look away. Too late to pretend she hadn't been watching her. Ben nodded faintly, as if they actually had met, and Courtney nodded back. The look went on for longer than a stranger's gaze might pass over another stranger's, and Ben felt the heat from across the room again. Courtney frowned, more in concentration than displeasure, and then Ben saw the transformation she'd come to recognize but had hoped, she realized now, she wouldn't see here. Courtney's eyes widened a little, her casual glance intensified, and as if suddenly aware she'd been caught looking, she averted her gaze.

Bennett watched her collect her take-out bag and leave without looking back. She sighed. Probably best they'd never run into each other again. Preconceptions almost always made things awkward and, all too frequently, disappointing.

❖

Courtney dug in the bag, found the familiar shape of the spinach and feta croissant, and pulled it out. She had a solid fifteen minutes until she needed to be at the hospital and planned to make the most of her last few minutes outside. Maybe she'd get lucky and pull a flight on the second Air Star medevac, which would give her a chance to grab some fresh air and a bit of daylight, but she wasn't counting on it. Best way not to be disappointed.

Angling across Main Street, the bag tucked under her arm, she alternately sipped her coffee and nibbled on the croissant, thinking about the woman in the café—the one from the court earlier.

Bennett Anderson.

That was her, she was sure of it. No wonder she'd been enthralled—that really was the word—watching her shooting hoops. She was just as mesmerizing as she had been when she played for UCLA. Lightning on the court, in every way—fast hands, exceptional foot speed, and surgically precise shot-making. She'd held the record for triple-doubles when she'd played as a senior in the Final Four. Courtney, a basketball fanatic forever, clearly remembered those games. Bennett hadn't changed all that much in appearance. She didn't look like a twenty-year-old anymore—she looked a hell of a lot better, the way women did when they grew out of their soft-faced early twenties. Court laughed. She wasn't that far past that point herself, but she could already see the same changes in her photographs that she'd noted in Bennett. A jawline that was more defined, cheekbones visibly arched beneath more defined cheeks, and maybe, for some people, a little weariness around the eyes. She didn't have that yet, but she probably would by the time she finished her five years of residency.

Bennett had that look—a little shadow around her eyes that only made her more attractive. She wasn't that much heavier than she had been in college, but her body looked fuller, stronger now. Yeah, no doubt, it was her. What the hell was she doing in town, playing basketball at five o'clock in the morning by herself?

Courtney started up Myrtle Avenue to the foot of the long winding climb to the hospital, trying to do the math in her head. She couldn't quite pinpoint the year when Bennett had been a college senior and everyone expected her to be a top draft pick, if not number one, going in the first few picks to a professional team. She couldn't remember which pro team Bennett had gone with, but her life was kind of falling apart and she hadn't been paying much attention to anything. That was just about the time when her father… She sighed. Yeah, not the best time in her life.

She'd been an angry teenager, a lot of it directed at her older cousin Val. In the last year she'd finally realized that wasn't fair, and thankfully, she and Val had made an uneasy truce that grew easier all the time. Whatever had happened to Bennett Anderson's basketball career, Courtney had lost track amidst the chaos of her own nearly upended life. One thing was certain—Anderson hadn't come here to play basketball. Maybe she was visiting someone, though if she had friends or family in town, someone probably would've mentioned her name at some point. All high school sports, but particularly basketball and football, were huge all over the region. Everyone rallied around the sports teams, whether they had kids on the team or not. It was a community pride kind of thing. Anyone connected to a top college ballplayer who went on to play professionally would've claimed bragging rights. Besides, she seemed to have a vague memory that Anderson was from somewhere in the southeast. Not likely she had family here.

The hospital came into view, and Court automatically checked the staff lot. Jane's motorcycle was there. So were a dozen other vehicles, including Brody's black Dodge pickup and a couple of others that she recognized as belonging to surgery staff and residents. The regular seven a.m. shift wouldn't start piling in for another hour. She had rounds to make, patients to see, X-rays to review, and probably a few emergencies to deal with before the OR.

The mystery of Bennett Anderson would have to wait.

❖

Ben finished the scrambled eggs and avocado toast, which she had been surprised and happy to discover chalked on the menu board in bright orange, and got another cup of coffee to go. Harper had set up a meeting with her and Flann at six thirty by way of informal orientation, since she'd interviewed by phone, and that had been pretty perfunctory. As Harper had put it on the conference call with Presley Worth, the CEO—who Ben later learned was Harper's wife—Ben had all the necessary creds, plus Harper could give her a personal recommendation right then. The whole interview had been a bit surreal with Harper essentially her boss now.

She should have been a year ahead of Flann and Harper in med school, but she'd started a year late, so they were classmates. She'd shared a cadaver with Flann that first semester, and that had led to study sessions together, which led to beer when they could get free at the same time, and eventually friendship between the three of them. With class, clinic, and studying, they rarely had a lot of free time to spend together, but the two Rivers sibs were the closest people she'd had in her life then. Closer than anyone since too.

She'd lost touch with them after they'd gone off to Maryland for their residencies and she'd stayed closer to home. She'd only ended up here because she'd seen the posting for a director of sports medicine, and for once, the timing in her life had been right, even though the circumstances had been anything but.

Pulling into the lot marked *Staff* at the top of the long winding road up from the village, Ben took in her new hospital. A circular drive bordered by rolling grassy lawn studded with shrubs and flower beds fronted the white colonnaded entrance to a four-story, ivy-covered, red brick building. Two symmetrical wings extended out on either side in a lazy U. Tall gracious windows would afford views worthy of a postcard down the mountainside to the village and beyond. So, this was the fabled Rivers—the dominion of Rivers physicians for more than a hundred years, where Harper and Flannery Rivers were now established leaders, Flann the chief of surgery and Harper in line to be chief of the medical staff when her father eventually retired. The stately facade and immaculate grounds spoke of an earlier era when medicine was the province of men, and the patients they tended only those who could afford the care. The grandeur, however assiduously maintained, told only part of the story of the Rivers—which now supported a level one trauma center, a medevac hub, the residencies to accompany their new divisions, and soon, a sports medicine center. Her sports medicine center.

Far from being intimidated, Ben registered the almost forgotten rush of anticipation that accompanied a good challenge. She was a stranger here, but she had the experience to head her own department, medically speaking at least. She'd just have to learn the administrative end of it in a hurry. Time was short. She hadn't mentioned she only planned to stay a year, and she wasn't going to do that this morning.

CHAPTER FOUR

Ben called the rental place, gave them the location to pick up the vehicle, then took her coffee with her as she walked across to the hospital's side entrance, where most of the people dressed in hospital garb appeared to be entering on their way to work. Just inside the door, a security guard in her midthirties, standing behind a counter-high desk that held a landline and a computer monitor, smiled at her and said, "Good morning. Can I help you?"

"Hi, I'm Dr. Ben Anderson. I'm starting work today, so I don't have an ID yet, but I'm supposed to meet Dr. Rivers…" She laughed. "Actually, two of the Drs. Rivers, in the auxiliary dining room."

The guard, whose name tag read Keema Watkins, glanced down at a printout on a clipboard. "I've got you here." She handed over a temporary visitor's ID. "Do you know the way to the cafeteria?"

"'Fraid not."

"Follow the red line all the way to the second intersection, and then you can either take the elevators to the second floor or the stairs. The staff dining room is at the rear of the main cafeteria area. You'll see the sign on the wall by the door."

"Thank you, Ms. Watkins."

The guard smiled. "Keema."

Ben nodded and clipped the visitor's tag to her shirt. "Thanks, Keema."

She followed the instructions, which she hadn't needed, since everyone seemed to be headed in the same direction, and at that hour, there could only be one destination. Clumps of hospital staff chatted as they walked, the snippets of conversation she could hear sounding like the usual Monday morning recounting of the weekend's activities. This place might be smaller than what she'd been used to, but the hospital milieu was the same everywhere. Small towns within towns, complete with all the drama, rivalries, factions, and cohorts of any other community. She might be new here, but she knew the terrain, and in an odd way, that made her feel at home.

She took the stairs at the end of the red line, smiling to herself when she thought how different the red line was here from what it usually signified in high-speed transit lines, and found the cafeteria with no trouble. She decided against hospital coffee after having had the real thing several times already and grabbed a bottle of orange juice on her way through the food area. After paying, she scanned the large rectangular eatery, an unadorned area crowded with rectangular tables that would seat eight or ten people, and a few smaller ones in front of a bank of windows overlooking yet more green—grass, shrubs, flowers, and in the distance, evergreen-shrouded mountaintops. The view was ridiculous—too beautiful to be associated with a hospital, at least none she'd ever been in. If she wasn't careful, she'd be seduced by the setting alone.

At the far end of the main cafeteria, a wide doorway led to a smaller dining room, which she guessed had once been reserved for doctors, as had been common in most hospitals in previous centuries. Now it probably served as an informal staff meeting area. Here the round tables seated six and were widely separated to afford privacy. Less than half were occupied, and Flann and Harper were easy to pick out at a table tucked into a shallow alcove by a bay window that overlooked a rose garden. Harper wore a casual, open-collared striped shirt, while Flann was ready for the OR in scrubs and a slightly rumpled lab coat. From across the room, they looked much as they had during their med school days—mirror opposites, one blond, one dark-haired, but looking near enough alike to be twins—both still lean and projecting an attitude of contented certitude that reached her at twenty paces. They were born to be here, and they knew it. She envied them that sense of belonging, of knowing they were doing just what they were meant to be doing. She'd never been quite so sure of her own path, believing she could follow one to eventually find another, only to learn differently. She'd never felt completely at home anywhere—except on the basketball court, and that had proved to be a fleeting illusion. Shaking off the past, she briskly threaded her way through the tables as they both rose and extended their hands.

"Ben," Harper said, shaking her hand first. "Great to see you."

"Harper," Ben said before turning to Flannery and gripping her outstretched hand. "Flann. Good to see you both."

"Looking good, Ben," Flann said. "Need anything? The food's not your usual fare here."

"Don't doubt it," Ben said, sitting opposite the two siblings, "but I'm good. I ate at the café in town."

"Then you've started out in the right place." Grinning, Flann leaned back and draped an arm over the top corner of her chair, her relaxed posture belying the sharp intensity of her gaze. Ben hadn't been fooled by Flann's laid-back, laissez-faire attitude for very long in med school. She was as much a shark as any of them, probably more, and now she had an entire surgery department to run. She had to be wondering why Ben had left a prestigious medical center to take a position light-years away, geographically and every other way, from what she'd been accustomed to. If she was Flann, she sure would be.

"So," Harper said, settling down before her coffee and bagel, "where you staying?"

"A motel by the high school."

Flann laughed. "The Bluebird? Good thing you didn't fly out here for an interview and land there. Might have scared you off."

"It's not so bad—clean enough, although the soundproofing could use a little upgrading."

"Uh, yeah," Flann said, still grinning. "Now, if Harper had let me in on the interview, I might've been able to warn you what you were getting in for."

Ben caught the question beneath Flann's tease. Did she really know what she had signed on for by coming here? Fair question, since her decision might seem odd to a lot of people.

"I'll admit," Ben said easily, "I did not look much further than what's been happening here since SunView bought in and the new CEO decided to turn this place into a regional medical center practically overnight." She paused. Might as well let them know she knew they were wondering. "Of course, it does look like you spend most of your time tending the gardens. I have to confess, I won't be much use there."

Flann raised an eyebrow at Harper. "You want to give her the bad news or should I?"

Harper laughed, and the familiar friendly competitive dynamic slid back into place again. They'd all been looking for residencies at the same time, competing with one another for the highest grades and the best clinical evals at the same time as they were studying together. Flann and Harper always knew what their future held. Ben had been completely the opposite. She'd had a very different picture of her future at one time, one that had abruptly ended. She'd pivoted as quickly as she could, as she'd had no choice. Meeting Flann and Harper soon after starting medical school helped her get through a year of upheaval and uncertainty. Medical school tended to make or break friendships, and these had held through it all and the years after.

"I take it the job isn't exactly as advertised?" Ben said, her unconcern genuine. She totally trusted Flann and Harper and doubted anything they required would be problematic.

Harper shook her head, her expression suddenly serious and entirely professional. "No, it's exactly as advertised, although the responsibilities might be a little different than what you anticipated."

Ben raised an eyebrow. "Details?"

Flann, being chief of surgery, was essentially her direct boss, although they both answered to Harper and the elder Dr. Rivers. Flann said, "The sports medicine department is technically a division of surgery, and as such, you and your residents, once we get you accredited, will need to take surgery call."

"Sports medicine residents will usually be ortho residents," Ben said, "although we could take primary care people with the right background. I'd like that option." In her experience, surgery chiefs were always looking for more residents to cover their patients at night and handle ER consults. No doubt the current surgery residents were looking forward to a little relief in the on call schedule with the advent of new residents in sports medicine too, which was fine, as long as her residents weren't expected to work outside their area of training. Apparently she was going to need to learn the administrative negotiation part of things on the fly and right away. "Our residents can't take trauma call solo."

"True," Flann said, "and we'll tailor the call responsibilities to suit their training, of course." She grinned. "And then, there's you."

"I expected to take call," Ben said, "but you know, I'm a bone doctor. You don't really want me cracking chests."

"True enough. You'll be in the ortho rotation, but given your status as chief of your own department, we'll try to keep your responsibilities more consultative."

"Appreciated, but not necessary." Ben shrugged. "I enjoy trauma, and I've had a lot of experience. I've got no problem taking ortho trauma call."

"Fine. You'll have some protection from ortho residents or, in the trauma situation, general surgery residents who'll be working with you."

"No problem."

"All right then," Harper said, clearly ready to shift the conversation. "We've already begun the accreditation process for the residency, and I don't see any problems with it. Presley has had several conferences with the accreditation board, and we've got the patient volume, the staff, the right mix of cases, and the intensive care requirements all covered. We've also got residents who are interested in positions."

"Can we get them credit if they come in late in the year?" Ben asked.

"If we bring them in before the end of the first quarter, we'll be able to adjust rotations over the length of the residency to make up for any shortfalls in cases and time served."

Ben nodded. "Good."

"We may also have a couple of in-house people who are interested in switching from general surgery," Flann said wryly, "although I'm trying to talk them out of wasting their life fixing torn ligaments."

Ben laughed. "We do a bit more than that, but it might be too complicated for you to appreciate."

"There's one other thing," Harper said before Flann could prolong the debate.

Ben cocked her head. So far everything had been as she expected. This sounded like it was going to be something unanticipated. "Shoot."

"It's kind of a community service sort of thing," Harper went on, "and the pay is lousy. As in zero. We need a team doctor for the high school sports events. The guy who's covering it has decided to retire. Considering that you are building the sports medicine program here, it's a great way to introduce the concept to the community, and it looks good on paper. Plus, you know, you have the professional creds."

"Those are a decade old and pretty meaningless now," Ben said slowly. They'd been meaningless from the moment she'd terminated her contract with the Storm before a year was out. "But as long as I'm only there in a medical capacity, I don't see a problem."

"Excellent," Flann proclaimed, pulling several sheets of paper from her lab coat pocket. "Let me show you the schedule."

Ben regarded the calendar warily before extending a hand, pretending not to notice the automatic surge of excitement that was as ingrained as breathing. After all, she wasn't a basketball player any longer. She was a doctor.

❖

"Margie," Taylor Richelieu called. "Wait up."

Margie stepped off to the side of the main throng, waiting for Taylor as she adroitly maneuvered her way through the crowded hallway and the rush of bodies hurrying between classes. As in so many things, any obstacles in Taylor's way—this time being other students—just seemed to melt away in the wake of her determination. Margie knew for a fact that Taylor earned every single honor and accolade she'd ever received, even if a few jealous people didn't. Just because Taylor made success look easy didn't make it so. She also couldn't help that her long, straight hair—perfectly and flawlessly blond—was totally natural, or that she had a brain to go along with her body. Today as usual she looked awesome in low-waisted skinny jeans, a cropped top that ended a few inches above her wide studded belt, and platform sandals with three-inch heels.

"Hey," Margie said when Taylor reached her, "I thought—"

"Over *here*." Taylor grabbed her arm and pulled her into a side hallway.

"What?" Margie sputtered.

"I heard Blake and Dave talking just a few minutes ago," Taylor said. "You have a date with Blake for the drive-in?"

"Um," Margie said, glancing at her phone. "We have to be in class in two minutes."

"Then you should hurry up and tell me. Is that true?"

"Well, not exactly. We're just gonna go to the drive-in on Friday night."

"You and Blake. The two of you. Not, you know, you, me, Dave, Tim, and Blake?"

"Well, yeah."

Taylor jammed both fists on her hips and glared. "How did I not know this?"

Margie hesitated. "Are you mad?"

"Not the point. Are we best friends or not?"

"Of course." Margie bit the inside of her lip. Blake had surprised her that morning, but the idea of going to the drive-in with him didn't seem all that much different than some of the other things they did together—like working in the clinic with Val, or Blake coming to Sunday dinner at the Homestead, or driving around in the truck talking. Except none of those things felt like a date, and this did. And she kinda liked that. She also would have wanted to know if Taylor was planning to go on a date—because, whoa, news. "I didn't know he was going to suggest it."

"Well, I hope not. Then I really *would* be mad." Taylor pretended to pout for a second, then grinned. "I love Blake, he's a sweetie, but not like *that*, you know."

"So you're not mad?"

"No, but I might be a teensy bit jealous just of the idea, you know?"

"I don't really think it's going to be anything other than what we would ordinarily be doing," Margie muttered.

Taylor rolled her eyes as they started walking toward class. "Uh-huh. Really? Then what would be the point of just the two of you?"

"I don't know, he just asked me, and I said yes, and well, now I don't know what to think."

"Just go with it." Taylor winked. "He is awfully cute."

Margie thought so too, but she said, "Yeah, but he's Blake. You know, one of us."

"And I suppose you've never looked at Dave and thought he was hunky?"

Margie stopped, gave Taylor a look, and said, "Actually, no. I *have* looked at you and thought you're hot."

Taylor blushed. "Get out."

"No, I'm serious. You are."

"So are we going to go to the drive-in alone?"

"Let me think about it," Margie said, not altogether unseriously. She did think Taylor was hot. She hadn't really thought about what that meant.

"Deal," Taylor said, and for once, Margie couldn't tell if she was serious or not.

"We're not going to let this change everything, are we?" Margie asked.

Taylor shook her head. "Caring about someone doesn't change the way you love your friends, does it?"

Margie squeezed her hand. "No way."

"Then we're all good. Just don't forget that we're all meeting at my house Friday night—so drive-in or no, you both need to be there."

"Deal," Margie said with relief. She had the night with Blake to look forward to, and she had her friends, and she'd figure out what she needed to figure out if and when.

CHAPTER FIVE

Court arrived at the hospital with a few minutes to spare and used the extra time to stow her gear in her OR locker, call the resident who'd been covering B service—her assigned surgical service for the month—to make sure there were no problems, and head back downstairs to radiology to view the images that had been done overnight. The more info she had on her patients when she discussed them with the attendings, the sooner decisions on care could be made—and the better she'd look, which was a nice side benefit.

As Court exited the stairwell, Brody Clark rounded the corner on her way toward the flight lounge. A little taller than Court, she wore the regulation navy-blue flight suit, zipped up the front and pockets laden with the usual paramedic paraphernalia of scissors, tape, stethoscope, and sundry other objects. Her dark hair was tousled and probably a little longer than she'd worn it when she flew SAR missions in the Army.

"Hey, Brody," Court said.

"Hi, cuz, how was your weekend?" Brody slowed and fell into step with her.

"Cousin by marriage only," Court said pointedly, "and *eww*, because, you know, for half a second pre-Val, I contemplated dating you."

Brody chuckled. "Couldn't have given it much thought in that amount of time, so I think we're non-*eww*."

"Well, when it comes down to me or Val, it's usually no contest." Court meant it as a joke, even though true, and hoped she hadn't sounded bitter. She wasn't...any longer.

Brody raised an eyebrow. "I can't see the two of you competing—well, maybe on some level, like academically maybe, both being doctors—"

"Val is a vet."

Brody laughed. "Yeah, and don't let her hear you suggesting you MDs have anything on the vets."

Court grinned. "Actually, I'm pretty sure she's smarter, but I'll never admit I said that."

"That's what I mean..." Brody paused at an intersection of hallways. "I don't see you competing for dates. There's a little bit of an age gap there, anyhow."

"Not all that much of one." A few years that seemed inconsequential now but which had seemed, along with Val's reputation of being the smartest, the sexiest, and the everything-est before Court even had a chance, like a huge obstacle to her high-school self. Not that she would bring that up now, especially with Brody, who didn't know the fine details of her and Val's past estrangement. Or, to be honest, good old-fashioned family feud. "And we never really competed. We both were raised knowing our fathers were warring, and that was enough to keep us apart. I didn't really know her then." She hesitated. "I might have blamed her a little for the family stuff, back then, but I know better now."

Not that she was certain Val believed that.

"I'm glad that's all settled." Brody slowed at the corridor that led down to the flight deck and the on-call lounge. "Because, you know, family. That matters."

"You're right," Court said, trying not to show the uneasy sensation that still surfaced when she thought about the past. She and Val had closed much of the rift that their fathers had created and passed down to them, but getting over a lifetime of resentment and, even though she hated to admit it, a little bit of jealousy wasn't all that easy to do. Thinking of Val as family rather than the enemy wasn't just a matter of understanding intellectually that her father's battle wasn't hers. There were feelings associated with the stories she'd heard, some of which she now understood were exaggerated or just outright fabrications. But she'd idolized her father and believed everything he'd ever told her, right up until the moment he walked out the door for a carton of milk and never came back. How trite.

And not something she wanted to talk about with her cousin's new love. She sucked in a breath and put on a smile. "So, how is Honcho enjoying her new territory?"

Brody's dark eyes softened, the way they always did at the mention of her retired war dog. "She patrols her perimeter every single time we let her out."

"So that means she likes it?"

"She loves it. And since our nearest neighbors are half a mile away, I don't worry about her running into anyone who might challenge her." Brody grinned. "Or vice versa. She won't go off our land. I showed her the borders the very first day we moved in. She understands territory."

"How's Val taking to country living?" Courtney asked, unable to keep the amusement out of her voice. Val might be a country vet, but she'd grown up in the swank suburbs of Saratoga Springs, the most affluent community within sixty miles.

"She might love it even more than Honcho," Brody said. "And the location is perfect for both of us. Close to Val's secondary office here, so it's easier for her to take her farm calls, and an easy drive for me. Perfect all around."

"I'm glad it's all worked out," Court said, and she really meant it. Brody was good-looking and interesting, but the dark places Court had had a fleeting glimpse of when they'd first met had been tempered by Val's love. They fit, and she doubted that she and Brody would have made as good a match. She didn't have Val's optimism or lightness of spirit. She wasn't really sure what she had, which was probably why she'd never been in any hurry to have a serious relationship. She liked the kind of relationship she had with Jane—the intimacy of sex without the worry that she might be missing some important cue that she'd end up paying in pain for. She'd certainly missed all the cues growing up, and that failure haunted her still. If someone walked out of her life now, she planned to make sure she didn't care.

Jane was likely out on the flight deck checking the helicopter right now. Court was just as glad she didn't have time to check, since dialing back on their relationship was the right call.

"I gotta get my butt upstairs and make rounds before the OR," she said. "Fly safe today."

"I will." Brody pointed a finger. "And you need to come out to the farm for a cookout soon. No more excuses."

Court backpedaled, nodding. "Sure. Totally. Whenever I have time. You know, the busy life of a resident."

Brody walked the other way, calling over her shoulder, "That excuse is getting thin."

Court skirted around the corner and out of sight before she had to come up with a rejoinder. She didn't begrudge Val and Brody their happiness, but it was weird, spending time with the cousin she still didn't know very well, but wished she did.

She made it halfway through her assigned floors when she got a text from the ER to call down. She finished the note she was writing on the post-op gallbladder patient and called.

"Valentine," she said when the phone was picked up.

"Hey, Court, it's Joe. We've been waiting on a surgery consult for almost an hour. Any chance you can come down and take a look at a guy with belly pain?"

Court groaned inwardly. Abdominal pain could be almost anything, and sometimes the workup required multiple X-rays and lab tests. Joe Antonelli was a PA student, and a good one. Chances were any patient he thought needed to be seen was the real deal. "Where's Musburger?"

"In the OR with Mary Anne Okonsky. You don't really want me to call up there, do you?"

Court smiled. Okonsky would tear a piece off Joe's butt if he bothered her resident in the OR. She was almost done anyhow and could see the last of the patients after her first case if she couldn't get to them before the OR started. They were both stable and likely to go home in a day or two. Musburger would owe her one too, which was never a bad thing.

"I'll be down there in five. Do you have labs?"

"Yeah, and an ultrasound."

"No CAT scan?"

"CAT scan's backed up."

"Great," she muttered. Not Joe's fault, but could something be simple, just once? "Okay. Name?"

Joe gave her the info on Mike Wells, and she pulled up his labs on her iPad before heading back to examine him. Relevant history:

a fifty-year-old man who had come in three hours previously complaining of the acute onset of pain in his upper abdomen that awakened him from sleep. Joe had already ruled out an acute MI, which, considering his age group, had to be excluded before anything else. The blood profile and electrolytes looked pretty unremarkable. No elevated white count suggesting an infectious or inflammatory process, and his general chemistries were normal except for a tiny bump in one liver enzyme—and that might be nothing at all. The abdominal pain could be anything—an ulcer, gastroenteritis, a blocked bile duct, or some vascular catastrophe. So—not simple. Surprise.

She slipped inside the curtain and held out her hand. "Good morning. I'm Dr. Valentine, one of the surgery residents."

The athletic-looking middle-aged man propped upright on the stretcher, oxygen cannula in his nose and an IV in his left arm, held out his right hand. "Mike Wells."

He croaked a little, and she suspected his throat was dry. The ER staff were well-trained and knew someone who might be going to the OR could not have anything to eat or drink. Another reason to get to the bottom of this asap. If he needed surgery, they needed to get him scheduled. If he didn't, he needed to be turfed to medicine.

"Mike, can you tell me what brought you here?"

He sighed.

"I know," Court said, raising a shoulder. "You've said it before, but I need to hear it from you myself. You never know—sometimes a little thing you might have forgotten earlier will make a difference."

He recounted basically the same story that had been documented previously. Healthy, ran five miles a day, rode his bicycle fifty miles on the weekend, no history of cardiac or blood pressure issues. Just this damn pain that woke him up.

"Weight stable?" she asked, resorting to autopilot and running down the standard questions when nothing popped from his story.

"Been trying to lose a little bit," he said vaguely.

She looked up. "You look like you're a pretty good weight. How much are we talking about?"

"Not much—ten pounds, maybe."

She bet the number was higher. "Any reason you wanted to drop weight?"

He looked away for a second. "Not exactly. Appetite's just been off a little bit, so I figured I'd take advantage."

If she'd had antennae, they would've been quivering. "How long?"

"What do you mean?" he asked.

"How long has your appetite been off."

"Couple months."

"How is your energy level?"

"Things have been busy at work—I'm a Realtor, and there's been a big boom in the area. Been moving a lot of houses."

"And?" Court pressed gently. He was nervous. More than that. A little scared.

"I might have been a little more tired than usual."

"Okay. Well, you need a CAT scan, so we can get a good look at everything that's in your belly."

"I just had an ultrasound."

"And I'm going to go take a look at it right now. As soon as I've had a look at you." She cranked the back of the stretcher down until he was almost flat and started with his chest. His heart and lungs were clear. He wasn't kidding about his exercise regimen—his heart rate was slow and steady, somewhere near sixty. His abdomen was basically flat, and as she first listened and then palpated, she couldn't immediately find any areas of localized tenderness. As she gently probed around the liver, she saw him wince a little. "Sorry. Does it hurt?"

"A little tender," he muttered.

A lot of things lived in the right upper quadrant besides the liver—most notably the gallbladder, the ducts that led from it, loops of small bowel and colon, and deep to them all, the pancreas. She quickly checked his distal pulses and didn't find any evidence of diminished blood flow to his lower extremities, ruling out any major vascular anomalies.

Finished, she stepped back and said, "The ultrasound is great for looking at the gallbladder and some of the organs in a general way, but nothing touches the CAT scan in terms of being able to show us fine detail in multiple planes. You need one, and it's going to take a little while to get. They're backed up downstairs. I'd rather not admit you until we have a more definitive diagnosis."

"I don't want to stay in the hospital," he said urgently. "I've got too much going on. Work and family stuff."

"I understand. Let's get some more information first, okay?"

"Yeah, sure."

Court eased the curtain open. "I'm going to discuss your case with Dr. Rivers as soon as I leave here. I'll do everything I can to speed things up."

"Edward?"

"No, Flann."

"Right, Flann's the surgeon. I sold her and her wife their new house. That'll be fine."

Court almost smiled. Better than fine. The best there was.

"I'll be back."

"Thanks, Dr. Valentine."

Court found Joe. "Where's the ultrasound?"

"I pulled it up on the monitor over there for you," he said, pointing to a computer at the workstation. She leaned against the counter and swiveled the screen to scan through the various images. Ultrasounds recorded differences in density between adjoining tissues and took training to read. She wasn't all that good at it, which was why they had radiologists to read them, but the report noted some thickening and fluid in the deep tissues in the upper abdomen. That she *could* see. Something, but not definitive.

She grabbed the landline and called down to radiology.

"Radiology, Murphy." The head CT tech sounded harried.

"Olive, it's Courtney Valentine. I need to schedule a CAT scan on a patient up here in the ER."

"How does Tuesday sound," Olive said.

"About twenty-four hours too late," Court said. "I need it this morning. Soon as you can."

Olive snorted. "Honey, we've got a waiting list down here. Three-car pileup at two a.m. We're still cleaning up from that."

"I get it. But I've got a guy with acute abdominal pain, and we wouldn't want him to perforate while we wait for a scan, would we."

"That sounds a little like blackmail."

"Possibly, but also true."

Olive sighed. "I can shuffle some of the in-house patients, but I've got to get the other emergency patients done first."

"Fair enough. Thanks."

When she had that arranged, she paged Flann.

"Rivers," Flann said when she answered.

"Dr. Rivers, it's Courtney. I'm in the ER."

"What have you got?"

"Fifty-year-old guy with new onset abdominal pain, so he says, but he also reluctantly admits to a fifteen-pound weight loss and fatigue. He's got a tender liver."

"Temperature? White count?"

"Nothing to suggest an acute inflammatory process. Chemistries are mostly normal too. They got an ultrasound, and it's a little edematous in the retro peritoneum. Gallbladder looks okay."

"What's the CAT scan show?"

"We haven't been able to get one yet. CT's backed up, but they promised they'd get to him this morning."

"What do you think?"

That was the question—the one that distinguished the clinician who had a sense for the whole patient from the technician who relied on labs and X-rays. She had a *feeling*, but she needed to show she'd considered all the possibilities. "He's not obstructed or perfed. No evidence of vascular compromise. Pancreatitis has to be high on the list, although not infectious in the absence of fever. He's not a drinker, and there's no evidence of jaundice, yet. He *could* have a stone that hasn't totally blocked the bile duct, and the pain is from that. Or there's a mass lesion."

"Where are you putting your money, Dr. Valentine?" Flann asked.

Court had kept her voice low as they talked, but she lowered it further. "We need to rule out a pancreatic lesion."

"Yeah, we do," Flann said. "Let's get the CAT scan. How old did you say he was?"

"Fifty."

"Otherwise healthy?"

"Perfectly."

"Then we don't want to miss anything."

"I know." If she was right, and she hoped she wasn't, a swift diagnosis and aggressive surgery were Mike Wells's best shot.

"Call me when you get the scan. I'm doing a bowel case at eight, but I'll get down there as soon as I can once we have that."

"All right."

"And Courtney," Flann said almost casually, "what are you doing in the ER? Aren't you on B service this morning?"

Of course Flann would know where all the residents were supposed to be.

"Yes, but Musburger is doing an emergency case with Dr. Okonsky."

Flann chuckled. "I see. Well, thanks for covering."

"No problem." She hung up and spun around, crashing directly into the person standing a foot away talking to the ER chief.

"Oh, sorry," Court blurted, staring into the amused eyes of Bennett Anderson.

CHAPTER SIX

"Courtney," Abby Remy said brightly. "This is Dr. Anderson, a new ortho attending and head of the new sports medicine division."

"Oh," Court said, off-balance in more ways than one. She hadn't expected to see Ben Anderson again, and for sure not here, definitely not as a new attending. "We've met."

Abby's brows came together, and her smile shifted to bemused curiosity. "Really, I hadn't realized that."

"Well, no, not really met-met," Court said, awash with gratitude that the floor hadn't yet opened to swallow her up in her acute embarrassment. "I meant..."

"Good to see you again, Dr...?"

Bennett hesitated and, before they were both embarrassed, Court instantly said, "Valentine. Courtney Valentine. Welcome."

She had the presence of mind to extend her hand, and when Bennett Anderson took it, the earth steadied instead of threatening to tilt. Bennett's grip was firm and warm, and for a second, Court envisioned her hands in motion on the basketball, fluid and swift and sure. Mesmerizing, like the woman. After a second, Bennett's fingers slipped away, and Court was left with the afterimage of her that morning still emblazoned on her mind's eye.

"I was just telling Dr. Anderson," Abby went on, as if the entire bizarre exchange hadn't happened, "how much I think the new department is going to add to the training experience as well as enhance patient care."

"I totally agree," Court said, on firmer ground now. "We used to just see training injuries primarily from overeager student-athletes, but now we're seeing the same thing in noncompetitive settings. More targeted treatment will be great experience for the residents too."

"Court is one of the coaches and a trainer for the Blazers."

Bennett frowned. "Ah, that would be...?"

Abby laughed. "Our high school basketball team. Made it to State last year—nearly took it all."

"Ah," Bennett said, glancing at Court. "I see."

"Assistant coach," Court added quickly, feeling the blush climb into her cheeks. Abby probably had no idea Bennett Anderson was one of the most accomplished college basketball players of the last two decades. Their little high school team and her role on it must seem incredibly provincial when compared to Bennett's experience. "Not a high-profile job."

When Bennett merely smiled, Court cleared her throat and said, "I was just finishing up a consult down here, and I need to get up to the OR."

"Oh, good," Abby said. "Would you mind walking Dr. Anderson up? She ought to meet the staff up there before she does much of anything else."

"Sure," Court said, a bit of heat flooding her cheeks again. Well, nothing like acting like a fangirl, but she couldn't help feel just a little intimidated, as well as curious about how Bennett Anderson, the rising pro basketball star, had ended up Dr. Bennett Anderson. And here, of all places.

Bennett fell in beside her, and after a few seconds of silence said, "Basketball coach, huh?"

Court really did want to be swallowed up now, cursing inwardly that despite not having the milk-white skin of some blondes, thanks to her mother's distant French ancestry, she still couldn't hide a blush if her life depended on it. "I'm mostly in charge of drills and keeping the playbook up to date," she said. "Anita Gold is the real coach."

"In my experience," Bennett said quietly, glancing over to catch Court's gaze, "assistant coaches often see a lot more of the personal side of things than the head coach, who's focused on a winning season. And young players are very malleable. A solid high school experience can land a kid a scholarship that will change their life. Not many places where we can do that."

Her gaze never left Court's as she spoke, and her voice, low and intense and utterly assured, slipped through Court like hot nectar. She couldn't have broken the spell if she'd wanted to, and she didn't.

When Bennett finally lifted her gaze, Court found her voice. "Sometimes we change lives here."

"We do." Bennett grinned and the solemnity in her eyes disappeared, returning a hint of the relaxed expression she'd had on the court that morning. "And we have fun doing it. Win-win."

Court grinned back. "Basketball and surgery—who would have thought they'd have so much in common." The words had barely left her mouth before she blurted, "Today must be my day for foot-in-mouth syndrome."

Bennett laughed, a sound both unexpected and appreciated. She cut Court a look as Court turned down an adjoining corridor. "It took me quite a while to appreciate the similarities."

"I ought to apologize for disturbing you this morning," Court said. No point pretending Bennett didn't know she'd been standing there staring at her.

"You didn't, and you don't," Bennett replied. "You're a surgery resident, I take it?"

That was a pretty obvious change in subject. So basketball was not a topic for discussion, at least not when it involved Bennett Anderson.

"Yes, first year," Court said.

"Thought about a specialty yet?"

"Not yet," Court said. Bennett was an attending, and the last thing she wanted was to come off as an insincere kiss-ass, so she wasn't about to admit that when she'd heard about the new sports medicine division and the open places for residents, she'd considered it. The more she coached and interacted with athletes, the more interested she'd become in the specialty. She'd also seen how valuable the right treatment and a sports-specific rehab program could be for the patient—any patient with a bone or joint injury. Not just athletes. But attendings talked, and she didn't want to burn any bridges by suggesting she might want to switch out of general surgery. She still had plenty of time to make a decision. "Right now, general surgery is my focus. I've got a lot to learn, and I can't imagine specializing without having a really firm grip on general first."

Bennett nodded. "I agree with you, and I think it's a wise plan. I've seen too many residents so set on a subspecialty that they never really got a good foundation, either technically or medically. You'll be a stronger resident, no matter what you decide on. Eventually, if you take advantage of learning to operate in any part of the body, you'll be able to handle any kind of injury that comes along."

"That's what I want." Court gestured to the elevator. "The OR is on the third floor. We can take the elevator or—"

"Let's hit the stairs."

Court sighed happily. She hated waiting for elevators, and besides, this way she got a little extra exercise in. "Absolutely."

She took the lead on the way up, aware of Bennett Anderson just behind her. She still couldn't quite come to grips with the fact that the image she'd had of Bennett was completely turned around now. She just couldn't help wondering too how Bennett had gone from being a pro basketball player to an orthopedic surgeon. The story had to be fascinating, and after actually talking with Bennett for just a few minutes, her curiosity was stoked even more. Watching her on the court that morning, basketball was so clearly in her genes. Bennett was a mystery she'd love to explore, but that wasn't about to happen. The new ortho attending probably wouldn't even remember her name in a few hours. Residents occupied an odd place in the hospital hierarchy—they were all highly trained and mostly intelligent, but unlike almost every other professional medical person, they came on the job with authority but very little real-world experience. The seasoned staff—from nurses to PAs—considered them students at best and hazards at worst. And the attendings often saw them as interchangeable.

No, she and Dr. Bennett Anderson did not exist in the same world.

"The OR central station's down this way," Court said, setting aside her pointless musings, "and the locker rooms and OR lounge are at the other end of the hall. SICU is around the corner."

"Where's the TICU?"

Since sports medicine handled traumatic injuries as well as reconstructive surgeries, Bennett would have patients in both the surgical and trauma ICUs. Court said, "Opposite wing on this level—the elevators lead right up from the ER/Trauma wing to this floor, no stops."

"Nice planning."

"Yeah," Courtney said. "It helps that when the ER was expanded, Dr. Remy had a hand in the planning."

"From the outside, this place looks like it belongs in one of those period dramas that are so popular right now," Bennett said. "And then you walk inside, and it could be any big city trauma center."

Court laughed. "Don't be too fooled. This is the Rivers—the place where someone from almost every family in this town has either worked, been born in, or died in for generations. This place has a soul."

Bennett slowed, regarding Court with a faint smile. "I think I knew that before I came. I'd heard about the hospital from Harper and Flann when we were students. They didn't phrase it quite so eloquently as you, though."

"Ah, well." Court bit her lip. She might have been embarrassed *again* if Bennett's expression hadn't been so intense she could feel it stirring quite a different sensation. One she rarely experienced in far more intimate situations, and *not* one she ought to be having right now and definitely not with this woman. Hadn't she just listed all the reasons why?

Abruptly, she pushed open a door into a large room with one wall of windows looking out into what was obviously the pre-op area, while an array of monitors crowded the walls above a U-shaped workstation.

A curly-haired redhead glanced their way and held up a finger as she spoke into a headset. "Manny, this is Patty in the OR. You can get Mrs. Fishbein ready to come down. We'll be sending transport in ten minutes. Thanks."

"Patty Sullivan is the OR supervisor," Court said as they waited for the redhead to finish a call.

Call ended, Patty spun around and said, "Hi, Court."

"Patty," Court said, "this is Dr. Bennett Anderson, the new head of sports medicine."

Patty smiled and rose with an outstretched hand. "Good to meet you."

"You too," Bennett said. "How many rooms are you running?"

"Fifteen," Patty said, "although right now we've got two on trauma hold."

Court'd heard the trauma alert just as they'd entered the stairwell. "Any idea what's coming?"

"Air Star's bringing two in from a barn collapse out in Hebron. Multiple injuries—that's all we've got." Patty raised a brow. "Trying to get in on the case, Dr. Valentine?"

Court grinned. "Always."

"Well, you might get a chance, because we just bumped *your* case."

"Oh, come on," Court said with her best sad face. "You don't want to make our bowel resection wait until this afternoon, do you? Can't you bump plastics or somebody?"

"Oh, I don't think so. I don't really want to hear about how Dr. Beauregard's abdominal reconstruction has been scheduled for two months and how we always give priority to the trauma service." She smiled at Bennett. "You know how that song goes."

"I do, and I'm just glad I'm ortho." Bennett laughed and looked at Court. "I don't think you're going to win this one, Dr. Valentine."

Court grinned. "Always worth a try."

"Looking forward to working with you, Doctor," Patty said, touching her headset. "OR—Sullivan."

When Patty was free again, Bennett said, "It was good to meet you. I'm sure I'll see you again soon."

"In all likelihood, sooner than you think," Patty said. "We've been backed up since midnight with trauma cases, and it sounds like more are coming."

The beeper on Court's hip pinged. "That's Air Star, and I'm on backup flight call." She glanced at Bennett. "Do you need—"

"Go, go," Bennett said. "Have a good flight."

"Thanks." Court met her gaze, caught for just a second by the deep blue intensity before she broke the connection and vaulted into the hall.

❖

Bennett checked the clock above Patty Sullivan's station. "I believe I have a staff meeting. Could you tell me the fastest way to get to the auditorium?"

"You'll want the main one on the second floor, just down the hall from the cafeteria. Take the same stairwell you came up, turn right, follow the hall all the way to the end, and make another right. The auditorium is the first door after you make the turn. There's a sign."

"Thanks, Ms. Sullivan."

"Patty."

Bennett nodded. "And I'm Ben."

"Glad to have you, Ben."

Ben followed Patty's instructions and found the auditorium, which was, in fact, a classic auditorium with twenty rows of tiered seating leading down to a raised stage. Each seat was upholstered in a plush blue fabric, and the arched coffered ceiling sectioned by elaborately carved crown molding. Rooms like this weren't often found in modern hospitals. She took a spot on the aisle halfway down, aware once again of casual glances sent her way as people passed. A man in a white coat, white shirt, black trousers, and shiny black wingtips strode onto the stage at precisely six forty-five. The resemblance to Flann and Harper was unmistakable. Edward Rivers. Chief of Staff. He made some general announcements, and when he moved on to routine business matters, Bennett tuned out. The morning had already been crammed with most of the critical information she needed immediately—all fairly standard hospital protocols.

What had been unexpectedly intriguing was Courtney Valentine. Ordinarily when she met a resident, she filed away the basics—name, training year, general impression of ability. Courtney Valentine was different, perhaps because she hadn't met her under the usual circumstances. They'd met, in a manner of speaking, on a personal level. Courtney saw her first not as a new attending, but as a basketball player. Recognized her as who'd she been. As who she still was, in her private moments. In an odd way, it felt as if they shared a secret.

Ben shook her head. The idea was just a fiction created by an odd set of circumstances that signified nothing. She would never know what Courtney Valentine thought while she'd watched her. Courtney had just embarked on the hardest years of her career. Her life would be a roller coaster of adrenaline-fueled highs and emotionally draining fatigue, and on occasion, a little rebellion. For some residents the fastest way to relieve the relentless tension was a few hours of escape with mostly harmless recreational drugs and mostly responsible sex.

She and Courtney would likely never have a personal conversation, let alone anything else. And given all the circumstances, that was for the best.

The meeting ended a little after seven, and Ben waited in the aisle as Flann walked up to join her.

"How's the orientation going?" Flann asked.

"I've met all the important people, I think," Ben said. "The ER chief and the OR supervisor."

Flann grinned. "That's about it. Come on, I'll show you where your offices are. Your department admin will have your calendar of patient appointment hours and your OR block time."

"What's the PA situation? Do we have someone assigned to our division?"

Flann chuckled. "We have some excellent PAs as well as a new training program. Right now, they're like gold. Everyone wants them. Most are in the ER, and if you try stealing any from my wife, I wouldn't lay money on your chance of survival."

"I wouldn't dream of it." Ben smiled. "Can we recruit?"

"We've got room in the budget for two. I'll see what I can do about getting you some resident coverage until we can bring in some from the outside."

"Thanks."

Flann grinned. "Don't thank me too soon. Every ortho guy we have is in the OR. You're it for now, so you're covering trauma and the ER."

Before she could reply, her phone buzzed. The text message was an unfamiliar number, but then every number in the hospital was unfamiliar. She glanced at Flann. "4-4-1-6?"

"That's the trauma unit, Dr. Anderson. Welcome to your first day at the Rivers."

Chapter Seven

The ER was a flurry of activity when Ben hurried through to trauma admitting. Residents, PAs, nurses, and techs hastily pulled on yellow paper cover gowns, tied masks around their necks, and slipped on disposable gloves. She didn't recognize anyone until Abby Remy hurried around the corner and stopped to survey the activity. When Abby spied her, she headed in her direction.

"I didn't expect to see you again so soon," Abby said while keeping a watchful eye on the preparations.

"I got a page, so I thought I'd just come on down."

"Everyone on call for trauma gets the page," Abby said. "I see that Flann hasn't waited very long to put you to work."

Ben smiled. "Just as well. Otherwise I'd be stuck at my desk all day looking at paperwork that I probably have no idea what to do with."

Abby chuckled. "You'll learn fast enough."

"What's coming?"

"Air Star is bringing in two patients," Abby said. "An adult male and teenage female, both blunt traumas from when a barn roof they were rehabbing collapsed. Multiple crush injuries."

"Do you have trauma fellows?"

"A first year, and when she's unavailable, trauma is covered by general surgery. General surgery staff also rotate with our new trauma attending—another new hire like you. My sister-in-law has been busy since she decided to put this place on the map." Her smile was fond. "We ought to have more fellows on board soon—we've had plenty of applications."

A rangy, sandy-haired woman with a lean runner's build and an unhurried, calm demeanor, wearing OR greens, paused by Abby. "Where do you want me, Abby?"

"Take the male patient with my resident. Make sure Costa gets the order of the exam right—it sounds like a C-spine fracture. I'll take Wakeem with me."

"You got it."

"Trauma?" Ben asked.

Abby shook her head as the woman strode away. "That's Glenn Archer—she's a PA and the director of our PA training program. She's also Flann's personal PA, and when she's not down here she's usually in the OR with Flann. You've been warned."

Ben laughed. "I'll stay clear, but I need one of my own."

"Don't we all," Abby said as a brunette, somewhere around Ben's age, in greens and an OR cover gown came down the hall with a young guy with curly dark hair in her wake, his expression halfway between anticipation and terror. Med student, Ben surmised.

"Let me guess," Ben said. "*That's* trauma."

"Yes," Abby said. "Hi, Grady."

"Abby." She nodded to Ben. "Grady McClure. Saw you at the staff meeting this morning. You're ortho, right?"

Ben held out her hand. "Yes, Ben Anderson."

"Welcome aboard," Grady said. "Sounds like we've got plenty of work for you. We'll two team if we can, depending on the injuries."

"Fine by me." Ben looked at Abby. "Can we get fast portables?"

"Yes, and they're usually excellent," Abby said. "You ought to have films good enough to work with."

"All right then. I'll stay out of the way until—"

The double doors at the entrance swished open, and a gurney carrying the male patient trundled in, propelled by a resident at the head with a medic and other ER staff running along on either side, one rhythmically squeezing a breathing bag attached to an endotracheal tube, and the other performing CPR.

Abby pointed to the first open bay as Grady ran to meet them. "Take one."

Immediately behind the first, a second gurney entered bearing a smaller figure nearly dwarfed by equipment, the face obscured by a cervical collar and an oxygen mask. That would be the female patient.

"In two, Brody," Abby called to the flight medic guiding the stretcher.

Abby and Ben followed Brody into the second bay, where staff immediately surrounded the patient, each team member slipping into the well-practiced routine of attaching monitors and IV lines, checking vital signs, listening for breath sounds, drawing blood and urine samples, and establishing that essential systems were all functioning.

Brody said, "Linda McCallum, eighteen years old, caught beneath falling debris when part of a barn roof caved in. She was on a scaffold when the support beams gave way, and she fell about fifteen feet. Part of the scaffolding protected her from being crushed. Alert but disoriented at the scene, blood pressure bouncing between 110 and 140 over 60, pulse 150. Obvious fracture, closed, right upper extremity. A distal left lower leg fracture, open. Both splinted in the field."

"Any sign of neurovascular compromise related to the fractures," Ben asked.

"Couldn't assess neuro beyond she withdrew to pain when we splinted her. Distal pulses were intact."

"Good." Ben made a visual appraisal as the PA, whose name tag identified him as Wakeem Watanobe, performed a quick but efficient physical exam as Abby ordered meds and labs. The extremities were of prime interest to her right now, although the entire skeleton would need to be assessed radiographically once the patient was stable. Vacuum splints had been applied in the field, as Brody noted, which would have helped control pain and reduce the likelihood of further damage from uncontrolled movement. They also obscured what was underneath them. X-rays would give Ben a view of the bones, but she needed to see the soft tissues as well.

The patient was semiconscious, although not terribly coherent, and unable to follow commands. She kept asking for her father, even though the PA had gently told her several times that her father was being taken care of nearby.

Ben would have to rely on whatever she could see and feel for now. The foot extending beyond the cast was normal in color. When she slipped her fingers over the pulse point on the dorsum of the foot, the pulse was strong and steady. A pretty good indication that the vascular supply to the leg was intact. She checked the right hand below the splint, and when she slid her fingers into Linda McCallum's palm, the girl squeezed with surprising strength. Her eyes opened and fixed on Ben's.

"Where's my dad?" she asked in an urgent tone.

Ben leaned closer. "Linda, I'm Dr. Anderson. You're at the Rivers. Your dad is just on the other side of the curtain, and he's being taken care of. How are you feeling—does your chest or abdomen hurt?"

"Sore," she muttered, and her eyelids fluttered closed.

Abby murmured, "X-ray's here, Ben."

"Great." Ben straightened. "I want to get the splints off and check the soft tissues. Let's get the films first, so we don't have to move her too much."

Abby said, "Wakeem, what have we got?"

"She'll need a head CT," the PA said, "but chest and belly look good. You can probably get the rest of the films you'll need once that CT's cleared."

"That's fine," Ben said. "We'll have plenty of time before we can get an OR room."

After the X-rays were done, Ben deflated the vacuum splints to examine the injured extremities. The midhumerus arm fracture evidenced the expected swelling and discoloration but was well-aligned and ought to do well with casting. The lower extremity was a different matter. A sterile wrap had been applied to the lower leg and ankle, and when she carefully exposed the underlying wound, she found a complex laceration most likely extending to the fracture site. An open fracture markedly increased the risk of infection.

"Can you get these re-dressed," Ben asked the PA when she was done.

"Sure," he said.

Ben found a computer and asked a resident how to access the X-rays that had just been taken. Abby came over as she reviewed them.

"What do you think?" Abby asked.

"The arm's not a problem," Ben said. "A cast will do. But this"—she tapped the displaced fracture of the distal tibia at the ankle—"will need a washout and then internal fixation."

"You're going to have a wait until the OR opens up," Abby said, "plus Air Star is en route to a multivehicle collision. We're going to have a few more coming before long."

"How's the other patient? Her father?"

Abby shook her head. "We're waiting on neuro, but he's got a high C-spine fracture. He's on vent support."

Ben sighed. In all likelihood, not a survivable injury.

Grady slipped around the curtain from trauma one to join them. "Talked with neuro. They're sending their resident down, but they want this guy moved to the head of the line for halo placement and possible internal stabilization. Can't wait."

"At this rate we'll be operating in the halls," Abby muttered.

"When do you close to trauma?" Ben asked.

"Never," Abby said, "short of an all-out mass casualty alert. We're the biggest level one for sixty miles. We'll just have to bump all the elective schedule."

Ben winced. Not what she really wanted to do the first day she arrived, but after everyone got over being angry, they'd understand.

❖

"What do we have?" Court said to Phil, the flight nurse who jumped into the medevac chopper behind her.

"First responders said three-vehicle pileup, multiple casualties. That's all we got."

Jane added from the cockpit, "Matt says we might have to divert to Albany, depending on what we get. We're backed up at the Rivers."

Courtney didn't like it. Added flight time always upped the risk that a patient with an injury that didn't appear life-threatening in the field could suddenly go bad as something unsuspected developed in midair. Medevac rescue was so effective at lowering trauma mortality because of the decreased time between injury in the field to definitive treatment in the trauma unit. Not her call, but she'd bet money Abby Remy would not send a critical patient on a long flight.

After adjusting her headset, she leaned forward and tapped Jane on the shoulder. "I thought you were flying first team today."

Jane didn't answer for a few moments, adjusting the throttle and checking gauges as they lifted off. Then she said, "Vinnie has some school thing for his kid later today, and I volunteered to take second shift. Figured I'd get a nap in this morning." She glanced at Court, grinning. "This will teach me."

Court smiled to herself as the chopper banked and headed northeast. She hadn't gotten much sleep either, but the unexpected morning's events had re-energized her. The brief conversation with Bennett Anderson stayed with her, as did the intriguing intensity in her eyes every time her basketball past came up. She rarely wanted to delve beneath the surface of a woman's secrets, but this time she couldn't help wonder what hid in Bennett's silence. She couldn't help thinking about how she'd been blindsided by a casual remark either. That happened to her exactly never.

Snippets of their time together kept replaying as she looked out the window, a view she'd seen many times but never tired of. A vibrant palette of rolling green pasture, solitary farmhouses standing at the intersections of winding country roads, flanked by barns that were often twice their size, and the small tan and white shapes of horses and cows clustered on hillsides. Vehicles, most of them pickups, glided along the pale narrow strips of road, seeming to move in slow motion as the chopper overtook them.

"Ought to be coming up on the scene pretty quick," Jane said as she brought the chopper up to clear a low crest and dipped down again into one of the many shallow valleys typical of the countryside. Court swiveled in her seat to take in the scene—fire trucks, police vehicles, and EMT vans with revolving emergency lights blocked the highway. She squinted against the morning sun's glare, searching for the involved vehicles. A pickup truck lay off the road on its side with a cluster of first responders ringing the wreck, another pickup crosswise farther down the highway, smoking from the front end but upright. Firefighters sprayed that one down with white flame-retardant foam. A third vehicle lay on its roof in the gully, emergency personnel at work there too. The EMTs and paramedics would already have ensured scene safety, triaged the injured, and begun extrication and emergency care of the victims. Her job would be to evaluate the injuries, stabilize the patient for transport, and render in-flight care. As Jane brought the chopper down, the scene came into clearer view, and the details crystallized. Her chest tightened, and she leaned forward as if getting closer to the window would change what she could see.

Oh my God.

"Jane," she said urgently, "do we have ID on the victims?"

"Nothing," Jane said as she set the chopper gently down just outside the ring of emergency vehicles. Phil unbuckled, pushed open the bay doors, and jumped out. Court followed automatically.

Courtney steeled herself. She might be wrong. No matter what, she had a job to do. A job that mattered now more than anything. She forced herself to follow protocol, identifying the paramedics already at work on a figure prone on the highway. She raced toward them, her pulse pounding in her throat.

"Air Star," she said, skidding to a stop and dropping to her knees. She took in the prone body in one quick glance. A young male, eyes closed, features slack, color waxen.

"Ejected from vehicle. No pulse or pressure when we arrived," the stocky, ruddy-faced paramedic said as he slid an endotracheal tube in and taped it. He gestured to the second paramedic performing CPR. "We've got a rhythm and pressure's coming up. But he's been down awhile."

"Stable to transport by ground?"

"Yeah." He tipped his head toward the overturned truck. "That one is no rush. DOA."

Court swallowed hard. The tightness in her chest was enough to make her heart stop. "What about the Subaru?"

"Single occupant. EMTs and fire rescue are working on extrication now. That one's for you." He grunted, rising to his feet. "The scene was a fucking mess when we got here. One of the locals came over for a look-see, said he saw those two trucks racing each other. Looks like they forced the Subaru off the road. Assholes."

"Thanks," Court said, the blood thundering in her ears on a dizzying wave of relief. She called to Phil as she ran for the Subaru. "Over here."

Neck, airway, circulation, extremities.
Extraction, evaluation, stabilization, transport.
She knew what to do. They all knew what to do.

❖

Ben sat at the trauma station to dictate her notes on Linda McCallum as Wakeem and a trauma nurse readied Linda for transport to the TICU. She'd be monitored there until an OR room opened up and Ben could treat her leg fractures. Linda's father, whose name Ben had learned was Curt, was already on the way to the OR. When Abby joined her, she said, "I'm on hold for now. I figured I'd stay—"

"Sorry," Pam Wendel, the charge nurse seated nearby, said, "but Air Star control is on the line for you, Dr. Remy."

Abby frowned and held out her hand. "Matt? We're just getting cleared out, but the OR's…What?"

The sudden strain in Abby Remy's tone caught Ben's attention. Abby grasped the edge of the counter, her grip on the landline turning white. "How serious?"

She glanced around the ER, her gaze clearly searching.

"Yes. Right here. ETA?…I know. I'll handle it. Where will you be?" She hung up and immediately redialed. "Patty, this is Abby. We need another room on standby right now. I don't care what you have to do—I need a room open and ready…Thanks."

Abby disconnected, took a deep breath, and walked over to Brody Clark, the flight medic who'd brought in Ben's patient. She grasped Brody's arm and said something too quietly for Ben to hear, but the reaction was clear.

Brody stiffened, a cascade of emotions flickering across her features almost too quickly to see. Confusion, shock, disbelief, and, finally, a hoarse shout.

"Brody! Wait," Abby called as Brody jerked from her grasp and raced toward the stairs.

Several staff stared after Brody, and a tech turned to Abby. "What's going on?"

"Air Star is five minutes out with another patient," Abby said, her features set in hard, determined lines. "It's Dr. Valentine."

CHAPTER EIGHT

"Hey, Blakey," Donnie Winslow said, coming up behind Blake, his shoulder bumping Blake's hard enough to almost throw him off stride. Almost. Donnie wasn't original in his taunts or his subtle physical assaults, and Blake had seen him coming around the corner as he'd headed down the east wing to chem class. He'd been expecting something like this and braced for it.

When he didn't answer, Donnie went on in a friendly tone, "Saw your name on the sign-up list for the Comets. You sure you didn't make a mistake and really mean the Blazers?"

Oren Miller, one of Donnie's crew, the kind of guy who could be always found in Donnie's shadow, snickered. Blake didn't even bother to look in his direction, just kept walking.

The Comets were the high school boys' varsity basketball team—the Blazers the girls'. When he'd enrolled as a new student after moving there between his sophomore and junior years, he'd enrolled as his real gender—male. The legal stuff like his birth certificate was taking longer to sort out, even though his mom was all over it, but his name change was legal, and besides, no matter what the paperwork said, he knew who he was.

"You know, the girls' team?" Donnie persisted.

"No, no mistake," Blake said. "The Comets."

"Because, you know, I heard you got some stuff removed," Donnie said, one hand making a suggestive gesture in front of his chest, "but"—his hand dropped to his crotch and mimed a little squeeze—"I don't think they're making these."

Blake didn't bother to tell him he was wrong about that, even if he wasn't going that way himself. He'd figured out pretty fast when he'd come out that some people didn't really want to understand or learn anything that might change their outlook or threaten what they believed. He'd never been able to quite figure out why that was, but Donnie Winslow was one of those people. Words were wasted on him. So was the energy to get angry.

"Making the team won't make you a guy," Donnie muttered, leaning close enough that his words didn't carry beyond the three of them. "I don't think you'll find any dicks in your equipment bag."

Blake sighed. Staying silent took a lot of energy too. "Thanks for the tip, Donnie, but I've got everything I need."

Donnie's eyes widened as if he hadn't quite expected that response, and it took him a few steps to come up with his next jab. "Some of the girls might think a little differently about what a guy needs. Margie, now, I bet she'd disagree."

Heat flared in Blake's chest, and he gritted his teeth. He could handle all the assholes in the world who wanted to insult him. But his friends, that was a different story. They'd stood by him, supported him, understood him. Nobody dumped on his friends. And nobody talked trash about Margie.

"You know," Donnie said, "I bet if you asked her, she'd probably even tell you she'd had some and li—"

Blake whirled, shoved both hands against Donnie's shoulders, and rocked him back against the lockers. Donnie was still a little taller, even after he'd finally had a growth spurt over the summer, but he got in Donnie's face all the same. "Shut up, Donnie."

Donnie's brows rose and his jaw worked, but no sound came out. His startled expression turned to a glower, and he shot a fist toward Blake's crotch. "Let's see what you really got."

Blake blocked instinctively, and Donnie twisted just right for Blake's knee to land soundly in his crotch. He went down, both hands between his legs, with a hoarse howl.

"What's going on," the distinctive voice of Pete Carlisle, the assistant principal, demanded.

Blake stepped back. "Nothing, just a misunderstanding."

Oren pointed at Blake. "He…he started it. He went after Donnie."

Blake clamped his mouth shut. Carlisle's expression said he wasn't buying it, though. Donnie was five inches taller than Blake and outweighed him by about forty pounds. Donnie also had the reputation of stirring up trouble, and everyone knew it. Blake had thus far managed to handle all the bullying without the episodes coming to the attention of the teachers or staff. Bringing them in would not make the bigots and bullies go away. He'd promised his parents he'd tell them if anything that happened seemed really dangerous, but so far, the worst had been taunts from jerks like Donnie.

"Blake?"

"Just a misunderstanding."

Donnie pushed himself to his knees. "You little asshole," he said, face red with rage. "You'll regret this."

"I don't think so," Blake said softly, looking Donnie squarely in the eyes.

Donnie lunged to his feet and gripped Blake's shirtfront, his other hand poised to punch.

"Whoa," Carlisle shouted, shouldering between them. With a grip on both their arms, he pushed them apart. "Okay, both of you, office."

Blake collected his backpack where it'd fallen during the altercation and hefted it over his shoulder. Ignoring the stares of the students gathered around, he didn't look at Donnie as he turned and followed Carlisle.

His phone started vibrating in his pants pocket almost immediately. He didn't need to see it to know he'd be the star of Instagram before lunch.

❖

It's Dr. Valentine.

Dread bludgeoned Ben's midsection with the force of a kick to the solar plexus. She spun to Abby. "Courtney? Courtney is the patient coming in on Air Star?"

Abby frowned, looking confused for a moment, then shook her head. "No. No. Not Courtney. *Sydney* Valentine. Brody's partner."

"Oh," Ben said, startled by the magnitude of her relief. She'd just met Courtney Valentine, but that didn't seem to matter. Courtney had appeared during one of those interludes when Ben left the present behind and returned to a time when only the rhythmic sound of a bouncing ball, the rush of her own breath, and the stretch and coil of her muscles eclipsed every other sensation. She'd looked up and known that the woman watching saw her as she saw herself, and when Courtney clearly recognized her from her previous life—on the court and in the café, even before they'd met at the hospital— that awareness built a bridge between the parts of Ben's life that had been abruptly sundered. Most of the people in her life, even Harper and Flann, knew little of those years of sacrifice and desperate dreams. Courtney had, and a link had been forged, at least for her.

Thinking Courtney had been hurt had shaken her as nothing had in years. She could only imagine—and didn't want to— Brody Clark's shock and terror when Abby had informed her of her partner's accident. Ben shied away from imagining just how terrible that news must have been. She'd seen agonizing traumas and tragedies in her life, and her training helped buffer the full brunt of the empathy that could paralyze. Now her job was to heal.

"Is someone on their way up to the flight deck to take charge of the patient? Because Brody shouldn't be up there alone when they land," Ben said. She didn't say *up there at all* because had she been in Brody's place, no one could have kept her away either.

"I know," Abby said. "Our trauma team is gearing up now to meet the helo. Glenn will look after Brody, and one of Brody's best friends is the pilot on this run too." She paused, her jaw tightening. "Oh God. I didn't even think of it—Courtney is on that helo, and she would have been in charge in the field. She shouldn't be responsible for that." She scanned the admitting area. "I've got a resident about to do a belly tap—I need to supervise her. I don't even have another resident free to send up to relieve her."

"I'm just waiting for an OR room," Ben said. "I can go. It'll just be till we get the patient down here. I think I can cover that."

"I'm sure you can," Abby said. "Thanks. This isn't usual for us. I appreciate it."

Ben shrugged. "It's why I'm here."

Abby called, "Glenn, take Ben and Sandy up to the flight deck. Get Brody down here, and have her wait in the private family room. If you could stay with her until I've seen Val, that will help. I'll let her see Val just as soon as I'm sure she's stable enough. Brody won't want to wait, but—"

"I'll handle it, Ab," Glenn said.

The ER nurse, a Black woman in scrubs, a cover gown, and Nikes, who looked like she ran marathons on her off days, joined them as they hurried toward the elevator.

"It's Val?" she said as the doors opened and they rushed inside.

"That's the report," Glenn said, her voice flat.

"Oh God," she muttered. "I hate when it's one of us. Did they say how bad?"

"Critical but stable—sounded like blunt chest trauma and extremity fractures." Glenn sucked in a breath, but her voice stayed steady. "She was conscious but disoriented in the field."

"Ah," Ben said carefully, "Val—Dr. Valentine. She's Courtney Valentine's sister?"

"No, cousin." Sandy stared at the floor numbers counting down in the elevator as if that might speed their ascent. "It's a good thing it's not Saturday, so the kids are in school this morning. God, they could've been with her."

"She and Brody have children?" Ben said automatically.

Glenn smiled as the elevator slowed and chimed, signaling the imminent opening of the doors. "No, two of our externs also work in Val's veterinary clinic. Blake Remy and Margie Rivers."

"I see." Ben *was* beginning to see. Remy and Rivers. So many lives here were somehow interconnected, in a way that most people never even thought about—generations of people had been born here, probably went to school together, knew each other's families, and when someone like Abby Remy arrived and married a longtime local like Flann Rivers, she was absorbed into the weave of the community as if she'd always been there. Friends and neighbors worked and played together. That phenomenon rarely happened in the city, where even your nearest neighbors were sometimes strangers.

Ben wasn't sure how she felt about that kind of interconnectedness. She didn't cultivate close relationships with people, not that she didn't like them. Growing up without sibs with all her focus on sports and getting an academic scholarship, her teammates had been all the friends she needed. More than friends, they'd been the family she hadn't had. When she'd moved from her high school team to college, she'd lost one family but she'd forged new ties, formed a new family. That lasted until she'd moved again to Seattle and the Storm. She'd lost another family and had just begun building yet another when her father had called, and it all had ended. Overnight she was homeless and effectively alone.

She'd been lucky enough to meet Flann and Harper during those first few chaotic weeks, and even in the midst of the competition and crushing tension of med school, they'd become friends. They weren't family, not like the women and men she'd lived with, trained with, and struggled with during her sports career, but they *were* friends. There hadn't been anyone else after they went their separate ways. Only a few short-lived affairs that she quickly discovered couldn't withstand the demands put on relationships by medical training. None of them had given her the intensity or connection she'd shared with her teammates, and letting work become her main source of satisfaction had just…happened.

"I'll look after Brody, and you two take care of getting Val transported down to the TICU," Glenn said as they exited the elevator. "Phil is with the flight team. He can give report. Tell Courtney she's relieved."

Sandy snorted but said nothing.

Glenn pushed open the door to the rooftop, and a gust of brisk air carrying the scent of motor oil and sunshine accompanied the rhythmic *whump-whump-whump* of rotors churning overhead. Ben halted just outside the landing zone marked out in wide bands of white paint on the flight deck tarmac, narrowing her eyes against the glare. The helicopter, nose tilted slightly down, swayed faintly as it slowly descended to the center of the landing zone. Brody Clark stood at the edge of the LZ, her body rigid, straining against the buffeting downdraft, poised to sprint toward the helo.

Glenn raced over to Brody, flung an arm around her shoulders, and shouted something to her. Brody gave a hard head shake and tried to pull away, but Glenn, still shouting, hung on. The helo had barely set down with a whoosh, rotors still whirling, when the broad bay doors slid open, and Courtney looked out. Ben lowered her head and shouldered through the still buffeting rotor churn, her gaze fixed on Courtney.

❖

Court crouched in the open bay by the head of the stretcher as Phil jumped down to take the other end. She squinted against the backdraft into the brightly lit landing zone. Figures moved into view, the person she hadn't expected to see capturing her attention instantly. Ben was there. The crushing fear threatening to overtake her eased a fraction. She didn't have time to wonder why. She didn't have time to feel frightened or wonder why seeing Ben calmed her or even to scream, although parts of her wanted to do all that and more.

Only one thing mattered.

Leaning down, she said, "Val, we landed. You're going to be all right. We're at the Rivers."

Val had been unresponsive when the EMTs and firefighters had finally cut open enough of the wreckage to extract her, the process taking so long Court could barely stop herself from exhorting them to hurry. Extrication was one of the most dangerous times during a trauma event for victims and first responders alike, but God, she just wanted them to get Val out of that twisted wreck. Out where she could *do* something.

Standing by, biting her lip to hold back the demands to *Hurry, damn it*, she'd felt as helpless as she had when she'd had to watch her father spiral into despair and her mother retreat from reality. No, no. That was wrong. She'd left all that behind—she was not helpless, and Val would not be just another victim this time. Once they'd gained access to the driver's compartment, now crushed into a narrow wedge barely resembling a passenger space, a paramedic secured the cervical collar while Val was still inside and meticulously maneuvered her onto a backboard. Only then did they extricate her from the wreck.

Court raced to them as they strapped Val to the stretcher. To her great relief, Val was breathing on her own, although shallowly, and both lungs sounded clear. The first blood pressure reading was alarmingly low. Seventy palp, and a copious amount of blood stained the right leg of her jeans and what Court could see of the driver's seat. The medics quickly inserted IVs, one in each arm, while still at the crash site, and started the resuscitation fluids running in full-bore. Court checked Val's pupils, experiencing another wave of relief when she found them to be equal and reactive. At least Val had no localizing intracranial injuries. A laceration just below her hairline, accompanied by pain and blood loss, likely explained her loss of consciousness.

"Let's move," Court shouted when they'd finished the initial stabilization.

Both medics nodded and lifted the stretcher. Court ran alongside, watching the monitors. Once inside the helo, she listened again for breath sounds, checked that the heart sounds were still clear and strong, and moved on to assess the rest of Val's body. Phil applied a moist saline dressing to the forehead laceration, secured it in place, and hooked up the EKG leads.

A ragged tear in Val's blood-soaked jeans extended from her right knee down to the ankle. Court viewed the fracture site in the mid-tibia exposed by a deep crushing wound, and for an instant, her stomach clenched. But she'd seen this before, and she concentrated on the work, refusing to allow herself to think about Val or her pain or what she might face in the weeks to come.

"We'll need a vacuum splint," she said to Phil as he adjusted the IV fluids.

"Got it," he said, swiveling around to extract the splint from an equipment case bolted to the inside of the helo.

Court wrapped the wound in sterile dressings and applied the splint from above the knee to the foot. The flight back passed in a blur as they monitored Val's vital signs. Just as Jane announced two minutes to landing, Val's eyelids fluttered, and she murmured something incomprehensible. Court took her hand and leaned closer.

"Val, it's Courtney," she said again. "We're on our way to the Rivers. You're going to be okay."

Val's eyes opened, the pupils unfocused and dazed. "Court?"

"Yeah, it's me, Val. You were in an accident, but you're going to be okay."

"How…bad?"

"Your neck and spine look okay," Court said, knowing that's the first thing she'd want to know. "You're banged up but stable. A leg fracture."

"Look after Brody," Val murmured faintly. "And Honcho."

Court swallowed hard. "Yeah, don't worry. They'll be fine. We'll take care of you and them."

Val grimaced and closed her eyes.

Court fought the helpless feeling again. All she knew how to do was what she was doing. The medicine she understood. She didn't have a clue about taking care of a person in emotional pain.

Bracing herself against the buffeting backdraft, she caught sight of Ben sprinting toward her. There was no reason for Ben to be there, but she was. And she couldn't help but feel, as foolish as the thought might be, that Ben was there for her.

CHAPTER NINE

Ducking as the rotors slowly settled, Ben jogged across the LZ and grasped the end of the stretcher to help Phil ease it to the tarmac. Courtney jumped down and lowered the other end.

Phil shouted to be heard above the engine noise as the pilot shut down the aircraft. "Stable vitals, head and extremity injuries, rule out closed thoracic and abdominal trauma."

Sandy grabbed hold on one side of the stretcher and Ben took the other, turning to Courtney as they propelled the patient toward the open elevators on the far side of the flight deck.

"Courtney," Ben said, "we can take it from here. Why don't you debrief with the flight crew."

"No," Courtney said, "I'm staying with her until we're sure."

They'd only taken a few steps when Brody broke out of Glenn's grasp and raced toward them. Ben briefly considered intercepting her, but keeping her away from her partner now was likely to be more traumatic than letting her see her. Brody was a professional, and she might be able to control her panic better once she saw that Val was stable.

"Val," Brody said, her voice low and urgent as she grasped Val's hand. "It's Brody, baby. I'm right here. Baby?"

Val's eyes remained closed, her face below the bandage on her forehead pale and slack. Brody stared at Courtney, raw fear in her eyes. "Did she talk to you, Court? Was she conscious? God, baby."

"For a few seconds, Brody," Court said as they reached the elevator. "She woke up on the helo. She knew me."

"What else—what are we looking at here?"

"BP's down to ninety," Sandy said as they pushed the stretcher into the elevator.

"Open up the IVs," Ben said calmly. "Courtney, would you please take Brody to the family waiting area when we get downstairs."

Court spared her a glance, her eyes flashing with resistance. "I…" She paused when Ben tipped her head in Brody's direction, and Courtney's expression changed to one of resigned acceptance. "Yes, of course."

"Thank you."

"I'm not leaving her," Brody said without looking up from where she leaned over Val, one hand brushing a smudge of dirt from her cheek.

"Brody—" Ben began.

Courtney broke in, "You need to let everyone work, Brody. You know that. Abby is waiting, and Glenn and Sandy and Ben have everything under control. You don't want to get in the way of them taking care of Val."

"I won't," Brody rasped, looking up, her eyes dark pools of anguish. "I swear. Please, Court."

Impressed with Courtney's gentle command but worried about how much more stress Courtney could take after handling a family member's acute injury, Ben said, "Brody, I want you to listen to Courtney. That's the best thing you can do for Val right now. Courtney will wait with you, and Abby will come talk to you after she's sure Val is stable."

Brody's shoulders sagged, and she nodded. "Do you promise to hurry?"

"As soon as Val is settled and safe, I swear."

Mutely, Brody nodded and went back to stroking Val's face. "I won't be far, baby. Just around the corner. You're going to be okay. Abby will take care of you."

Abby, not Courtney.

Courtney winced, but when the elevator doors slid open, she said, "Come on, Brody. Abby's waiting for them. She's going to be well taken care of."

Of course Brody would put all her faith in Abby. Who wouldn't?

She was just a resident, after all, and barely family, no matter how playfully Brody called her *cousin*. She squared her shoulders. None of this was about her or her hang-ups anyhow. She was a doctor, no one else. Her guilt over her crappy treatment of Val nearly a decade ago didn't matter right now.

Brody brushed a hand over Val's hair and looked up at Courtney, her narrowed gaze angry now. "Tell me everything you know about what happened out there."

Courtney drew in a breath, her chin lifting. "I will. As soon as we get to the waiting room."

The doors opened, and Court stepped back from the stretcher as Sandy and Glenn checked lines and Ben scanned the monitors to be sure nothing had changed on the short ride down. She took Brody's arm, wary that Brody might resist leaving at the last minute. Ben glanced at her and nodded again.

"Let's go, Brody," Court said, firmly grasping her arm.

Brody leaned down and kissed Val's cheek. "I won't be far. I love you."

When she stepped back, her eyes dark and unwavering, Court glanced at Ben. "Will you be sure someone comes to talk to us?"

"As soon as possible. I promise," Ben said. "And Courtney— you need some time to decompress too. That was a tough situation out there, and you handled it."

Courtney stared, relief and gratitude threatening to crack the wall she'd put up to keep her fear and worry at bay.

As if Ben could see her wavering, she said, "Good work."

"Thanks," Court whispered as Ben hurried away.

In addition to the main trauma waiting area, several small private rooms had been designated for families of acute care trauma patients. No one other than Court and Brody occupied the small, windowless space furnished with the ubiquitous blue wear-forever fabric sofa and matching chairs, a low oak-veneer coffee table, and a tiny corner stand bearing tea bags, packets of creamer and sweeteners, and instant coffee next to a hot-cold water cooler.

Court said, "Do you want something to drink?"

Brody shook her head, pacing in a tight circle on the beige industrial strength carpet. She halted abruptly, her eyes blazing.

"What the hell happened out there? I only caught the tail end of the alert. Three-vehicle collision? On a country road with almost no traffic?"

"I…" Court hesitated. She didn't know all the details, didn't even know the name of the deceased or the patient being transported by ambulance. "I don't know, Brody. Besides Val's SUV, I saw two pickups off the road. I'm sure the sheriff will fill you in as soon as they know more."

Abruptly, Brody sank into a chair and put her head in her hands, staring at the floor between her black flight boots. "Yeah. Like it really matters."

Helplessness was not a feeling Court tolerated very well. She'd chosen medicine and then surgery so she could *do* something about a problem. Assess, recommend, treat. Lots of professions might have fit the bill, but surgery had a built-in caveat that suited her perfectly. Distance. The OR was a sanctuary where she could do the very best job possible while the patient slept. So far her dependence on emotional remove had not been tested. Even her worry over Mike Wells's abdominal pain—and God, how long had it been…she needed to check that he'd gotten his CT—had not been something she shared with him. She cared—so she could fix, not comfort.

And she was failing big-time now.

"Brody," she murmured, resting a hand on Brody's back. "Val is going to be okay."

"You don't know that," Brody whispered.

Court discarded all the platitudes they both knew were meaningless. "She's at the Rivers, Brody, and that's all that matters."

Brody held out a hand, and Court took it. Wordlessly, they waited.

❖

When they rolled into trauma admitting, Abby said briskly, pointing to an open bay, "In there."

While Sandy and Glenn directed Val's stretcher inside, Ben waited and gave Abby a brief rundown of Val's status. The swarm of activity had already begun, the choreographed symphony of everyone working in tandem, knowing what needed to be done. Ben deflated the vacuum splint Courtney had placed while the primary trauma team worked. A jagged laceration extended from just below Val's knee halfway to her ankle. When she gently palpated the surrounding tissue, motion at the site confirmed the fracture. Grimacing, she plucked a shard of metal and a scrap of blue denim from the depths of the wound. When Abby was happy that Val was stable, Ben asked the X-ray technician to get the portable X-rays she needed.

A few minutes later, she stood in front of another array of X-ray images, studying the comminuted fracture in Val's lower leg. Abby appeared at her shoulder and peered at the screen.

"Hell. That's not going to be stable in a cast. Can you plate that?"

"Not right away," Ben said. "Too contaminated to risk infection. This will need a washout and an external fixator until we're sure the wound is clean. Then bone grafts and internal fixation."

"What's the prognosis?" Abby asked.

"Overall," Ben said, "good. She'll need a fair amount of rehab."

"How big a rush on the washout?" Abby asked. "She needs to go down for a head CT, and that could take an hour or more unless I push."

"I'll order the antibiotics," Ben said. "She ought to go up before Linda, though."

"Let the OR know that," Abby said.

"Sure."

"Dr. Remy," one of the ER staff called, "we need you in one."

Abby blew out a breath. "That's the belly tap. I gotta go. Can you talk to Brody? I'd rather it was one of us."

"Of course."

Ben double-checked that Val was stable and headed down the hall before realizing she didn't know where she was going. She stopped a tech passing by. "Excuse me, I'm looking for the private family waiting rooms?"

The tech frowned. "I'm sorry, who are you?"

"Ben Anderson, ortho staff."

"Oh," he said, his expression clearing, "sorry, Doc. Yeah, right around the corner, first door on your left."

"Thank you."

She knocked on the door, opened it, and stepped inside. Brody and Courtney sat side by side on a sofa. Courtney held Brody's hand. No one else was in the room.

Both shot to their feet.

Brody took a step forward, her shoulders tense, both fists bunched, as if readying for a fight. Her gaze locked on Ben's, wary but blazing.

"Abby's with another patient, but your partner is stable," Ben said immediately. For some family that would be enough—enough for the frantic fear to dissolve into tears of hope and relief. It wouldn't be for her. Or Brody. "Vital signs are good. There's blood on standby, but so far her pressure has responded to fluids. She's not fully conscious yet, but her neuro exam doesn't show anything focal. Chest and abdomen exams are negative. She'll be going down for the head CT and the rest as soon as things open up there. She's got a comminuted fracture of the right tibia which is going to require surgery, also as soon as I can get her upstairs."

Brody said, "Can I see her now?"

"Abby said to tell you yes, for a few—"

Brody barged out the door, leaving Ben and Courtney alone. Ben wanted to ask Courtney how she was doing but held back. She didn't want to give Courtney the impression she didn't think she could handle an emergency, even though this one was far from ordinary. She wouldn't ask anyone else that question, but she cared about Courtney more than anyone else, and that left her asking why. Not a question she had time to examine. Plus, despite the connection she sensed between them, their link was fragile—woven as much from what they *hadn't* said as from what they had. Theirs was merely the first tentative tether between strangers who touched each other in an unusual and unexpected way. Most of all, she didn't want to intrude. She didn't want to go where she wasn't welcome.

"I should get to the OR," Courtney said into the silence. The adrenaline surge from the trauma alert hadn't abated, leaving her pupils dilated and a fine tremor coursing through her hands.

This Ben knew what to do about. "You need something to eat. The OR can wait."

Courtney grimaced. "The OR can never wait."

"Sometimes it has to. Besides, these are exceptional circumstances."

"Aren't they all?" Courtney said with a dullness to her tone that Ben hadn't heard before.

"Sometimes it seems that way," she repeated. She held out a hand, not touching her, just gently beckoning. "Come on. I'll buy you breakfast. I haven't eaten either."

Court followed her a few steps toward the door, then hesitated. "Yes, you have. At the café."

Ben grinned. "Well, that was yesterday, wasn't it?"

"Feels like it." Courtney gave a shaky laugh. "I'm okay, but thanks for the offer."

"Look," Ben said. "I'm waiting on a call for my first case in the OR. Once I get started, I don't know when I'll get done. So I'm in need of fuel too."

"Okay."

Courtney nodded more briskly this time, as if hearing that Ben needed something gave her permission to admit she did too. Funny how that worked. One of the first axioms Ben had heard when she'd started her residency, which truly *did* feel like a lifetime ago, was that to ask for help was a sign of weakness. She understood the theory behind it and subscribed to it herself, up to a point. Self-sufficiency, the imperative to learn to make decisions and to trust those decisions, was a critical part of the training. While essential, it also fostered a sense of isolation and an unwillingness to admit fatigue, fear, or uncertainty that could lead to bad decisions. Residency training was long and intense to allow for balance between independent, safe decision-making and supportive teaching.

Courtney said, "I should call my chief and let him know where I am."

"Do that. I'll call the OR and see what the time estimate looks like," Ben said.

They made the calls before they left the cocoon of the secluded waiting area. Ben held the door for Courtney, and they walked away from the muted cacophony drifting from trauma admitting.

"I saw Syd's car from the helo," Courtney said into the burgeoning silence, her tone that same flat monotone, so different from the animated, vibrant voice Ben had heard earlier. "I panicked. My mind went completely blank, and all I wanted to do was run away." She snorted. "Being five hundred feet up in a helicopter might have been the only thing stopping me."

"Yeah, I know that feeling," Ben said.

Courtney shot her a glance, a little suspicious, a little...relieved. "You do?"

Ben nodded. "Not for the same reasons, but I remember..." She shook her head. This was about Courtney. "Never mind."

"No, tell me," Courtney said urgently, as if she needed to hear what Ben had to say.

Maybe she needed to know someone else had felt that terrifying vulnerability. Maybe that would erase some of the bitter self-recrimination in her voice.

Ben took a breath. "I was senior on call in the house, and I got a stat page from a service I wasn't even covering. Head, neck, and throat surgery. Blown carotid."

Courtney's eyes brightened a little, the dull haze giving way to a spark of animation. "Whoa. How far away were you?"

Ben grinned. "I was still in pretty good shape, even though I hadn't run a full-court press in..." She caught herself. "Well, I could run, and believe me, I *ran*. It was three in the morning, and the halls were empty, and of course, the ENT ICU was all the way in another building. I must've made it in under a minute."

"You can pump a lot of blood out of the carotid in under a minute," Courtney said, her gaze riveted, and their steps slowing as they talked.

"The nurses were good and had pressure on it. But there was a hell of a lot of blood."

"And?" Courtney said.

"I got on a pair of gloves, put my hand over the nurse's, and she slid hers off the pressure bandage. When I lifted the gauze, I got hit with a gusher. That convinced me what it was, and for just a second, everything stopped. I didn't know who I was. I didn't know where I was. And I didn't know what the fuck...excuse me..."

Courtney laughed. "Oh yeah, right. Like I've never heard it before? Come on—what happened?"

"Like I said—when it really hit me that I was supposed to know what to do, I panicked."

"What changed it?" Courtney asked quietly.

"His eyes were open," Ben said, caught in that moment in time again. "He knew it was bad."

"Man, that's tough," Courtney whispered. "What did you do?"

"I stuck my finger in the incision, right on the carotid, and the bleeding stopped."

"Yeah, but—"

"Yeah," Ben said, nodding. "I couldn't move because he'd bleed out. Of course it was the middle of one of the worst thunderstorms we'd had in a while, and it took half an hour for the attending surgeon to get in. So I just stood there, with my finger in his neck, waiting."

Courtney shoved the stairwell door open. "No elevators, right?"

Ben smiled. "Right. So—what did it for you? What got your head straight?"

"I saw the Subaru, and even though the clinic logo on the side was almost scraped off," Courtney said as they started to climb, "I knew right away. Like you said—I wanted it to be someone else in that car. Anyone else. But I knew. *I* wanted to be somewhere else. Anywhere else. But I was trapped in the helo with Jane and Phil. Phil is really good and so is Jane, but it was my responsibility. My job."

"Yeah."

"And I thought, if Val knew it was me, she might be afraid I wouldn't take care of her."

Ben didn't ask why. That was a different story, and one Courtney would have to decide to tell her. Or not.

Court took a deep breath. "And I needed her to know that wasn't true. No matter who was in that car, I would do my best, but for Val, I'd do anything. Anything at all. I had to be sure she knew that."

Ben said, "Traumas like that are pretty terrifying, no matter what. But when it's family…" She shook her head. "You did great, Courtney. You did exactly what you were supposed to do in the toughest of situations."

Courtney stopped in the middle of the hall and faced Ben. The bustle of cafeteria noises carried through the open doors twenty feet away as people passed on either side. The chestnut brown of her eyes blurred for an instant, and Ben's chest tightened. Courtney's pain was so bright that anywhere else, with anyone else, she might have been compelled to touch her, but she couldn't. Shouldn't. Not when Courtney was so vulnerable, and for a dozen other reasons.

"Courtney," she murmured.

"No—I'm good," Courtney said, the light returning to her voice. "I am. Thank you. You didn't have to tell me that. Any of it."

Ben didn't correct her, didn't say she'd had to do something, anything, to help ease the pain Courtney didn't deserve. Instead she said, "You're welcome. Now can we please eat?"

Courtney laughed, and the sound was magic.

CHAPTER TEN

The intercom crackled to life in Flann's OR room, and Patty Sullivan said, "Dr. Rivers, there's a call for you."

Frowning, Flann stared over at the intercom as if Patty could see her face. "I'm a little busy here, Patty. Page one of the residents for whatever it is."

"I know that. I can see you working on the monitor," Patty said with just the slightest bit of asperity in her voice.

Flann smiled behind her mask. Patty wasn't even ten years her senior, but she'd been the OR supervisor since before she'd gotten her MD. Patty ruled the OR, and Flann shuddered to think what might happen if Patty ever decided to retire. There was likely to be bloodshed over who had rights to OR time.

"Take a message, would you?" Flann said, pointing to the ends of bowel that needed to be reconnected. "Start at the corner with that first suture, Brewster."

"I would do that too," Patty said, sounding a little less hassled, "but it's the high school, and they want to talk to you or your wife. I checked, and Dr. Remy is in the midst of multiple traumas downstairs. Can I tell them when you will be able to call back?"

Flann's stomach tightened. She'd been apprised of the situation in trauma admitting by Grady McClure. Abby had several patients who needed emergency surgery—one of whom was Val—and Flann had to somehow find OR rooms where rooms just didn't exist. She had zero time to spare, but the school did not call for no reason during the middle of the day.

"Did they say it was an emergency?"

"No, and I asked. Not a medical emergency, but they'd like you to call as soon as possible. That's all they would tell me."

"I've got twenty minutes here until I can step out."

"I'll give the operator the number you'll need."

"Thanks, Patty."

The intercom static disappeared, and Flann glanced across the table at Doug Brewster, a fourth-year resident. He had good hands and a level head, but she couldn't leave him alone until the bowel repair was done. "I'd like to get this anastomosis done before tomorrow, Dr. Brewster. Let's say we pick up the pace a little."

"Can do," he said quietly, continuing in his methodical and careful way to place the sutures exactly the way she had shown him.

Flann approved. Hasty surgery was never wise. If that's the pace he needed to be certain he was doing a good job, then that's the pace they would go.

Twenty-five minutes later, they'd completed suturing the abdominal fascia, leaving only the skin and tissue directly beneath it to close. From there on out it was routine, and she'd be less than a minute away if she left him to finish.

"I'm going to go take this call. Then I'll be in the lounge. Call me when you're ready to extubate."

"Will do," Doug said.

Flann stepped back from the table and looked over the anesthesia screen. "You good up here?"

Claire D'Angelo, the nurse anesthetist, nodded. "Not much blood loss. She's stable."

"He'll be about fifteen minutes with the rest of the closure. Any problems, I'll be right outside."

"That's fine." Claire was an Army Reserve colonel, and if Flann or one of the family needed surgery, Claire would be high on her list of who she'd want administering anesthesia.

"Thanks." Flann stripped off her gown and gloves, tossed them in the bins, and left the OR. At the nearest wall phone, she rang the operator and said, "It's Flann Rivers. Patty Sullivan left a number with you. Can you connect me?"

"I will do that, Dr. Rivers," the operator said briskly, adding, "I have the message from Patty with the number right here."

The line rang twice and was picked up by a young man who

said, "Central County High School, Mr. Carlisle's office. How may I help you?"

The principal's office. That was unexpected, and a hell of a lot better than the school medical office.

"This is Flann Rivers. I got a message to call. Is my son all right?"

"Hold on just a second, Dr. Rivers. I'll get Mr. Carlisle."

Flann gritted her teeth. She understood protocol and hierarchy, but really, would it have been so hard for him to simply say Blake was all right?

She was already feeling a little heated when Pete Carlisle came on the phone, saying, "Flann, Pete Carlisle. Thanks for getting back to me."

"We're in the middle of a hell of a morning over at the Rivers, Pete. What's going on?"

"Well, we're having a bit of a morning here too," he said in his usual laconic, unruffled tone. "Blake and Donnie Winslow got into a little tussle in the hall."

"Donnie Winslow," Flann muttered, her temper rising a notch. "Blake's all right?"

"He's fine. There's not a mark on either one of them, other than perhaps a little ego bruising."

"This isn't the first time Winslow has messed with Blake. If Donnie Winslow put his hands on him, I'm going to bring charges."

"Whoa, slow down a little bit, Flann," Pete said, "and I'll tell you what seems to have gone down. At least what we know. Neither boy is saying much."

Apparently, Pete hadn't witnessed the whole altercation, so exactly who made first contact wasn't clear, and neither Blake nor Donnie would say. Oren Miller, Donnie's henchman—okay, maybe that description was being a little extreme—insisted Blake started it.

"That's not Blake's style," Flann said. "He's steady. He's got a cool temper. Donnie Winslow is not the first little asshole who's called him names. Isn't there something you can do about that? I thought the school district preached zero tolerance for bullying."

"We do, and we mean it," Pete said with an edge to his voice. "And if I'd witnessed it happening or someone brought a complaint to me, I would investigate it. If proven, we'd suspend the students involved. But that hasn't happened in this case." He grunted. "Or in any case to date."

"Come on, Pete," Flann said, annoyance adding more heat to her temper. "You know these kids aren't going to come to you and complain. That would earn them more social ostracism than the bullying. You remember how it was. Kids will swallow a lot not to appear like losers in front of their friends."

"But you know that Blake has had some issues."

"Sure, he's told us. What we haven't seen for ourselves."

"Then you can make a complaint in his place."

Flann snorted. Nice move, throwing it back on her. "Right. And what will that do to the trust between me and my son?"

"I get it," Pete said. "It's not an easy issue. We're always struggling to balance what's best for the student in terms of their safety versus their sense of autonomy."

"I understand it's a thin line that separates the two, but they're still kids. They still deserve to be protected. And Blake..." Flann sucked in a breath. "Blake is in a particularly vulnerable situation."

"Blake isn't the only queer kid," Pete said reasonably, "and the teachers and staff are sensitive to those issues."

"He's the only trans kid."

"Maybe," Pete said, "but we don't know that. Not unless they self-identify publicly, and sometimes they can't. Not every family is as supportive as yours. You know that."

Flann rubbed the bridge of her nose. None of this was Pete's fault, and she knew he was sympathetic. But feeling as if her hands were tied made her nuts. "Yeah, I know. I know. God damn it. What's wrong with people?"

Pete sighed. "I can't answer that, and I can't change it. We have to deal with what we have in front of us. Right now, it's two boys involved in a little physical roughhousing in the hall. I don't want to suspend either one of them. But I need you to come on down while I talk to Blake about it. I need your backup here, Flann."

"You've got it. I want him to tell us if this thing is escalating. But we really are up to our ass in emergencies here, Pete. I don't know if Abby can get free, but as soon as one of us is available, we'll be there."

"I appreciate it. For now, Blake is going back to class, just like Donnie."

"You should probably know that Blake is trying out for the Comets. I've played pickup ball some with him—he's good. Quick hands and covers the court in a flash. In any other world he should make the team. If he does—or if he doesn't—it could spike some controversy from both sides."

Pete was silent a moment. "He's really pretty fast?"

"Faster than anyone I've seen on the floor for the Comets so far."

"Point guard fast?"

"Plenty enough."

"We could use some speed there."

Flann laughed, the humor bittersweet. As if it could be that simple. In any other scenario, the coaches would be *recruiting* Blake to play—instead of all of them wondering if his gender identity was going to create a barrier. But this was Blake's reality—*their* reality—and simple was not in the cards. "Just giving you a heads-up."

"Appreciate it. I might drop by for the tryouts."

"Thanks." Flann disconnected and sighed. Whatever had happened, it wasn't just Donnie Winslow taunting Blake. That was old news, and Blake was used to it. The fact that he had to be used to it made Flann's head pound every time she thought of it, but she and Abby tried to follow Blake's lead in all of this. There were limits to that, though, and they'd find out if the line had been crossed once she or Abby could get to the school.

First she needed to deal with the OR situation. She picked up the phone and punched in the number for the medical chief of staff.

❖

Ben and Courtney had just started along the cafeteria line when their phones buzzed simultaneously. Ben pulled hers from her pocket. 2420. That number she knew. "It's the OR. I better get it."

Courtney checked hers. "Flight deck. I gotta get this too."

A young woman with short black curls and warm brown skin, who looked about twenty but whose name tag read Aurora Comfy, Medical Resident, said from behind them in line, "Go ahead. You can jump back in after you call."

"Owe you, Aurora," Courtney said.

"Thanks," Ben said, stepping out of line in search of a quiet corner to call from.

Call finished, Ben gestured to Aurora. "You should go ahead of us."

Courtney nodded to the guy in rumpled green scrubs and tired eyes behind Aurora. "Thanks for letting us cut back in."

The guy shrugged. "No problem. I'm going home after this."

"That was the OR," Ben said as she opted for oatmeal and blueberries. She'd already had her allotment of morning fat at the café. "Patty Sullivan said she found me a room. Something called the amphitheater?"

"Wow, really?" Courtney said. "I can't ever remember anyone operating in there."

"At this point I'd operate anywhere. I'll be able to get your cousin up in about an hour—just waiting for an anesthetist."

Courtney said softly, "That's great."

"Everything okay with Air Star?"

"Oh yeah. That was Jane, the Air Star pilot who brought Val in. She's Brody's best friend. She's going to come down and join us if you don't mind."

"No, of course not."

They found a small table by the wide wall of windows overlooking rolling lawns and shrubs still green with the last valiant heat of September. She sighed and started in on her oatmeal.

"You okay?" Courtney instantly winced as if wanting to take the words back.

Surprised, Ben said, "Yes, why?"

"Um…" Courtney flushed. "Jeez, this is embarrassing."

"Can't be that bad. You don't know me well enough yet to say anything truly offensive." She smiled when she said it.

Courtney's blush seemed to deepen. "You sighed. I don't know, it just sounded…sad. And, wow, am I humiliated now."

Ben sipped her coffee, buying a little time. She couldn't

remember the last time anyone had asked a personal question of her. "I'm not sad. Nostalgic, maybe." She gestured to the window. "I've always had this thing about the end of summer. It's always seemed a little bittersweet to me. And this place is a little disorienting—not in a bad way, just an unexpected way. I've never seen a hospital like it. Walking in was a little bit like being tossed back in time."

"I forget you've just started here," Courtney said. "It seems like you've always—well, anyhow..." She looked away, shaking her head. "Everybody who grows up in the village knows the Rivers family and their history with the hospital. We all knew that the Rivers kids were going to be doctors, but this place defines all of us in some way. It's our past and our future."

"I've heard this before," Ben said, laughing softly. "From Flann and Harper when we were students. Apparently, it's something in the water here."

Courtney laughed. Again, that burst of music unlike anything Ben had heard before. "You went to school with them?"

"I did, by chance, really—I wouldn't have been in their class since I had a deferral to join the WNBA draft but—" Ben caught herself. "Anyhow, I think I understand what you're saying about this place."

Ben paused when the blonde from the café appeared by Courtney's side. Ben hadn't seen her come up. She'd been too engrossed in Courtney.

"I don't want to interrupt, Court," the blonde said. "I just wanted to check in after this morning. Are you okay?"

Courtney smiled. "I'm good—we all did good out there."

Jane nodded. "We did."

Gesturing to a chair, Courtney said. "Sit down."

The blonde held out a hand to Ben. "Jane Montgomery. Air Star."

"Ben Anderson. New guy."

Courtney snorted and Jane laughed.

"Usually new guy means, like, first-year resident," Jane said, "and I could be wrong, but you don't have that vibe."

"Oh?" Ben said.

Jane nodded seriously. "Yeah, I don't see any panic, fear sweat, or fake bravado."

"I'm really glad to hear that." Ben smiled. "I'm ortho staff, but I *am* the new guy."

"She's more than that," Courtney put in. "Ben...sorry, Dr. Anderson is the head of our new sports medicine department."

"That's great. With what we're bringing in from the field these days, we'll need that kind of rehab." Jane glanced at Courtney. "Anything yet about Val?"

Courtney took a long breath. "She's stable, but she'll need surgery as soon as a room clears."

"What about Brody," Jane said softly. "I didn't want to intrude, but this is gonna be tough."

"She's with Val right now. She's okay. Shook up."

Jane nodded. "Listen, I told Matt to find a replacement for me for the rest of my shift. Someone's going to need to take care of Honcho, and she doesn't like strangers. She knows me. Could you tell Brody when you see her that I'm heading out to her place."

"Oh my God. I didn't think about Honcho. I should have." She blinked before squaring her shoulders. "Val even said—look out for Brody *and* Honcho. Of course she would think of the dog. I don't know why I didn't."

"You were pretty busy out there." Jane shook her head. "That scene was a mess. The accident investigators are still working, but there was an eyewitness. It's pretty clear the two pickups were in some kind of race, or maybe road rage. Looks like Val swerved but had to go off the road to avoid them when they crashed into each other."

Ben said, "It's probably best that Brody doesn't hear about it just yet. The sheriff's people will talk to her at some point."

Courtney nodded. "Once Val is awake and can talk to her, she'll be a hundred times more rational."

"Okay, good." Jane rose. "I've got keys to their place so I can feed Honcho when they're both out on emergencies. I'm going to head over there now. I just wanted to check in."

"Hey, thanks, Jane." Courtney slid her hand onto Jane's arm and squeezed.

Jane smiled. "No problem, babe."

Ben caught the easy intimacy between them. Something there, like she'd figured earlier. Not surprising. Courtney was vibrant and bright and beautiful…why wouldn't she be involved? Ben blinked and brought her focus back to the patients she needed to care for. "I ought to get back to trauma admitting."

Courtney stood quickly. "I have a CAT scan on a patient in the ER I need to check."

On her way to leave her tray on the conveyor, Ben's phone buzzed again. So did Courtney's.

She checked the number as Courtney checked hers.

"Trauma admitting," Ben said, the familiar surge of adrenaline accompanying the expectation of a new problem.

"Me too," Courtney said.

Ben called down, listened for a moment, then disconnected and glanced at Courtney. "That was Abby. Val's awake and wants to talk to me."

Courtney's brows rose. "That was Brody. Val wants to talk to me too."

CHAPTER ELEVEN

When Court and Ben got to trauma admitting, Brody was waiting for them outside the automatic double doors. Despite appearing like she'd lost ten pounds in the last hour, Brody looked better than the last time Court had seen her. Some of the color and vitality had returned to her face, and her eyes had lost their desolate, haunted sheen.

"She's awake," Court said, squeezing Brody's hand. "That's so great."

"Yeah," Brody said, her voice still raspy, as if she hadn't used it for a while or had been straining to hold back tears.

Court's heart twisted. If only she could do something, say something that would help. Brody had to be scared still, knowing all that lay ahead for Val, even if everything went perfectly. Brody was a veteran of war, abroad and at home—a double-edged sword at times like this. She wouldn't panic or be overwhelmed by the complexities of Val's care as many non-medical professionals often were, but she'd also know all the things that could go wrong. And she'd know better than most how much Val would have to go through before she put all this behind her. Court didn't doubt, though, that Brody would be there for Val every step of the way—while *she* would have to be happy just offering what she could, her support and medical assistance.

As the doors swung open, Brody asked Ben, "Do you know when you'll be taking her up?"

"Within the hour," Ben said.

"And what do you need to…" Brody ran a hand through her hair. "Never mind. I'll find out when you tell Val." She grinned fleetingly, her expression a little wry. "Val is awake but just barely. Abby says we've got five minutes. She's taking a tough stand on visitors."

"That's the protocol," Ben said, her tone light and her smile easy. "And it's the right way to do this. When medical people cut corners for family or friends, even bending rules as simple as visitors, mistakes get made. We don't want that."

"I know," Brody said, "but it's so damn hard to leave her. She's…" Brody looked away, her jaw tensing. "She's hurting."

Court's throat tightened. Ben was right, and Brody knew it. So did she. Gently, she said, "We should go see her. We're on a time limit, after all."

Brody laughed softly, a gratifying sound, and the bees swarming in Court's stomach eased off a little. This was horrible, and she needed to be a whole lot more together, starting now. She'd been through the worst of it, after all. She'd witnessed Val lying in the twisted wreck, helpless while the rescue team worked feverishly to get her out. Here in trauma admitting, Val was as safe as she could possibly be. Everyone in there was focused on making sure of that.

Court glanced at Ben, who was watching her. She lifted her chin and held Ben's gaze. After a second, Ben nodded and looked away, apparently satisfied with what she'd seen in Court's eyes. A surge of pride chased away the last of Court's uncertainty.

The curtains were closed around two of the trauma bays. The low murmur of many people talking at once emanated from bay three, signifying an alert in progress. That was probably the other victim from the accident.

Brody opened the curtain around bay one, moved to the side of the treatment table, and said, "Honey, Court and the ortho surgeon are here."

Court followed Ben around to the opposite side of the table.

Two steps in, she froze, her breath caught in her throat.

The scene was completely familiar—bright, too-harsh lights shining down on a patient supine on the table, nearly invisible beneath an array of tubes, monitors, dressings, and splints. Why she'd expected Val to be sitting up, regarding them with her usual intense, appraising expression, she didn't know. This was Val as she had never known her—not accomplished, always certain, successful Sydney Valentine, DVM. This was a severely injured woman who had to be frightened and in pain, leaving Court with one less anchor in her frequently shifting world.

When Ben moved forward and leaned over into Val's line of vision, Court recognized her role—she was a resident, and she was here to learn as well as to treat. She eased closer to hear what Ben would say.

"Dr. Valentine," Ben said quietly. "I'm Ben Anderson, one of the ortho surgeons. How are you doing?"

"Seen better days," Val said in a voice Court didn't recognize.

Ben chuckled. "I can totally believe that. Let me tell you what's going on with your leg."

Court had heard similar explanations hundreds of times before as others informed patients about their injuries, outlined treatment plans and options, described possible complications and projected outcomes, but this time every word made an indelible impression in her brain. She was part of Val's medical team now.

As Ben talked, Brody stiffened. As if realizing what she had done, she visibly took a deep breath, and her shoulders relaxed. Like Court, Brody was hanging in there for Val.

When they finished talking, Val said slowly, "How long before I can walk?"

"I'll be able to answer that better after the surgery," Ben said.

"I'm a vet…If I can't stand up and walk…I can't work."

"Once we're able to put in the internal fixation devices and the wound heals satisfactorily," Ben said, "we'll get you into a walking cast."

"When—"

Ben went on, her tone still mild and matter-of-fact, "My number one goal is to restore the function in your leg and get you back to the things you were doing before the accident. However long that takes, whatever we need to do, I'll keep you informed. Right now, we need to get the wound cleaned up and the bones stabilized."

"I want…Court…there," Val said, starting to drift.

Ben cocked her head and leaned closer. "Sorry?"

"In…OR. Courtney."

Ben gestured to Court to come forward.

Court edged closer until Val could see her face. "Hey, everything's going to be okay."

Val's eyes, normally so sharp and intense, blurred with a combination of pain and the meds she'd been given. Her unfocused gaze roamed Court's face. "Thanks. For out there."

Court swallowed and nodded.

"You'll…assist?"

"Right now," Ben broke in smoothly, "we need to get out of here so the trauma folks can get you ready for the OR."

"Brody," Val murmured, "go with them."

"No way, baby." Brody kissed her cheek. "I'm staying until Abby kicks me out."

Abby Remy slipped into the bay. "That would be now. Brody— go get something to eat while we take care of things here. It's already been a long day, and it's not quite noon." She gave Brody a quick hug. "And Val needs to rest."

Brody hesitated, then kissed Val's cheek. "I'll see you upstairs before they get started. I love you."

The intensity in Brody's voice made Court shiver. She'd seen Brody and Val together, even though she avoided invitations to their house. The past still stood too firmly between her and Val for casual interactions. Brody's love and commitment reverberated in her every word and action. Court was certain she'd never experienced anything like it, but unlike in years past, she wasn't resentful of Val's good fortune, even as she doubted she'd ever have the same.

❖

Court, Ben, and a reluctant Brody left the trauma wing and headed into the main hospital.

Brody said, "I should talk to Matt about covering my shifts and— Hell, I've got to get someone to feed Honcho tonight. I'm not going to leave until Val's out of recovery."

Court said quickly, "Matt knows to rearrange the flight schedules, Brody. And Jane is going over to your place now. She'll look after Honcho, and if she can't, she'll make sure she sets someone else up to do it. You don't have to worry about that stuff now."

Brody rubbed her face. "I know Val's okay. I mean, I know she *will* be okay." She glanced at Ben. "There's nothing else I need to know, right?"

Ben shook her head. "No. I told Dr. Valentine and you everything I can right now. When I know more, I'll tell you both." She paused by the stairwell. "I'm going up to the OR to get an update on the room situation."

"I know Val said she wanted me to scrub," Court said, "but if you want one of the ortho residents—"

"I'm fine with it if you are," Ben said. "You took care of her in the field, and she wants you there. It's not only a good learning experience for you, but it matters to her. If you feel all right about it."

"I'm fine," Court said, and she really was. The greatest moment of fear had been when she'd first realized it was Val, and she hadn't been thinking like a doctor then. She'd been thinking like a friend and family member. The last thing in the world she wanted was Val to be hurt. But now it was all about treating Val's injuries and helping her on the road to recovery. She was secure in that path, and although she wouldn't say so out loud, she wanted to scrub with Ben Anderson. She wanted to see her in the OR, to get a glimpse of the other side of her. She'd been intrigued years ago by the basketball player and all over again before she knew who she was, in those fleeting moments on the court at dawn. The idea of working with her in the OR excited her. "I feel totally fine. I want to scrub. I'll make sure the ortho residents are okay with it, but I think everyone is already on a case."

"Good," Ben said, "then—"

"Brody!"

Ben turned to see a tall, statuesque woman step out of the elevator and hurry in their direction. "Flann just called me. I'm so sorry I wasn't here sooner."

Ben needed only a glimpse to guess who she was. Her dark hair, bright blue eyes, and angular jaw were the mirror image of Harper's. She was a Rivers, no question, and Ben would bet she was Flann and Harper's mother. She might easily have been Brody's mother as well from the way she opened her arms, and Brody, who'd been a coiled spring seconds from snapping since Val was brought in, went into her arms and pressed her forehead to the woman's shoulder.

"There now," the woman said in a rich alto with a hint of the South in the melody, "Val is going to be just fine. And so are you."

She stroked Brody's hair, and Brody's shoulders shook for a few more seconds. Then Brody straightened and stepped back, brushing her hand across her face. "I'm really glad you're here."

The woman slipped her arm around Brody's waist with a shake of her head and a fond smile. "And where else would I be?" She looked past Brody to Courtney. "How are you, honey?"

"I'm fine, Mrs. Rivers."

The woman's brows shot up. "Courtney Valentine! Brody and Val are family, and so are you. It's Ida."

Warmth fluttered through Courtney's belly. She knew Brody had grown up with Harper and Flann and had left home young for the Army. She'd returned not long ago and was as much a Rivers sibling as Harper, Flann, Carson, and Margie. And now Val was part of the clan too. That Ida would extend the invitation to her meant more than she could have guessed. She didn't have much of a family anymore. Her mother was there, in her way, but more and more dependent every year.

"Thank you." Courtney gestured to Ben. "Oh, Ida Rivers, this is Dr. Bennett Anderson. She's—"

Ida, still holding on to Brody, or possibly holding her up, smiled at Ben, an open, warm smile that spoke of heart and generosity. "You would be Flann and Harper's friend from medical school. I was always trying to get them to bring you home."

Ben felt herself flush, remembering the many invitations she'd turned down. She hadn't been totally honest with them about why. "And I'm grateful for all the invitations and very sorry I couldn't visit, especially after all the stories I've heard about your cooking."

Ida laughed, obviously delighted. "Then I expect you for dinner very soon."

"That's very kind of you," Ben said.

"It isn't kindness. It's a pleasure for me, so you would be doing me a favor," Ida said. "Where are you staying? Have you found a place already?"

Ben hesitated but couldn't think of anything to say except the truth. "I am temporarily at the Bluebird Motel, the one out on—"

Ida's eyes narrowed. "Does Flannery know that?"

"Ah, I'm not sure I mentioned it."

"Good, because I raised her better than that."

"Well, I—"

"My house was built a long time ago when families were large. I had a large family myself, but all of them have grown and left except for Margie. I'm overrun with empty rooms. I'll expect you to move your things in tonight, until you've found a place of your own. And there won't be any hurry on that. You'll be far too busy doing more important work."

"Well, I…" Ben said, having difficulty with her vocabulary, something that wasn't usually a problem. "That's very kind of you, but I wouldn't want to impose."

"How could it be an imposition? You would be providing me with something I'm sorely lacking these days—conversation, company, and someone to appreciate my cooking. I don't see my children near enough to satisfy all of that, and my youngest, being in high school, is rarely about."

Ida smiled, her tone friendly and easy, with enough steel for Ben to realize she didn't have a lot of choice. She really didn't mind. The idea of moving out of the Bluebird was a welcome one. And besides, it would only be for a few days.

"Well then—"

"Good." Ida turned Brody toward the elevator. "Now I'm taking Brody to the cafeteria and getting her something to eat. And you will be taking care of Val, right?"

"Yes," Ben said. "Courtney and I will be operating very soon."

"Good. We'll want to hear all about it as soon as you're finished."

"Of course," Ben said.

"We'll be in the surgical waiting room just down the hall from the OR," Ida said.

"I'll find you."

"I'm sure Val is in capable hands."

Ida whisked Brody away, and Ben turned to Courtney. "What the hell just happened?"

"You've just met the one person in the Rivers family no one ever says no to." Courtney laughed. "If you're not careful, you'll end up getting adopted into the clan."

Ben doubted that would ever happen—she just wasn't cut out for family.

CHAPTER TWELVE

"A bby," Pam Wendel called, "Flann's on the phone. Can you take it?"

"Ask her to hold on a minute," Abby told the charge nurse. She took another quick look to be sure Val was stable, comfortable, and ready for transport to the OR before ducking her head into the second bay. Grady McClure and PA Mari Mateo directed the assessment of their remaining trauma patient, for the moment at least. When a day started like this, it often presaged a nonstop trauma circus.

Grady observed while Mari assisted a first-year resident in inserting an intravenous catheter into the subclavian vein just below the young man's collarbone.

"That's a good angle," Mari murmured. "Just keep negative pressure on the syringe until you see venous blood, and then advance it a few millimeters more. That's it…go ahead with the catheter."

Grady watched a few more seconds, then joined Abby.

"How's it going?" Abby asked.

"He's stable from a general surgical point of view," Grady said, "but I'm worried about his head. He was unconscious in the field, and we can't identify any local injury. I've called for neuro to come down. We'll need the CT, but I also think he's going to need a bolt and a transfer to the neuro ICU for monitoring."

"Mari and Wakeem can keep an eye on him until neuro gets here," Abby said. "I'm sure you've got plenty waiting upstairs."

"More than enough," Grady said with a weary sigh. "Sometimes I wish we'd never invented automobiles."

Abby grinned ruefully. "Or guns, airplanes, ATVs, and skateboards."

"Yeah, I guess if that was the case, we'd find some other ways to mess ourselves up."

Abby squeezed her arm. Grady had been up all night operating, and even the most stalwart got tired after a while. "You need to take a break. Who's your backup?"

"Annie Jacobs, and she's been here since two a.m."

"Well, with a new baby at home, she's probably used to being sleep-deprived."

Grady laughed. "I'll tell her you said that."

"Flann's on the phone," Abby said, "so I'm going to leave you to it. If anything changes—"

"Everything's okay here, Abby," Mari said.

She smiled. "I know. Thanks."

Pam handed her the landline when she returned to the nurses' station. "Hey. It's me."

"Listen," Flann said, "can you get free for an hour or so?"

Abby looked around. Pam had gone down the hall to check on a patient, and no one else was close. "Baby, if you're asking for a nooner, the heart is willing, but…"

Flann laughed. "I'm so there, but no. Everything is fine, but Blake got into a little tussle with Donnie Winslow at school. Pete Carlisle wants to talk to Blake with one of us there, and I can't get free up here for at least another three or four hours."

An icy wave coursed through Abby's middle. "He's all right?"

"Yes, it doesn't sound like it came to blows, but I think there was a little more than just verbal jousting this time."

Abby checked the ER/Trauma board. Mercifully almost clear. "We're just getting things under control down here. I'll see if Mike Carrera can cover things for me."

"He's back from paternity leave?"

"Just this morning."

"Bet he wishes he was home changing diapers."

Abby laughed. "I should be down there in a few minutes."

"I'd go myself, Abs, but—"

"It's fine. That's why we're lucky there's two of us, right?"

"You got that right," Flann said. "I love you."

"I love you too."

Abby called Mike, who answered after a few seconds. When

she told him what she needed, he said, "We're good here, Abby. You go ahead."

"I'll owe you one."

"The next time my older son has a dance recital, I'll take you up on it."

She laughed. "Done."

Abby hurried out to her car and five minutes later pulled into the high school parking lot. She hadn't thought to call and did that as she walked to the school. "This is Abby Remy. I'll be there in a minute or two."

"I'll let Mr. Carlisle know," his assistant said.

"Thanks."

Abby hadn't grown up in the village, but she'd been to the high school when she'd enrolled Blake, talked to the school counselors, met with the principal, and attended some functions enough times to know her way around. When she reached the principal's office, his assistant, a young man who looked to be about thirty in a subdued plaid button-down collar shirt and dark pants, greeted her with a smile. "I'll take you in to Mr. Carlisle."

Pete rose from behind his desk when Abby came in and held out a hand. "Hi, Abby. Thanks for coming."

"Pete," Abby said. "Flann didn't have much of a chance to tell me what's going on."

"I thought we'd wait until Blake got here, and you could hear it from him."

"All right."

A minute later, the door opened again, and Blake came in. Abby scanned him, head to toe, the way she would when a trauma patient first arrived in trauma admitting. She wasn't looking for blood, but she *was* looking for bruises, any other physical signs of injury, and most importantly, his expression. Blake was many things, and one of the things she loved best about him was how open and emotionally available he was. His feelings never embarrassed him. She wasn't foolish enough to think he didn't have secrets. He was a teenage boy, after all. Of course he had secrets. But from the time he'd come to her at fourteen and told her that he'd always known who he was, and that he wanted, *needed*, all of him to fit who he was—his words—he'd talked to her about his hopes and fears.

His gaze met hers now, and she read embarrassment, a little chagrin, and a spark of anger. That was interesting. For everything he'd been through, the loss of friends, the disdain directed at him and others like him in the media, and the taunts of strangers, he'd rarely lost his temper. But today, it seemed, he had.

"Hi, honey," Abby said.

"Hi, Mom. Sorry you had to leave work."

"That's okay." She gave him a quick kiss on the cheek and squeezed his hand.

"Why don't you both sit down," Pete said, gesturing to the visitors' chairs in front of his desk as he settled in behind it. "I asked your mom to come in, Blake, so we could talk about what happened. Do you want to tell your mom?"

Blake said, "It wasn't anything." He lifted his shoulder. "Not anything new, anyhow."

"Details?" Abby said.

"Just Donnie Winslow being an ass—jerk," he said, glancing at Pete.

"More details," Abby prodded.

"Just the usual," he insisted.

"Blake," Abby said, putting a little doctor-mom into her tone, "I know it's the code that what happens between you and your classmates is something you want to handle on your own, but you wouldn't be here in Mr. Carlisle's office if it wasn't a little more than the usual."

Blake let out a breath and turned away from Mr. Carlisle to face her. "Donnie was just giving me a hard time about the basketball tryouts. He won't be the only one, Mom. We talked about it, remember?"

"We did, and I thought we all agreed that there might be some pushback, some dickheads…" She glanced at Mr. Carlisle and smiled. "Sorry, you can pretend you didn't hear that."

He smothered an obvious smile and nodded.

"So was it harder to take than you thought?" Abby said gently.

"No, it wasn't." Blake laughed a little humorously. "I generally run through possible scenarios, to think about how I might feel about it. Guys like Donnie don't bother me…well, they do, but not all that much. Because then I remember what it was like before I transitioned. Everyone has to pay some kind of price for being who they are, don't they?"

Abby's heart twisted. "I wish that wasn't true, but probably, on some level it is. I'm proud of you, you know. Every single day."

"I know." If Blake had been standing, he probably would've shuffled his feet. He was mature beyond his years, but he was still a teenager, and his mother could still embarrass him.

"So all that being the case," Abby went on, putting her doctor voice on again, "exactly what escalated things?"

For the first time, Blake looked uneasy. He faced Mr. Carlisle. "It was my fault. I mean, I shoved him first."

The admission surprised her. Blake had been through a lot, and physical confrontation wasn't his thing. She'd enrolled him in a self-defense class before they left Manhattan to be sure he could protect himself. She wasn't naive enough to think the world was a safe place under the best of circumstances, and it would be even less so for her son. But he didn't initiate fights.

"What did he say?" Abby said quietly.

The muscles in Blake's jaw tightened. "Nothing."

"Oh," Abby said, "so you just decided to push him around because he was just doing what he's always done. Being a dickhead?"

"Yeah, pretty much."

"Blake," Abby said gently, "I love you to pieces, but some things are unacceptable."

Blake wasn't telling her everything, and he knew she knew. His shoulders sagged just a little, and then he squared them. "He said something about Margie."

Abby glanced at Pete Carlisle. Donnie Winslow was one of those teenage boys who grew to their near-adult size while in high school, which made it easy for them to physically intimidate everyone, boys and girls alike. Margie was five four and a hundred pounds.

"What did he say, son," Pete said, his usual easygoing tone replaced by hard-edged iron.

"He said something about her being with other guys and... liking it."

Abby had a feeling Pete would've cursed if they'd been in any other place and Blake wasn't there. She certainly felt like it. God, teenage boys could be such assholes. And sometimes they could be dangerous.

"And so you shoved him," she said.

"I should've punched him," Blake said softly.

"No, actually you shouldn't have," Abby said, lightly squeezing his arm. "I don't have to tell you that's no solution."

"No," he said. "But I still should've."

Pete leaned forward. "I appreciate your honesty, Blake. The school has a no fighting policy, and under ordinary circumstances you'd be suspended for two weeks."

Abby shot up straight. "And what about bullying and provoking an altercation? What about spreading malicious rumors about a classmate?"

"Mom," Blake said softly, "it's okay."

"No, Blake, it's not." Abby kept her anger and disgust under as much control as she could, but where was the justice here? What good were rules and policies that ignored the simple clarity of right and wrong? This was Blake's school, and he needed to not only survive here, but be valued and supported. "What about all the incidents that led up to today, Pete?"

"Unreported incidents," Pete said with a heavy sigh. "And I am considering the prior events I've heard about. I intend to speak to Donnie and his brother, Wade, who is now his legal guardian, and make it very clear that any further instigations like today will carry a heavy penalty. For now, considering both boys had a share in initiating the episode, the two-week suspension will be in-school."

Blake sucked in his breath. "What about basketball tryouts?"

"Since those are school-sanctioned events that you wouldn't be able to make up later, unlike classroom studies—which you will be responsible for—you will be able to go to tryouts."

Blake's shoulders relaxed and he glanced at Abby. "It's fair."

"All right," Abby said, willing to accept the compromise. "There's one other thing, Pete. I'd like Blake and Margie Rivers to be excused from school early today. It's a family matter."

"All right," he said immediately. "Margie's next class ends in ten minutes. Michael will tell you where she'll be."

Abby and Blake rose. "Thank you."

"What's going on, Mom?" Blake whispered while they waited for Pete's assistant to look up Margie's class schedule.

"Let's wait until we get Margie," Abby said, setting a hand on Blake's shoulder.

By the time they reached Margie's classroom, they only had a minute to wait. When she saw them, she hurried over. "Hey, what's going on?"

"Val has been in a car accident, but she's doing okay," Abby said as she shepherded them away from their other classmates toward the exit. "She's at the Rivers and will be having surgery later today. The family is gathering."

"Oh my God," Margie said. "She's really okay?"

"What happened?" Blake said.

"We're not entirely sure, but there were a couple of other vehicles involved."

Blake looked at Margie. "Honcho."

"Yeah," Margie said, "and all the boarders at the clinic. We're going to have to take some time off from school, Abby."

"That was quick," Abby said admirably as they all piled into her car. "I think we'll work it out so you can help out at the clinic *after* school."

"Maybe Honcho can come and stay with us?" Blake said.

"We'll talk to Brody about it. I think once Val's surgery is over, Brody will able to handle everything, but we'll all make certain of it."

Blake nodded and glanced at Margie. "For sure. That's what families do."

❖

Ben poured another half cup of coffee into the disposable cup and carried it to the sofa in the OR lounge, mentally reviewing the surgery ahead. Val's injury was fairly commonly seen in motor vehicle accidents, and she'd done hundreds of cases like it. All the same, she pulled up the image of the fracture site in her mind, thinking about the specifics of the break, the incision placement, and her game plan. Half a dozen other people sat scattered around the room, some chatting, others leaning back with eyes closed. A few of them had likely been up all night or a good part of it and were napping. Just a typical day in the OR.

Courtney came in, saw her, and headed over to join her. She'd lost the strained tension around her eyes and looked fresh and re-energized. And despite the ubiquitous scrubs, sexy. Caught off-guard by a surge of attraction, Ben reminded herself that close to eight years separated them, and Courtney was a resident. Not strictly forbidden, but not the wisest situation and one she definitely planned to avoid. That she was even thinking about why she shouldn't be thinking about Courtney Valentine set off alarm bells.

"Hi. How's your patient in the ER?" Ben said, setting a safe course of business only.

Courtney's face clouded as she dropped onto the sofa beside Ben. "I just went over his abdominal CT with radiology. He's got a mass lesion in the head of his pancreas."

Ben grimaced. "Probably not inflammatory?"

She shook her head. "Probably malignant."

"How's the liver look?"

"Clean so far." Courtney sighed. "He's fifty years old."

"It sucks no matter what the age," Ben murmured, "but that double-sucks."

"Yeah, it does. I didn't say anything to him. I'm waiting for Dr. Rivers—Flann—to see the films and talk to him."

"If he's clear everywhere else," Ben said, "he's got a chance."

"That's what I'm hoping." Courtney seemed to visibly shake off the melancholy, a good sign. Compassion was essential, as long as the empathy didn't incapacitate. Courtney was far from the usual first-year resident, able to balance caring with the clarity needed to effectively treat the sick and injured.

Ben wondered what past trials had forged her impressive resilience and quickly pulled herself up short. She wasn't going to think about Courtney Valentine, the woman, no matter how strong the urge. That was a sure path to disaster.

"They've called for Val," Ben said.

"Great. I had X-ray make hard copies of her leg films."

Courtney indicated the oversized manila folder under her arm. "I'm not sure the amphitheater's even hooked into the internet."

Ben frowned. "Sorry?"

Courtney grinned and went from attractive to sexy in a nanosecond. "You haven't seen it yet, have you?"

"No," Ben said, annoyed with herself for noticing the playful light in Courtney's eyes. "I just got done talking to Patty."

"Come on, I'll give you a tour while we wait."

"Okay." That sounded like the kind of distraction she needed right then. Sitting beside Courtney for another thirty minutes trying not to notice the way the light played in her eyes when she laughed or the curve of her lips when she smiled or her intriguing blend of enthusiasm and intensity when she focused on a case was a losing game plan.

Courtney led Ben through the OR, out into the perimeter hallway, and then up a narrow flight of stairs that looked as if they'd seen a hundred years of wear, despite being polished to a high shine.

"I'm starting to get a little worried here," Ben said. "How exactly do the patients get up here?"

"Don't worry, I'm taking you the back way. There's an elevator that opens right across from the amphitheater. They'll bring Val up that way."

"Okay," Ben muttered as they reached a long, wide, marble-floored corridor with a row of columns running down both sides and leaded glass windows in between. The twelve-foot-high ceiling held three chandeliers that lit the gallery.

"In here," Courtney said, pushing open carved walnut doors that looked like they ought to be the entrance to a museum or a theater from another century.

Ben stepped through and stopped, her gaze sweeping around the two-story domed operating theater. Courtney grabbed masks from a cart inside the door and handed her one.

"You've got to be kidding me," Ben murmured as she tied the mask.

"It's amazing, isn't it?" Courtney said.

The main floor looked much like any other operating room, although all the modern equipment had obviously just been brought in. Rolling racks of supplies lined one wall, and an OR table sat next to an anesthesia machine in the center of the gleaming wood floor. Electric cords and anesthesia gas lines snaked across the floor to an open cabinet, where they disappeared into the wall connections. A woman in scrubs and a mask sat on a stool by the gas machine, adjusting dials. She glanced over and waved.

"Hey, Courtney."

"Hi, Claire."

The anesthetist nodded to Ben. "I'm Claire D'Angelo. You must be Dr. Anderson."

"That's me," Ben said, still slightly stunned. Unlike any other OR she'd ever been in, this one soared two full stories to where a translucent skylight centered the domed ceiling. A semicircle of tiered theater seats ringed half the room around the base of the dome. Doors to either end of the seating area probably led to the corridors by which observers could come and go.

"Is this place for real?"

Courtney chuckled. "Totally. This was the main operating room until the late 1940s, and then with the expansion of the hospital and modern anesthesia, the other ORs were slowly added. This one was still used for teaching and demonstration surgeries when visiting professors operated, right up until the end of the last century."

Ben cocked her head. "And you know this how?"

Courtney's blush, visible above her mask, was unexpected and more than a little charming. "I, uh, like medical history."

"Do you?" Curious, Ben resisted the urge to ask more. "Are we likely to have observers today?"

Courtney frowned. "I guess we could. I could put signs out by the doors saying no observation."

"Dr. Valentine will probably be awake when she comes in," Ben said. "We can ask her."

Courtney said quickly, "I'll do that."

"Good, thanks," Ben said, taking in the tiers of empty seats. "Looks like a little stadium."

"Yeah," Courtney said, turning in a half-circle as she looked up. "I guess you're used to that."

Surprised, Ben said, "Pretty much. Not like this, though."

"Did it bother you? All those people watching you play?"

"No," Ben said. "By the time I graduated high school, I'd learned to shut out the people and the noise from the stands. The crowds got bigger every year, but by then I barely registered them."

"There's a lot of traffic in the OR too, I guess," Courtney said, "but usually no one is chanting your name."

Surprised again, and unaccountably amused, Ben laughed. "For which I am thankful."

Ben could tell Courtney was smiling behind her mask, and the pleasure that rippled through her was both foreign and enticing. Refocusing, she said to Claire, "Are all the other ORs still running?"

"Every one of them," Claire said, "and nothing's going to open up very soon."

"Then we're not giving up this one. I've got two more cases to do." Ben turned to Courtney. "And unless someone comes looking for you, you're with me today."

Courtney's eyes gleamed. "I'm all yours."

Ben couldn't help but grin back. "Hell of a first day."

CHAPTER THIRTEEN

Val was groggy from the pre-op medications when two of the trauma staff brought her up to the OR. Courtney met them at the door and helped transfer her to the OR table. As Claire got ready to administer the anesthesia, Courtney squeezed Val's upper arm and leaned down. "Val, it's Courtney. How are you doing?"

Val's eyes flickered open, her pupils unfocused and glazed. After a few seconds her gaze cleared, and she fixed on Court's face.

"Ready…to get…this over," she said slowly but clearly.

Court smiled. That was just like Val. If there was a problem, she was all over it. She'd never seemed scared or unsure, even as a teenager. Maybe she wasn't. Maybe having a father who stuck around made a difference. And maybe *she* was still wishing she'd had Val's life. Which was just pathetic. "You're in the amphitheater. You okay with observers?"

"Sure." Val laughed. "Gotta…be good karma."

Courtney nodded, her throat a little tight. Did she have to be so damn brave? "That's what I think too."

"Brody?"

"Ida is with her. She'll keep her busy."

Val closed her eyes. "Good. Have…fun."

"You know it." Court laughed to cover the catch in her voice. "You'll be fine. Talk to you soon."

She stepped back as Claire placed the mask over Val's face to begin the induction. After waiting to be sure all went smoothly, Court joined Ben at the scrub sinks. Unlike in the new OR where the scrub area overlooked the OR room via a window, these were tucked into an alcove in the hallway.

Ben said, lathering her hands and forearms with the antiseptic scrub brush, "Everything okay?"

"Yeah, she's good."

"I meant you."

"I'm good," Court said. Ben was asking about the case, of course—checking to see if she was ready for it—but a little part of her couldn't help warming to the idea that Ben was asking about her personally. "I'm glad I'm here."

"All right then," Ben said after a pause, "why don't you walk me through the case."

Court took half a second to settle herself. This was the first real test Ben had presented her with. Even though she wouldn't be in charge of any important decisions in the OR, or anything at all, really, one day she would be, and she had to act as if now was that day. Continuing to scrub, she described what they'd be doing, not letting herself second-guess what she was saying. She'd be right or she'd be wrong, but she'd be sure. The time for indecision ended at the door.

Ben turned off the water with the press of her knee and stepped back, the last drops dripping from her elbows as she held her hands up in front of her. "Good. What's the long-term treatment?"

Courtney followed her in as Ben shouldered through the door. "Ah—internal fixation and bone grafting."

"That's the plan," Ben said. "When?"

Court had had the basics of orthopedics, just like every other medical student, but nothing very detailed. And the morning had been way too busy to review the specifics of the case. Now she'd be guessing, and if she guessed wrong, all she'd be doing was making herself look unprepared. She thought about the options and finally worked through them out loud. "But I'm not sure of the best answer."

Ben nodded. "A lot's going to depend on how much of the bone appears devitalized and the state of the soft tissues," Ben said. "But we want to get the fixator off, the fracture internally stabilized, and a cast on in the next ten days. Two weeks at the outside."

As Ben spoke, she scanned the gallery. Courtney looked up, double-checking that Brody had not somehow given Ida the slip and snuck in to watch the surgery. Brody didn't need more stress, and even though the surgery was going to go fine, Brody didn't need to see it. As Court suspected, with almost all the residents tied up in the operating rooms, there were only a couple of people up there. One of them was Jane. Their eyes met for a second, and Jane raised a finger in salute.

Court tipped her head to Jane before turning to Mark Chesney, the scrub nurse, who held out her gown.

"I see you've got a fan club," Ben said.

"Just a friend," Court said, feeling the damn blush climb into her cheeks. Jane had always said she wanted to see Court in the OR, even though she'd seen her work in the field plenty of times. Jane was like that—paying attention to the little details that made a person feel special. Jane would make someone a great girlfriend. Someone else. Although Ben might think Jane's being up there meant they were more than friends. And what did it matter if she did?

Jane *was* a friend, more than that still, and none of that could possibly matter to Ben. That it mattered to her what Ben surmised was just her wishing for something that couldn't be. A bad habit of hers.

Ben said, "Go ahead and prep," and the gallery disappeared from Court's mind, as did everything else except the injury they'd come to treat. As she and Mark placed the sterile drapes in a rectangle around Val's lower leg, leaving the fracture site exposed, that became her only focus. An hour and a half later, she wrapped the incision lightly in the sterile gauze and got ready to stabilize Val's leg as they transferred her back to a gurney.

Ben came back in after having stepped out to check with Patty about the next case.

"Everything okay?" she said to the room in general.

Claire said, "Doing fine."

On Claire's count, Court, Ben, and Mark transferred Val to the ICU bed. An ICU nurse joined them to assist Claire in transport.

"Still some time to grab lunch before the next case," Ben said, glancing at the clock. "I don't suppose there's any chance of street dogs?"

"Hot dogs?" Court dumped her mask in the trash and grinned. "You mean like from the carts you see in New York City?"

Ben gave her an amused look. "I mean the carts you pretty much see in any city with a population over a hundred thousand."

"We don't have any of those," Court said, laughing. "We're shy of the population requirement by about 97,500."

Ben's brows rose. "You're not kidding, are you? About the population, not the street vendors?"

"Nope. Although since Presley showed up and expanded this place, we've got a lot more people in the area working here. Most of them are commuting from a couple of the bigger cities around here, though. Not everyone likes how quiet it is here."

"You mean people would like to be able to eat out at ethnic restaurants, shop at brand retailers, and maybe watch a movie without driving an hour and a half?"

"Hey, you exaggerate," Court said, feigning indignation. "Twenty-five minutes will get you all of that. That's just a nice drive in the country."

"Really? You'll have to tell me where," Ben said as they walked toward the OR lounge. "I'm all for burgers and pizza, but every once in a while, I'd like sushi."

"You're in luck," Court said. "There's a good sushi place not that far from here."

"Define *not that far*," Ben said.

"Half an hour. When you're up for it, I'll give you directions."

"Why don't you show me?" Ben said. "Sushi is one of those meals meant to be shared."

Court caught her breath. The invitation was so unexpected she almost didn't know what to say, but before Ben could take it back, she hurriedly said, "Sure. Just let me know when."

She glanced at Ben out of the corner of her eye. Ben stared straight ahead. "I'll do that. Thanks."

The sudden silence was a pretty good sign Ben already regretted the impulsive invitation.

"Well," Court said, not wanting to add to the embarrassment for either of them, "I'll head over to the ICU to check on Val."

"I'll speak to Brody and Mrs. Rivers while you get her settled," Ben said, still not looking at her. In the next instant Ben ducked into the stairwell and disappeared.

Court couldn't shake the feeling that Ben was trying to escape. Great. Talk about an emotional roller coaster. First she gets hit with an invitation for dinner—she wasn't making that up, either, that was an invitation—one that Ben obviously instantly regretted. So from breathless one minute—in a good way, from a rush of excitement that she hadn't felt in a very long time—to confusion and disappointment sixty seconds later. She didn't know what had just happened, but she was sure of one thing. She wouldn't be going out for sushi anytime soon.

"Court!" Jane called, jogging down the hall to join her. "Sorry I didn't ask if that would be okay, me being up there. I didn't think you'd mind, but I should have asked."

"It's fine," Court said, trying to put Ben Anderson and questions she couldn't answer out of her mind. "Could you see much?"

"Yeah, it was neat. You looked...cool."

Court laughed. "Cool?"

"Different than I'm used to seeing you." Jane leaned closer as they turned the corner into the main hallway and lowered her voice. "Very commanding."

"Really." Court shot her a look. "Are you saying I'm not usually."

"Let's just say it's a different side to you than I've seen before." Jane grinned. "And seriously, the whole thing was fascinating."

"Well," Court said, "Ben let me do some of the easy parts, but I was mostly assisting."

"She's pretty hot," Jane said casually.

"She's attractive," Court said, fighting a flash of irritation.

"Do you know anything about her? Is she involved?"

"Are you planning to ask her out?"

Jane's brows rose. "Just curious. Aren't you?"

Court forced a smile. "Who has time, and I don't know anything about her personal life."

"Give it a few days," Jane said. "The grapevine will know." She stopped at the elevator. "I'm going to let Matt know I'm back. Honcho is good for now, and Blake called to say he and Margie would check her later. I'll probably take the evening shift on the flight deck, so I can't make dinner tonight."

"No problem," Court said. "I probably won't either."

"So I'll catch you soon," Jane said as the elevator opened and she stepped inside.

"Text me," Court called as the doors started to close. Jane was right—Ben *was* hot, and interesting and charming, and she'd be noticed. A lot of new faces had appeared at the Rivers in the last few months, but the hospital—the whole village—was still a small place and not that many newcomers were single. She had no idea if Ben was available or not, but if she was…

And there she went, fantasizing about possibilities where none existed. At the end of the day, she'd be the last person on Ben Anderson's mind.

❖

Ben hurried away before she could dig herself into a deeper hole of irrational impulsivity. She'd just asked Courtney Valentine to go to dinner with her. What the hell? She'd escaped just in time, shuddering to think what she would have said if she'd spent another twenty-five minutes sitting next to her in the OR lounge. Told Courtney her life story?

She didn't do casual friendships with women. She liked women, but she didn't hang out with them. Well, not since the women on her team, and their ties had been more about shared goals than anything else. When they got together on the road for a meal in some strange hotel or spent hours crammed together on a bus, they talked about their training, their coaches, and their next competition. Not much about family, or boyfriends or girlfriends, and not much about feelings. That had been fine with her. She didn't want to remember, let alone think, about family. And after, in medical school, Harper and Flann had been her go-to companions. They'd all shared the same goals too. Funny, how that's what she was comfortable with. Sure, Flann and Harper talked about their family, but mostly about the hospital and their plans for when they finished training. They didn't push when she didn't talk about her family. That was good. That was how she'd wanted it.

With the women she occasionally dated casually, an evening out to dinner or some other event was often a prelude to sex. She didn't talk about anything personal, and if that wasn't what her date had in mind, she could thank her for the evening and walk away.

With Courtney, the pattern didn't hold. She hadn't been thinking about sex when she'd mentioned dinner. While the parts of her that were alive and breathing might have been aware of how damned sexy Courtney was, she was old enough to keep those under control. She'd mentioned going out to eat because she liked spending time with her. Their brief conversations—the ones that *hadn't* been about medicine, and when did she usually have any of those—were easy and comfortable. Even so, enjoying a woman's company was no reason to invite her out, was it? Not when it was a mistake, and she knew it. Fortunately, she didn't have to carry through on the idea. But she did have to be a lot more careful around Courtney.

With that settled, Ben walked into the surgical waiting area to take care of her duties to someone else's family. Brody sat with Ida, along with two teenagers, and everyone jumped up at the first sight of her. Ben didn't have to guess the teens' identities. The boy had a hint of Abby Remy's jaw and her smile, although his hair was dark where hers was blond. The strawberry blonde beside him had Ida Rivers's bright blue eyes and the direct, appraising stare that all the Rivers siblings seemed to have. Blake and Margie. Ida put a hand protectively on Brody's back.

"Everything went fine," Ben said, her usual opener. She found if she didn't allay the basic fear that all families had no matter what kind of surgery their loved one was undergoing, they rarely heard anything else she had to say. Sometimes they still didn't. "Dr. Valentine is on her way to the recovery room, and from there she'll go to the trauma intensive care unit. The TICU is—"

"I know where it is, thanks," Brody said. "How did the fracture look?"

Ben explained what she'd found and how they'd treated it. "I'll bring her down again in a few days for another washout and to assess the wound. If things look good, we can think about scheduling the definitive repair."

Brody let out a long breath. "Right…okay. Thank you." She held out her hand, and when Ben grasped it, she squeezed it and held on. "Thank you so much."

"Not at all. It'll be a couple hours before you can see her."

Brody glanced at Ida. "You don't have to stay."

Ida merely smiled. "Nonsense. Once you've seen Val, we can talk about dinner." She fixed Ben with that same smile. "Don't forget I'm expecting to see you at the Homestead tonight with your luggage. Most anyone can tell you how to get there. Dinner will be later than usual—around seven. If you can't make it by then, there'll be a plate in the oven for you."

Ben swallowed. "Ah, I…" Ida's smile never wavered, nor did the hint of steel in her gaze. "That sounds great. Thank you."

Ida nodded and said, "Come sit down, Brody. You just need to wait a bit more, but Val is fine. Remember that."

Ben left them and returned to the OR lounge. When she walked in, Courtney and Jane sat talking on the sofa. Ben hesitated. Although they were angled toward each other like any two people having a conversation, Jane's knee touched Courtney's, one of those telltale signs of body language that suggested…what? Courtney had said they were friends. Friends could mean almost anything, and whatever it meant, it was none of her business. Courtney looked over, saw her watching them, and that faint color rose to her cheeks again. Ben imagined Courtney hated that emotional tell, but she found it appealing. And as appealing as she found it, she wondered what it meant. And wondered at herself for wondering. Turning, she got coffee and sat down alone at one of the tables. When Jane rose after a few moments, squeezed Courtney's shoulder, and left, Courtney didn't join her. She was waiting for an invitation, and Ben thought it best not to send one.

Chapter Fourteen

A middle-aged woman with a round face and smile lines around her eyes, wearing maroon scrubs and a yellow cover gown, appeared in the entrance of the waiting room, took a quick look around, and nodded in Brody's direction. "Brody, you can come back to see Dr. Valentine now."

"Thanks, Latisha," Brody said, jumping up to join her, leaving Margie, her mother, and Blake alone.

"Mom," Margie said as Brody disappeared with the ICU nurse, "I can get dinner started if you need me to."

"Thank you, honey, but I think I can manage," Ida said, giving Margie a quick squeeze. "Once I'm sure that Val is fine and Brody will be all right here alone, I'll be able to head home. I do think the two of you should help with Honcho, though."

Blake said instantly, "Absolutely. We're on it."

Ida smiled. "Good. You're invited back for dinner too, Blake."

He grinned, already pulling out his phone. "Thanks! I'll text my mom and let her know."

"Tell her to collect Flann and come along too, if they can."

"Okay," he muttered, tapping quickly. He looked up a second later, his expression the serious one he got sometimes when he was worried. "Are you sure you don't want us to stay for a while? Jane said she checked Honcho this morning, so we have time."

"No," Ida said, "you two go on ahead. Honcho is bound to be upset that Val hasn't come home yet, and Brody will be late too. More visits is probably better than fewer."

Margie said, "She's right, Blake. We won't be able to see Val until she's out of the ICU anyhow. And the first thing she's going to ask us is how Honcho is doing and what's happening at the clinic."

Blake grinned wryly. "That is way true."

"Okay, we should go," Margie said, grasping Blake's hand and pulling him toward the hall. "See you soon, Mom."

Ida waved good-bye, and Margie and Blake hurried toward the stairs. Margie hadn't had a chance to talk to Blake alone since they'd left school, and now that the crisis seemed to be passing, she had time to mull over what Taylor had hurriedly told her between classes.

"Blake got pulled into Mr. Carlisle's office," Taylor whispered as she rushed along beside Margie to English class.

"What? Why?"

"I heard he punched Donnie Winslow."

"Blake? No." So surprised, Margie almost stopped dead in the hall. Only the throng of students right behind her kept her moving. "Did he really?"

"That's what I heard, and he wasn't in chem lab." Taylor leaned closer. "And Artie Nibbs said they saw Abby Remy down here earlier today."

"I hope he's all right," Margie said, catching her lip between her lower teeth.

"Me too," Taylor said. "If you see him first, tell him we were worried. And then text me what happened."

"I will. You too, if you get any more info." She smiled at Taylor. "And thanks for finding me."

Taylor smiled back. "Hey. If one of us has an issue, we all do, right?"

"Right."

Pushing out through the hospital exit closest to the parking lot where she'd left her pickup, Margie glanced sideways at Blake. He seemed physically all right. If there'd been some kind of fight, he hadn't been hurt. He hadn't seemed upset the past few hours while they waited either—except for worrying about Val and Honcho. Well, Brody too, but her mother had that covered, and Blake knew it. Honcho and the animals at the clinic—that was their thing. But it must have been something serious for him to end up in Mr. Carlisle's office.

"So, what happened with you and Donnie Winslow?" Margie said as soon as they were out of earshot of any passersby.

"You heard," Blake said glumly.

"Taylor told me."

He winced. "Talk about embarrassing."

Margie didn't see how anyone could think news like that wouldn't be all over school in the time it took to text, but she felt bad for him. She'd hate it if she was the topic of conversation too. "I'm not sure how far the story has gone. Taylor mentioned something because, you know—it's us."

Blake groaned. "Which means she heard it from someone else. Someone who probably wasn't..."

"Sympathetic?"

"Yeah—wishful thinking, right?" He blushed. "It'd just be nice not to have everyone I know hearing about it. Especially when most of them are going to hear something that didn't even happen."

"Most people aren't going to take Donnie's side, whatever that is. Everyone, even his friends, knows he's a jerk," Margie said as they crossed the parking lot crowded with secondhand trucks, Jeeps, and muscle cars. She unlocked her doors remotely and got behind the wheel. Blake climbed into the passenger seat and buckled his seat belt. Margie clipped hers in and started the truck. "So? What *did* happen?"

"I feel like I've been repeating this all day. You know they called both my parents."

Margie winced. "They called Flann?"

Her second-to-oldest sister could be a little overprotective sometimes. As in ready to kick someone's butt if they messed with anyone she loved. Most of the time Margie was good with that, but then Flann wasn't her parent. If she was Blake, she would *not* want her parents in the middle of her private stuff. "Are you going to tell me what happened?"

With a sigh, Blake recited the story in a monotone.

"Wait," Margie said as she drove out of town, "you *shoved* but didn't punch Donnie Winslow."

"That's right. Although I was about an inch away from doing it at the end. I wish I had."

"So what happened to telling me the part where he said

something that ticked you off so much that you shoved, not punched, him?"

"Just some bullshit," Blake muttered under his breath.

"Just some—why am I not seeing that?" Margie gave him a look. "If it was just Donnie and his usual dumbass comments, you would've ignored him like you've done about a million times already. And if he threatened to do something that you thought was really dangerous, you'd tell someone about it. So why are you hiding the details?"

The silence stretched until finally Blake said, "Donnie's an asshole. He says things about everyone."

Margie swung off the two-lane onto a narrow unpaved road, one of the many back-country lanes in the county that had never been paved because the farmhouses along the routes were several hundreds of years old, spaced many more hundreds of acres apart, and rarely drew enough through traffic to warrant resurfacing. The dust kicked up in a small cloud behind them as Margie drove toward Val and Brody's new home. Val planned to renovate the old barn that was no longer needed for dairy cows for a clinic and hospital, but for now the boarders and any overnight patients were housed in a big air-conditioned RV that Val generally used as a mobile hospital.

"If it was just Donnie being Donnie, why aren't you telling me what he said?" Margie persisted as the farm came into sight.

Blake blew out a breath. "Donnie made an asinine remark about you and sex."

"Me?" Margie jerked her head around and stared. "Oh God, he didn't say I had sex with him, did he? Like I would be that low?"

Blake grinned. "No, he didn't."

"Then what? It must've been something if it made you mad enough to push him around." She frowned as Blake tried to smother his grin. "And it's not funny. Donnie Winslow—so…just, no."

Blake instantly grew serious. "Jeez, I know, I'm sorry. It was just…never mind. I'm sorry."

"Tell me," Margie said flatly.

"He was just trying to get under my skin. Anybody who might've heard him never would've believed it." Blake reached across the seat and touched her knee. "I swear."

"I have a right to know if people are talking about me,"

Margie said softly. She hadn't really imagined that anything Donnie Winslow said could be taken seriously by other people, but then again, some kids believed anything. She didn't like the idea of being the topic of gossip, but everyone she knew who knew her, or who she cared about, wouldn't believe some stupid rumor. Blake would know that, but maybe he thought she didn't. "Blake?"

"Donnie started out bugging me about the basketball tryouts."

Margie couldn't quite make a connection between basketball and her and sex, so she just made a *hmm* noise and waited.

"That I wasn't really a guy because, you know, no guy equipment."

"Oh, for fuck's sake," Margie said. "He is such a dick."

Blake smiled. "You know, not everyone gets it the way you do. That it's not about that."

"I know." Margie glanced at Blake then back at the road. "I'm sorry."

"It's okay. It matters a lot that you and the rest of my friends get it."

"That's because we *are* your friends. And we're not dicks."

Blake laughed, and he sounded like himself. "That's true."

"So you said you didn't let that bother you."

"No more than usual."

"Then how did we go from you not being bothered by Donnie's usual dumbass remarks to him talking about me?"

"I guess he thinks we're kinda, you know, a couple."

"Oh," Margie said, suddenly on uncertain ground. They weren't, that part she was sure of. But then there was the drive-in thing. That was different—the two of them. "So he said we were having sex?"

"No," Blake said, a little bit of flush rising on his neck above his T-shirt. "I would've punched him then."

"Why? You wouldn't be embarrassed if we were, would you?" Margie was a little bit embarrassed by the whole topic herself. Making light of things helped a little bit.

"Well, no, but it's not the sort of thing that somebody says about a girl."

Margie rolled her eyes. "Oh. I guess I didn't realize it was a *guy* thing."

"Cut it out," Blake said, grinning.

"So what did he say?" she said, emphasizing every word.

Blake took a deep breath. "He said you'd like a big...you know..."

Margie slowed and gaped at him. "Dick?"

"Yes, yes. Please, can we stop now?"

She burst out laughing. "Oh my God. It's such a boy argument. That made you mad?"

"Yes...and he was saying that you, you know, had done it with other people."

"Oh." Margie thought about that. Whether or not she cared. Then she decided she did. "He's an asshole."

"That's not news. And everyone knows it." Blake was silent for a few seconds. "I'm sorry."

"For what? You didn't start anything."

"I probably made things worse, though. Jumping on him for saying that."

"It was a real dick thing to say," Margie muttered.

"Nobody's going to believe it."

"Some people probably will. But not the people who matter." She pulled into the driveway in front of the traditional two-story white frame house with its wide front porch, long red barn at the end of the drive, and big yard surrounded by acres of plowed fields. Honcho ran out to the drive and paused between the house and their vehicle, watching them, ears alert and her lithe muscular body poised to spring forward.

Margie rolled down the window. "Hey, Honch, it's us."

The dog relaxed and sat, her tail gently swishing as she waited.

Margie shifted on the seat and regarded Blake. The distance between them was only a few inches. "Thank you for caring about what he said, and what other people might think."

"You're welcome," Blake said, seeming suddenly shy. He was never shy around her.

"But I'd rather you not fight if he says something like that again about me." She hesitated. "It's not true, you know."

"Jeez, Margie! That's none of my business." Blake went from shy to strident in a second.

Margie shrugged. "I'm just saying. Even if it was, it's nobody's business. Either way—you don't need to defend me. I can do that for myself if he says anything where I can hear it."

Blake let out a sigh. "Yeah, I mostly just reacted."

"Are you doing okay? You know, with the other stuff he was saying?"

"I've heard it all already. Or seen it on the internet. Almost everybody in the world thinks that your body parts define who you are. Not everyone, which helps some, and I know it's not true. Every trans person understands what it's like to look at their body in the mirror and be surprised, or confused, or sometimes…horrified."

He looked away, and Margie stayed still and quiet.

"I knew I was not the person that my body said I was. And now I know that my body is just my body, and who I believe myself to be and how I live with that…that makes me who I am."

Margie tapped Blake's leg with her toe. "You know, you're really cool."

"Uh, I don't know about that. But it would be a lot harder if you didn't understand me." He spoke very softly, and when he looked at her, his eyes glistened.

"If there's something I don't get…ever," Margie said softly, "you can always explain it to me."

Blake shifted closer and now their legs touched. His hand rested on her shoulder. She wasn't sure how it got there.

"You know," Blake murmured, "the best thing that happened to me since I moved here was meeting you."

Blake was so close Margie could pick out the tiny gold flecks in the blue of his irises. They were so mesmerizing she forgot to answer. Then his lips touched hers, softly, and didn't move away. Her insides buzzed, as if her middle had suddenly turned into a giant beehive, and she pressed her lips more firmly against his. The softness and the tingling lingered for a moment, and then he pulled away.

"Um," Blake said.

Margie took a long, slow breath. "That was…nice."

Blake grinned. "Yeah. Okay."

Margie said, "Honch is waiting."

Blake bobbed his head vehemently. "Yeah."

"We should get out, walk her around. Check the mobile. Make sure everything's okay."

"Feed her," Blake said.

"Yes, definitely."

"Okay." Blake didn't move.

Margie leaned toward him. "In a minute."

Blake's smile widened as his arm came around her shoulders. "In a minute."

CHAPTER FIFTEEN

Ben finished her third trauma case shortly after five p.m. Her beeper had been quiet since late afternoon, and now all she had to do was check her post-op patients before she left for the night. With an hour to kill before her last patient—a fifteen-year-old boy who'd fractured his elbow sliding into second base in an afternoon practice—would be out of recovery and settled in a room, she might as well tackle whatever waited in her office for her to review. She took a last look around the amphitheater. Claire had removed the anesthesia machines, the scrub nurses had pushed their instrument tables out into the hall, and the gallery had emptied hours ago. The space echoed, not with emptiness, but with the memories of all the lives touched within over a century. Chances were she would never operate there again, and she was glad she'd had the opportunity. She'd probably never feel the way about the history of the hospital—of the whole village, really—that those who'd grown up there like Flann and Courtney did, but she'd shared in a little bit of it in that room. Courtney, she discovered, had more than a passing interest in local history, sharing stories of the town, the hospital, and the changing economy as the area had moved from a farming region to manufacturing with the growth of foundries and mills along the river, and finally back to farming again as the industries died out. Through it all, the hospital and its vital role in supporting the community remained.

Today she'd felt a small part of that continuing drama. The day had been full of surprises, Courtney not the least of them. Courtney had worked with her all day and had proven to be a tireless resident, handling all the small details required to get patients ready for the OR and settled after and, on top of that, was an excellent assistant in the OR. Unlike many young residents who had too many responsibilities and were too often in situations where more was expected of them than they had the tools to perform, Courtney was capable and confident and eager. All in all, Ben couldn't have asked for better company or assistance in the midst of a hectic day.

Not that she ever did. She enjoyed teaching and relied on the residents to help her provide timely care to patients, but she didn't seek them out. Didn't *enjoy* them the way she had Courtney. If asked, she would have sworn she just didn't connect that easily. But she had—for her part at least—connected with Courtney. Had to be a coincidence—they just shared a few common interests. Basketball, surgery, an interest in history she'd never even known she had. Nothing unusual in any of that. Nothing to worry about.

Ben stopped to change in the locker room. She still had to decide what to do about Ida Rivers's command invitation to stay at her home—the Homestead, she'd said—until she made permanent arrangements. She hadn't lived in close proximity with anyone since she'd started med school. Her social skills, never all that honed to begin with, were rusty.

"I definitely don't want to offend Mrs. Rivers," she muttered as she pulled on her trousers and slid into her loafers.

Patty Sullivan came around the row of lockers from the adjoining aisle and smiled. "Since I can't pretend I didn't hear that, if you mean Ida, I'll just say you're not likely to. She's impossible to ruffle and one of the kindest, strongest people I know. She's my godmother, by the way, so I know what I'm talking about."

Ben stared. "You're making that part up."

"Nope." Patty's eyes sparkled. "My mother and her are besties—since kindergarten."

"Wow." Ben shook her head.

"So my advice—not that you're asking—is follow Ida's. You won't go wrong."

"Thanks," Ben called as Patty shouldered her go bag to leave. Small-town living was going to take some getting used to. She hadn't shared this many personal exchanges since she, Flann, and Harper went their separate ways in the third year of med school rotations.

She made a couple of wrong turns on her way to the administrative wing but finally found the corridor where her office was located. Her footsteps echoed in the deserted warren of cubicles and darkened rooms. The support staff left at five, and surgeons generally didn't spend much time in their offices. The door to hers was standing open, and a quick glance from anyone walking by would suggest the space was unoccupied. No photographs, prints, or calendars hung on the walls, and the trash can next to the standard issue plain wood veneer desk was empty, as were the windowsills and bookshelves. A multiline phone sat on the right-hand corner of the desk, which she assumed was mostly for calls coming through the hospital operator, as she used her cell for all her calls, as did most people. The only other sign of occupancy was the three-inch-thick pile of papers stacked neatly in the middle of her desk. She stood in the doorway, eyeing them as she might a strange serpent, coiled and waiting. With a sigh, she flicked on the overhead lights, blinked in the bright glare of the fluorescents, and promptly switched the lights off again. She would need a desk lamp if she was going to work at night.

The leather swivel chair was comfortable enough, and she leaned back and closed her eyes, letting some of the adrenaline of the day seep away. Until today, she'd thought nothing could give her quite the same pleasure as mastering a difficult case and knowing that while she drew satisfaction and personal enjoyment from the operation, she was also doing a service to someone else. She had all that and more during her cases *and* in between today. And the reason why seemed never far from her mind. Courtney Valentine.

Ben opened her eyes and leaned forward. Thinking of Courtney's company was a very bad idea. She'd already almost asked her out to dinner—okay, she *had*, but not really dinner-dinner. And no date had been set. Thankfully there wasn't much in the way of entertainment available in the village, so she couldn't accidentally suggest a movie or play or…anything she ought not to be considering.

Resolutely determined not to travel any farther down *that* road, she pulled the stack of papers closer and began scanning and signing all kinds of memos, HR forms, health insurance applications, and other departmental paperwork. Almost none of the paperwork pertained specifically to her new department, although the final folder was the projected division budget provided from the chair of the department. That being Flann. Those spreadsheets were going to take some serious study and probably more mental sharpness than she had right at the moment. Between her inadvisable contemplation of Courtney Valentine and her paperwork, she'd managed to spend an hour.

Her patients all should be settled now. One final check and she'd be free for the night. She almost laughed, thinking that before she'd arrived in town a free night would have meant a solitary workout on the court and a book. Tonight, with the unknown situation at the Rivers home looming, freedom had taken on a very different shape.

She left the office door ajar as there was nothing of value in the room. Anyone who wanted that stack of papers would be welcome to them as far as she was concerned. Happily back in the hospital proper, she first saw the post-op patients on the regular patient floors, leaving the ICU until last. At the unit, she badged her way through the security door and pulled on a cover gown.

Courtney sat behind the desk tapping on an iPad. She looked up when Ben came in and nodded, her expression more reserved than Ben had seen all day. Ben hadn't expected to see her, and the swift kick of pleasure stirred a smile she couldn't hide. Courtney instantly smiled back, and Ben worked not to show how glad she was to see her.

"How is everything?" Ben asked, pulling a chair over next to Courtney.

"I just checked on Val," Courtney said. "She's extubated and hasn't had any problems, but she's pretty sedated. Her vital signs are good."

"No significant fever?"

Courtney shook her head. "No. One hundred point three."

"Keep your eye on that. Have the nurses call you if she spikes. After a washout like that, bacteremia is not unusual. If she spikes, she needs to be cultured."

"I'll let the resident on call know before I leave." Courtney tapped a note in her iPad.

"You're not on call tonight?"

Courtney shook her head. "No. Allie Masterson is."

"Then what are you doing here now? We finished that last case almost two hours ago."

"Oh, I was helping clear up some of the scut for A team. They got really hammered today."

"Admirable of you," Ben said, not at all surprised that Courtney would put in extra time at the hospital, "but make sure you get a break too."

"Oh, I'm outta here after this," Courtney said, her eyes sparkling. "Ida Rivers invited me to dinner, and that is not something I want to miss."

Ben winced. "Yeah, I'm not surprised."

"And you're supposed to be moving in there tonight, right?" Courtney said with just the slightest bit of laughter in her voice.

Ben frowned. "There's no way I can get out of it, is there?"

"Well, I don't think she'll come after you and force you bodily to move in, but..." She cocked her head. "Why wouldn't you want to? She's great, it's not that far from the hospital, and it's going to beat the hell out of the Bluebird Motel."

"She doesn't know me."

"You're friends with her kids—you're a doctor at the Rivers. You don't need any more of an introduction."

"I'm gonna be a terrible houseguest. I'm not all that talkative."

"I never noticed that." Courtney managed to make the observation sound both teasing and ever-so-slightly seductive. If someone wanted to take it that way. Which Ben didn't.

"Well, I talk to you but..." Ben swallowed the words. And she should learn to keep her mouth shut. Totally without her volition, she was caught up in another conversation with Courtney that was already out of her control—and her comfort zone.

"I *did* notice that, actually." Again, Courtney grinned. "And since you're good at it, I'm not sure why you think you aren't."

"Today was an oddity. Definitely not a normal circumstance," Ben muttered.

"I think I'm a little stoked about that, then. But you won't be required to converse at the Homestead, if you don't want to. There'll be plenty of people around to take up the slack."

Ben didn't even want to contemplate what *plenty* meant. And putting off the inevitable wouldn't change anything. Plus she really needed to free Courtney up to leave. "So, do you think Val will be ready for transfer to a regular floor tomorrow?"

Instantly, Courtney's playful look morphed to the completely professional. Ben found the change disappointing. But necessary. She just needed to keep reminding herself of that.

"I think so if her temp is good. Her post-op numbers are great." She read off the pertinent lab results and went on, "The foot looks good, and the dressings around the external fixator are clean and dry."

"I agree," Ben said. "Make sure you check her...oh, right, sorry, you're not actually assigned to my service." She grimaced. "I'm not entirely sure anyone is."

"I could be," Courtney said quickly. "I mean, I'd *like* to be if Dr. Rivers and you agree."

Ben needed a resident, and she'd worked with Courtney all day. She wasn't all that experienced, but she was definitely reliable and responsible—both more important than experience at times. And, if Courtney was her resident, that would make keeping a rational distance much easier and provide a certain solution to her errant and unfounded fascination.

"I'll talk to Flann tomorrow," Ben said before she could change her mind.

"Thanks. I'll check on Val first thing in the morning, no matter what."

Ben nodded. "I'm going to take a look at her, but you should get out of here now."

"Are you headed out to the Homestead after this?" Courtney asked.

Ben sighed. "That's going to be a bit of a problem. The rental was picked up today, so I'm without transportation. I was planning to get a car...sometime, but since the hospital is so close, it wasn't high on my list. I'll have to call tomorrow to arrange for another car if I'm living out of town. So until then, I can't actually move."

Courtney said, "That's not a problem. I'll follow you over to the motel and wait while you pack up. As long as you don't have more than three suitcases, I can put your things in my trunk. Then we can both go to dinner." She looked at her watch. "We should just about make it."

"I..." Ben couldn't think of a gracious or valid reason to refuse. Just because the longer she spent with Courtney, the easier it became and the more she enjoyed herself was no reason to turn down a friendly offer. "If you have other plans..."

"No," Courtney said quickly. "I don't have any plans at all."

❖

"This will only take me a couple minutes," Ben said as Courtney pulled her car into the Bluebird Motel parking lot. She pointed down the row of green doors. "I'm number seven."

"Do you need a hand?" Courtney asked.

"No, but you're welcome to come in and wait if you want while I throw some things in my suitcase."

"Sure." Courtney shut off the engine. "If you're okay with it, I'll call Sam's Auto while you pack—they're just down the road. Sam can drop off a loaner for you tomorrow. They're good that way if your car goes into the shop for repairs or whatever."

"That would be...great." Ben couldn't argue that the plan made sense, even if having someone else worry about her problems, and offer to fix them, left her a bit off-balance. To cover her uncertainty, she hurried to unlock the door and held it open. "Sorry the accommodations are a little spare."

Courtney settled onto the chair and looked around with a wry grin. "Nice."

Ben laughed.

Courtney, still in her scrubs, propped her backpack against the leg of the chair. "When you're done in the bathroom, do you mind if I duck in and change?"

"No, I'll just be a minute." Ben grabbed a clean pair of jeans and a plain black T-shirt from her suitcase and stepped into the tiny bathroom. She quickly changed and gathered her toiletries into her bathroom kit. Holding the door open for Courtney to pass, she said, "All yours."

"Thanks."

Courtney brushed by her close enough for their shoulders to touch. Ben stood shoulder to shoulder, hip to hip, with practical strangers every single day in the OR, but this faint contact shot through her like lightning. She just barely managed not to gasp. The whole scene was oddly intimate, although there was absolutely nothing suggestive about any of it. Just having Courtney there in her room felt...personal.

Hurriedly, she abolished the thought—and the lingering sensations—and occupied herself with repacking the few things she'd actually unpacked. When Courtney came out, she said briskly, "All set."

Courtney cocked her head and pointed to the basketball sitting by the door. "Don't forget that."

"Oh, it's not mine. I'll drop it off in the office before we leave." Ben tucked it under her arm. "Borrowed it from the manager. You'll have to tell me where to go to find a sports store at some point."

"No problem," Courtney said, "although I've got a couple extra. You're welcome to one. Very good shape."

Ben grabbed her suitcase in her free hand and nudged the door open. "Right, assistant coach. If you've got one lying around somewhere, I'd be grateful."

"I suppose it would be too forward for me to suggest shooting hoops sometime?" Courtney asked as they walked out.

At the word *forward*, Ben's brain had taken a leap to somewhere not involving sports, and it took a second for her to decipher the innocent question.

"Sorry, that was pushy," Courtney said quickly, waving a hand as if to brush away the request. "I imagine people are always asking you to do that. It must get pretty tiresome."

"Actually, no," Ben said as she opened the door and held it once again for Courtney to precede her out. "I'm not that famous. And, sure, I'd be happy to. It's hard to get enough exercise with our schedules."

"You sure?"

"Yes. I'd like that."

Courtney brightened. "Great. I'll pull up in front of the office while you drop the ball off."

Ben tossed her suitcase in the trunk and took the basketball to the office. The manager wasn't there, so she grabbed a pen from the mason jar on the counter, folded over a flyer from the rack on the wall, and wrote *Thanks, checking out, plans have changed. If I owe you anything, call me.* She wrote down her phone number and left. Courtney was parked right in front of the office and she climbed in.

She'd surprised herself by agreeing to shoot hoops with Courtney, although she ought to be used to acting out of character around her. Every time she turned around, she was doing something she never did or saying things she never talked about with her. She wasn't thinking—that was the problem. Some strange instinct or compulsion seemed to take over whenever they were together. That couldn't be a good thing, but the pulse of anticipation that stirred every time Courtney was nearby was hard to ignore. Or deny. Courtney's company was addicting, but she couldn't find any reason to say no to such a simple invitation. Or maybe she just didn't want to.

CHAPTER SIXTEEN

Courtney wished there was some way to make the ten-minute drive last an hour. Maybe in that amount of time she could figure out how to ask the million questions she had of Ben Anderson. Most of them—no, all of them—totally inappropriate. Like, why did she quit the Storm. And why did she leave Nashville. And was she single? Oh, that one was really, really not appropriate. Along with why did seeing her shake her up—in a good way—more than going out on a date with a woman she was hoping to spend the night with. More than some of the women she *had* spent the night with. And how about asking if the way Ben watched her, so focused and intense, even when they weren't working, meant what she hoped it meant. That Ben was interested in her in the same totally non-work way. If the situation had been even a little bit different—if Ben was a woman she'd met on a road trip while traveling for a game, or with a group of friends out for a night, or at a party celebrating after a big win—she wouldn't have been shy in letting her interest show. Even at the café this morning she might have asked if she could join her, just to make casual conversation. Why not? That's how people met, after all.

But they hadn't officially met outside the hospital, and despite the conversations they'd had that weren't about work, there were still the formalities to consider. Ben was staff, and that was an unspoken barrier. Not because of impropriety—all adults here, after all—but more about the implied hierarchy. Like the dividing line between the up-side of town and the other side of the metaphorical tracks. She felt it more keenly for having grown up as the poor relation—all, according to her father, because he had been unfairly shunted aside by his father and stepmother for Val's father. The anointed son. True or not, the stamp of not being quite good enough had marked her. She'd left a lot of that self-doubt behind as she'd made her way in med school and into her residency, but the unwillingness to put herself out there only to be rejected was hard to overcome. Maybe that was why she chose to keep her relationships short and simple.

She glanced at Ben's profile, sharp and calm as the evening sun cast its last golden rays into the vehicle. Ben was a whole other level away from Courtney's world in just about every way. But then Ben turned to her and smiled, and Courtney didn't care.

"I'm a general surgery resident, you know," she said. Might as well address the elephant in the room—at least the one she could see.

"Yes, I know." Ben shifted until her back was to the window, facing Court as if waiting for her to make the next move. Which she guessed she would have to, since she'd made the first one.

Court kept most of her attention on the curving two-lane, which she could drive with her eyes closed in a snowstorm. Even a quick glance at Ben distracted her. Out of scrubs, out of the hospital, she was just a great-looking, sexy, interesting woman who Court wanted. She blinked. Thankfully twilight had crept up on them as she drove, and her blush wouldn't be visible. She hoped. She'd been ignoring the twisty beat of urgency low in her belly for the last few hours, which hadn't been so hard to do when she'd been busy taking care of patients. Now—not so much. Like, not at all. Well, okay. Nothing wrong with a little healthy lust, even if it absolutely wouldn't go anywhere, perhaps ever. Confused at the pulse of disappointment at that thought, and even more in a quandary as to why she seemed so affected when she usually had so much more control in situations like this. Except she couldn't quite come up with the memory of another situation like this, one where she was so taken with a woman she wasn't even trying to be cool about it.

"So," Court went on, making the move. Hey, why not? "Not that it would matter to anyone, anyhow, but since I am thinking it would matter to you, there isn't any reason we couldn't…" She risked a glance at Ben's face. Ben watched her with that intense you-have-all-my-attention look that shot right into the center of her. Her throat felt dry, and the heat she'd been ignoring doubled, hard and fast and damn unsettling. "Have sushi."

For a long moment the silence lingered, and Court's heart plummeted. She usually judged a woman's interest well enough that a refusal wasn't all that common, and when it came, rarely bothered her. Nothing ventured, nothing lost—right?

"I'm not sure when I'll have a free night," Ben said quietly.

"Right, of course. You're just getting settled." Court focused on the lights of the Homestead flickering up ahead.

"But I'm sure I could manage time for a burger," Ben added just as quietly.

And just like that, the heaviness in Court's chest disappeared. She stifled the urge to laugh, the happiness bubbled so high inside. Instead she merely smiled. "I know a great burger place."

❖

Ben eased back around in the seat until she could look out the windshield and not at Courtney. Every single argument she'd constructed since they'd met as to why getting to know Courtney personally was a bad idea lost its power when Courtney was a few inches away and smelling like a spring garden—fresh and full of life. How Courtney managed that after a day of hard work, she didn't know. The combination of effortless sensuality, confidence, and emotional openness was impossible to resist. The latter, Ben was certain, was unintentional, but one of the most appealing of Courtney's many intriguing sides. She'd said yes to a burger—that could possibly just be considered a friendly meal between acquaintances, after all—because she liked being around her, and pretending otherwise was merely self-deluding. She'd vowed to be done with that.

While she was at it, she admitted to herself that the heat stirring in her middle whenever Courtney smiled was welcome too, even if so foreign as to seem brand-new. More than welcome—addicting. If they hadn't been pulling up behind a long line of vehicles that included a Jeep, two trucks, and an SUV, she would have been tempted to find a way to make her smile again. Just to experience that pleasurable heat coiling through her. When Courtney shut off the ignition and turned to her, Ben had to press both hands to her thighs to stop from reaching across the few inches that separated them to brush her thumb against the corner of that smile.

"Are you ready for this?" Courtney asked.

"Not in the slightest," Ben answered, amazed at the gravelly edge in her voice.

"I promise it won't hurt." Courtney's lids flickered lazily as she met Ben's gaze, her tone playful and ever so subtly inviting.

"I'll take my chances, then." Ben opened the door before the air between them grew any heavier and she did something she might regret.

Ben closed the car door and paused to take in the place everyone referred to as the Homestead. She could see why—the long winding gravel drive passed between fields of tall corn, their golden tassels fluttering in the breeze like pennants, and ended at a three-story white farmhouse that commanded the crest of a hill above the river that edged the village. In the fading glow of a late September sunset, the slanting rays glinted on the many-paned windows and reflected off the blue-gray slates of the roof with glittering shards of color. Huge locust trees that had to be hundreds of years old shaded the house on the far side before giving way to vast fields of hay and alfalfa awaiting the harvest. A huge red barn stood at some distance past the house toward the river. Somewhere a dog barked. She took a deep breath and smelled lush fields, the tangy breeze off the river, and the tantalizing scents of food cooking.

"This is gorgeous," she said softly.

"Yeah," Courtney said, coming up beside her. "I have to say this is kind of my dream house. The doctors, Flann and Harper, I mean…they're older than I am, so we weren't friends in school, but a few times a year on big holidays or as part of special village events, the family held open houses and everyone around came. I was here enough times as a kid to covet the place." She laughed a little self-consciously. "I suppose I still do."

As they walked slowly toward the porte cochere at the rear of the house, Ben said, "I can certainly see why. After spending hours inside at the hospital, it would be amazing to come home to a place like this at night."

"I have a little place of my own right now," Courtney said with a soft laugh, "which would fit in about a quarter of this place. But it's mine, and one day, I might go bigger."

"How about family," Ben asked. "Do you have a whole clan like the Rivers too?"

Courtney laughed sharply. "Pretty much the opposite. There's just me and my mother—well, of course, my cousin Val, but we weren't close growing up." She hesitated, then added, "My mother had pretty serious postpartum depression, which I never appreciated until I was much older, obviously, and she never completely recovered."

"Ah," Ben said, "that's hard. I'm sorry."

Courtney picked up her pace and said quickly, "She's doing better now that she's in assisted living with a great support staff and friends she can see every day."

"That's great." Ben noticed there was no mention of Courtney's father, and now was not the time or place to ask. Not everyone had the kind of family that made for pleasant conversations, even though where Courtney was concerned, she wanted to catch every little glimpse of who she was, past and present.

They rounded the corner to the back of the house in silence and approached a wide porch populated by several high-backed wooden rocking chairs, low tables scattered around them, and, at present, Flann Rivers and Abby Remy.

"You made it," Flann said, her gaze tracking from Ben to Courtney. "Just in time. My mother announced the roast is ready to come out of the oven, and Harper informed us we are all due in the kitchen promptly."

Ben and Courtney returned the greeting as they climbed the steps. Flann narrowed her eyes and said to Ben, "Aren't you supposed to have luggage?"

Still unsure and more than a little uncomfortable, Ben ran a hand through her hair. "It's in Courtney's car. I just figured, you know, I ought to wait to be sure it's not inconvenient—"

Abby laughed. "Court, didn't you explain to Ben the only

possible difficulty would be if she turned down the invitation to stay here?"

"I tried."

Court grinned in Ben's direction, and Ben muttered, "I surrender."

Flann swung an arm around Ben's shoulders and herded her toward the door. "Good thinking. You can get your bags after dinner. If we keep everyone waiting, there might be bloodshed. There are teenagers about."

"Uh, right." Ben tried to shake the tension from her shoulders as she followed Flann into a slightly warm, very crowded kitchen that smelled better than any place she'd ever been. Courtney, thankfully, stayed close by, which somehow eased her sense of being totally out of place—and out of her element. The kitchen was the biggest one she'd ever seen, running what looked to be the entire back of the house. An oak table that would hold at least a dozen people held center stage. The mouthwatering smells emanated from several ovens, including the ones below the eight-burner stovetop and another set into a red brick wall at the far end of the room. Wide multipaned windows above the counter provided sweeping views across the sloping lawn to the river.

Ben sat down where Flann indicated, and Courtney settled beside her. Glancing up and down the table, she was able to place most of the faces. Harper carved a huge standing roast at the far end of the table while Blake Remy and Margie Rivers set out platters of potatoes and vegetables.

Abby Remy sat across from her and said with an amused smile, "Busy first day."

Ben nodded. "Yeah, you could say that. Good day."

"The busy ones always are," Courtney said, reaching for a hot roll from a basket Abby passed to her.

Ben nodded, finding it a rare pleasure to be understood without explanation.

Footsteps crossed the porch, and Edward Rivers, in a white shirt—still crisp-looking despite what must have been a long day at the hospital—and sharply creased black trousers, walked in. He kissed his wife on the cheek, glanced around his packed kitchen, and said congenially, "Good evening, everyone. I hope I didn't hold up dinner."

He walked to the far end of the table and took a seat. "Dr. Anderson. Excellent to see you. I understand you've had a full day."

Ben didn't wonder how he knew who she was or how he knew what kind of day she'd had. She doubted if anything that happened at the Rivers escaped his notice. He had the calm, confident air of a man who knew his precise place in the world and embraced it. Just like Flann and Harper always seemed to have known.

Ben had envied them that. Tonight, though, after a day of rewarding surgery and unexpectedly meeting a woman who grew more intriguing by the hour, she couldn't ask for more. "Yes, sir, it was an excellent introduction to everything the Rivers has to offer."

"I trust you will find many more as time goes on."

He smiled at Ida, who took the seat at the far end of the table opposite him, and food was passed around. Conversation drifted away from medicine to the happenings in town, discussions about books, and side conversations. Ben didn't know these people, but she felt comfortable anyhow. Another unusual circumstance for her.

As she ate the excellent food that lived up to all the acclaim, she offered the occasional comment, all the while aware of Courtney close beside her. Now and then, Courtney's knee would touch hers, and every time that happened, a frisson of unexpected excitement tingled along her thigh. She'd been so absorbed by the heady sensation, she hadn't even noticed the dessert course being handed down the line of diners.

"So, Ben," Flann said, passing her a plate of fresh strawberries, biscuits, and cream, "how about a pickup game after dinner?"

Ben froze, her spoon halfway to her plate. The suggestion was innocent enough—natural, even—but the reluctance to drag the past into the present was ingrained, and she needed a moment to dismiss the knee-jerk reaction. She cleared her throat, aware of several people, Courtney included, watching her. "Sure."

"Good," Flann said blithely and pointed her fork around the table. "Blake, Margie, Court...you in?"

After the chorus of enthusiastic yeses, Courtney leaned a little closer. "You okay with this?"

"I'm good." Ben met Courtney's questioning gaze and was caught off-guard by the concern and understanding she found there. Reflexively, she rested her hand on Courtney's thigh. "Thanks."

The muscle beneath Ben's fingers tensed, and Courtney's pupils flared. Ben would have said she was sorry, but before she had a chance, Courtney's warm palm pressed hers for a fleeting second.

"Good," Courtney said. "This will be fun."

"I think you're right," Ben murmured, even if she suspected they weren't talking about the same thing.

CHAPTER SEVENTEEN

Following Courtney's lead, Ben carried her plate over to the counter and placed it with the others that were stacked and waiting to go into the dishwasher. Margie slid a platter covered in foil into the fridge and leaned against the counter next to her.

"Flann said you played professional basketball." She took a plate, rinsed it, and passed it to Courtney, who'd appeared on her other side and deposited it in the dishwasher without a word.

"I did, for a few months." Ben picked up a bowl with a colorful rooster in the center and handed it off to Margie. They worked in silence a few moments, an easy rhythm that Ben found soothing and oddly relaxing.

"For the Storm, right?" Margie asked eventually.

"Yep."

"Did you like it?"

The question wasn't quite what she expected. Usually when her short professional career came up, the questions circled around why she'd left. Of course, most people likely figured she just couldn't cut it.

"I was still getting used to it," Ben said. "Playing professionally is a lot different than college ball. Faster, and I thought I was pretty fast before I got there." She laughed. "And the coaching is different. Suddenly I wasn't a student athlete anymore. I was just the rookie, and I had to prove myself in a way I hadn't had to do before."

"Huh," Margie said. "Kinda like being a first year, right, Court?"

"Sounds like it." Courtney looked past Margie and caught Ben's eye. "Without the TV cameras recording every move, though. Not sure how I'd like that."

"You probably wouldn't notice once you focused on the ball—literally," Ben said. "You didn't have any trouble with that today."

Courtney flushed. "Thank you."

"I think it's neat," Margie said matter-of-factly, "that you had two careers like that—that you didn't have to choose."

Ben nodded. "You're right—I was lucky I got to play basketball all that time."

"Here now," Ida said, stepping up beside them with a swat to Margie's backside. "How did you rope these two into doing half your chores tonight?"

Margie grinned. "They got here first!"

"Well, you can finish up and let these two go socialize."

"Yes, ma'am," Margie said, still grinning.

Ida turned to Ben. "When you bring your luggage in, take it up the front stairs—Courtney can show you the way—to the second room on the right. You'll have a nice breeze from the river across the cornfields. You can sleep with the windows open most nights until November if you don't mind cool fresh air."

"That sounds great," Ben said. "And I appreciate it very much."

"Well, so do I. Most days it's too darn quiet here in the morning."

"Ah, is there anything I should do or not do if I'm leaving early?" Ben said, painfully aware that she hadn't lived with anyone since her student days, and even then she'd only had a roommate for a short time.

"If you somehow manage to get up before me," Ida said, "you can start coffee."

Ben glanced at the percolator presently sitting on the stove, with the coffee bubbling in the small glass knob on the stainless steel lid, and swallowed hard. "Um, I have no idea how to work that."

Ida laughed. "Neither do any of my children, or my husband, for that matter—at least not well enough to make a proper pot." She pointed to a nook at the far end of the room. "You'll find an automatic coffee maker there, which we usually use when there's a crowd. You're probably familiar with that."

Ben laughed. "I think I can manage."

Courtney leaned around Ida and said, "If I were you, I'd wait for Ida to make coffee on the stove. You've never tasted anything like it in your life."

"Actually, that's totally true," Ben said. "And from the way it smells right now, I'm pretty well convinced that I should try it."

Ida grabbed a dish towel and wiped an enormous blue ceramic bowl that Margie handed her. "We'll manage a cup together one of these mornings. Now, I'm going to find my husband and remind him it's time to sit down with the family before he gets busy returning patient calls. Courtney, take Ben outside."

Ida disappeared, Margie right after her, leaving Ben and Courtney alone. Ben let out a breath. "Do you think it would be really, really rude if I hid under the covers until I smelled coffee in the morning?"

"You don't have to worry. Unless you're up before four, at least. I'm pretty sure that's when Ida gets up."

"If I'm up before four, I'll be at the hospital drinking really bad OR brew." Ben grinned. "You'll probably be there yourself, now and again."

"I hope so," Courtney said fervently. "I want to be there if there's an emergency case going on."

"Let's see if you say *that* in a year."

Courtney's eyes flashed. "Bet?"

Amused, Ben shook her head. "I'm not a betting person, especially not when the odds are against me."

"Sometimes taking a chance is worth it," Courtney said, and the way she held Ben's gaze, steady and intense, sent a shot of adrenaline straight to every nerve in Ben's body.

"Maybe—"

Luckily Flann came through the kitchen door just at that moment, the screen door slapping shut behind her, interrupting what Ben'd been about to say—what she'd been thinking about *doing*. Courtney drew in a shaky breath, as if she'd read what had been in Ben's mind.

Flann said, "People will be finished with coffee and dessert in five or ten minutes. You ought to grab something if you want anything before the game."

Courtney murmured, "I'm good."

Ben gave herself a mental shake and pulled herself out of the mesmerizing depths of Courtney's gaze. "I think I better pass too, if I'm gonna have to play soon."

"Are you pissed I put you on the spot about playing ball?" Flann asked after a moment.

Ben laughed. "No. It's fine."

"Because now that I think of it," Flann said, "you usually managed to avoid any of the pickup games when we had five minutes of free time."

Ben lifted a shoulder. "Well, I was behind in the studying end of things, if you'll remember. I hadn't been planning on med school for another few years."

Aware of Courtney nearby, Ben hesitated for a second but, oddly, didn't mind talking about it with her there. "I'd been figuring on at least five or six good years playing professional ball before I got too slow or I started to hear complaints from med school that I needed to get started. You know, they were willing to defer my enrollment for a while, but it wasn't going to be indefinite anyhow."

"Well, that year hardly put you behind," Flann said, "but I can see why playing pickup with a bunch of amateurs probably wasn't going to be the most enjoyable thing you could do right about then."

"I needed not to play for a while," Ben said quietly, "until I really got that I was done."

"Look," Flann said, "if you'd rather not—"

"Too late now," Ben said quickly. "I want to see what you've got, Rivers."

Flann brightened. "Excellent. I talked Harper into playing, so we've got three on three."

"One-point shots," Ben said.

"Fine. We call our own fouls."

"None on game point," Ben added.

"Of course. I'll captain one team," Flann said, "and you can captain the other."

Courtney snorted. "Wow, why does that not surprise me."

"What," Flann said, feigning innocence. "Seniority and all that."

"Whatever happened to drawing straws, or rock-paper-scissors," Court said. "And experience ought to count more than age, anyhow." She pointed to her chest. "Coach here."

"She's got you there," Ben said.

"Okay. I yield to the coach." Flann grimaced. "So, there's one other thing. Our son Blake, he's trying out for the high school varsity team."

Ben said, "I get first pick, by the way. I imagine he's good."

"Yeah, well, I think so. I've been trying to practice with him as much as I can, doing, you know, drills and that sort of thing. If you notice anything we ought to be working on, I'd appreciate it." She glanced at Courtney. "That's fair, isn't it? Not cheating in any way? I mean, I know Ben's an expert and all."

Courtney shook her head. "Hey, if Ben was a coach, then I'd say no way, but she isn't. There's no rule, unspoken or otherwise, that says Blake can't get input from people who know the game. I won't say anything to him, just to keep things totally clean."

"Okay, thanks." Flann let out a breath. "I just want him to be as ready as he can be. It's gonna be a tough go for him, I think."

Courtney said, "You don't think that Chuck Rossi is going to have an issue, do you?"

"I would've said no, but you know politics being what they are, and some of the little...some of his *classmates* might give him a hard time." Flann looked at Ben. "Blake is trans, and he's been out for a few years. He's also a new kid here, which has its own challenges. He's already caught a little flak about trying out for the basketball team."

Ben said, "Is he going to be the first trans kid playing on one of his school's teams?"

Flann nodded. "As far as we know."

"If the coach is a good coach, he'll handle it," Ben said.

"Chuck is good," Courtney said, "plus he's been really vocal about the girls' sports teams getting equal funding for equipment and training space in the school district, so he's likely to be sensitive to Blake's situation too."

"I hope you're right," Flann said. "I just want Blake to have a fair shot. And hell, to have some fun."

"We ought to be able to help with that," Ben said. "Let's go play ball."

❖

Court won first pick after all and took Blake and Flann for her team. Ben had Harper and Margie. Flann would at least have a good time trying to muscle Ben out of the paint and was physical enough to do it, while Blake was quick and wily and fast off the dribble. As for herself, Ben had an inch on her in height and a whole lot of an advantage in skill, but she had a good three-pointer, and even though she'd only get a point for a deep basket, she planned on hitting as many of them as she could. Court hadn't seen Harper play since they were all younger, but she'd probably be on par with Flann in terms of skill. Margie could play on the high school team, from what Court had seen of her in the recreational games. All in all, their teams were well-matched—except for Ben.

But hey, it was just a game, right? Yeah, right.

Court pulled Flann and Blake aside. "Keep the ball away from Ben. Once she has it, she'll be able to shoot from most anywhere. Flann—you need to get in her road. Blake—steal off Harper or Margie if you can, and take your own shots whenever you're open."

"Right, Coach," Blake said, bouncing on his toes.

"I'll stick with her," Flann announced optimistically.

Court put a hand out for Flann and Blake to grip, and they headed onto the hard-packed earth court in front of the barn with a whoop.

While the night drew down around them like a blanket, floodlights on the barn eaves lit as bright as day the area beneath the basketball hoop clamped to the side of the barn. The river and the wind rushing through the corn provided a steady murmuring backdrop to their shouts, occasional catcalls, and cheers for the first scores.

A few minutes into the game, Court could tell Ben was holding back. She passed far more often than she shot, even though she almost always worked her way into a position to score. Instead, she got the ball to Harper and Margie, giving them the chance to shoot. When their side got the ball, Flann tried to tie Ben up so Court and Blake could work a pick and roll. They kept the score close until Margie yelled, "Come on, Ben, shoot the ball. Let's bury them."

Ben's laughter held a challenging note Court had not heard before. They'd spent time together in almost every circumstance—tense moments in the emergency room, quiet focused interludes in the OR, and, after the sudden release of stress at the end of a case, lighter moments when conversation flowed easily. They'd talked over meals in the cafeteria and while drinking coffee in the OR lounge waiting for a case to start. But she'd never heard Ben really laugh as if an idea thrilled her. She liked the sound of it.

"I am shooting," Ben yelled, passing the ball to Harper, who drove for the basket and would've made an easy layup if Court hadn't planted herself there first and taken the charge. She almost went down on her ass when Harper shouldered by, missing the shot in the process, but no one called foul. It was pickup, after all.

She managed to regain her balance, and Ben flashed her a questioning look of concern. She grinned and waved her off. Then, riding the adrenaline high and the pure joy of the competition, she mouthed, *Chicken.*

Ben pressed her lips together, and the ball suddenly came to life in her hands. She cut around Flann and broke for the basket. Almost faster than Court could follow, she shot off the dribble. The ball arced, streaking through the crescent of light cast by the floodlights as it rose and soared and dropped through the rim.

"Woo-hoo," Margie yelled. "That's the ticket!"

"Show-off," Flann shouted.

Ben merely grinned. She didn't repeat it but went back to feeding the ball on almost every opportunity. Even with her not playing full-out, when Margie hit a jumper from midrange, Ben's team reached the final score with a margin of two. Cheers erupted. Court, Blake, and Flann clapped good-naturedly.

"Great game," Harper said, leaning over with her hands on her knees, catching her breath. "I think I need to do that a little more often. I'm getting out of shape."

"That's what happens when you have a desk job," Flann said, wiping sweat from her forehead with the sleeve of her T-shirt.

Harper shot her a look. "Yeah, yeah."

"Another game?" Margie asked brightly.

Harper groaned.

Flann shook her head. "Not on a school night, kiddo."

"Oh, come on," Margie said. "It's early yet."

"Hey, I was talking about me," Flann said, tossing an arm around her shoulders and squeezing. "I've got an early case tomorrow, and Abby's on days. We need to be getting home."

Ben said, "I need an early night too."

Flann clapped Ben on the back. "We need to get you on our team, next time there's a pickup game."

"I'm going to go find Presley," Harper called. "Night!"

When Blake and Margie went on ahead, Flann stayed back with Court and Ben.

"So, Blake is good, right?"

Ben nodded. "If he shows up at the tryouts ready to play and puts himself out on every drill, shows some spirit, I think he'll do fine. He's got good speed and handles the ball well. Make sure he's hitting his free throws."

"Thanks." Flann waved and jogged off toward the house.

Court strolled by Ben's side as everyone else disappeared. Once out of the circle of light in front of the barn, the night was suddenly upon them—the scents, the sounds, the warm night air like a dream she never wanted to wake from.

Ben said after a moment, "Nice game, by the way."

"Back at you. I love to watch you play."

Ben looked startled. "Really?"

"Well," Court said, "you're beautiful when you move."

Ben stopped. "That's not the kind of thing people usually say."

"Maybe most people aren't looking at you while you're making basketball magic. I happen to like to."

"Courtney…" Ben murmured.

"You know, my friends call me Court."

"I think Courtney is a beautiful name," Ben said quietly, "but I'll remember that."

If she put her arms around Ben's neck right now and stepped in to her, if she kissed her, Ben would kiss her back. She knew it. She wanted to do it, and that kept her rooted to the spot. The want was so unexpected, coming from someplace she didn't recognize, she couldn't take the chance. Oh, she recognized lust and the healthy, wholesome, fun sex that followed. This was different, an ache, a yearning, and a desire so sharp she felt she could almost put her hand over the pain. A need that powerful was terrifying.

"I got a text from Sam," Court said to break the spell. "He'll have a Volvo for you here in the morning. In plenty of time for you to get to the hospital."

"Thank you for doing all that," Ben said. "I guess I better grab my luggage so you can get out of here. Long day."

"Yes," Court said.

A few moments later, she led Ben back through the kitchen, along the hall in the quiet house, and up the stairs to the second floor. The door to the bedroom stood open, and moonlight illuminated it brightly enough that neither of them tried to turn on a light. Ben stepped inside and set her bag down by the foot of the big four-poster bed. Court stopped just over the threshold. With the muted light from a lamp at the far end of the hall behind her and the silver glow of moonlight behind Ben, they were trapped in twilight.

"Thanks for everything today," Ben said.

"Thanks for having me scrub—"

Ben took a step forward and cupped Court's face in her hands. "I wasn't talking about the OR."

CHAPTER EIGHTEEN

Ben's palms along Court's jaw were soft and strong, her fingertips just grazing the edge of Court's hair at her temples. Court leaned into Ben's hands. Ben was going to kiss her. No danger there. Court liked kisses—they came in so many shapes and forms, light and playful or demanding and eager. No matter the form, she knew where they were going. Kisses were a prelude to sex—a stepping-stone to the fast and the furious and the fun. She'd been wanting that kiss for hours.

Ben's mouth was warm and firm when it finally met hers, her lips silky soft and tasting a little of salt. Ben's fingertips slid into her hair, and the pressure of the kiss changed, deepening, breaking away for an instant and returning with an edge of hunger, as if the kiss was everything Ben needed to survive. Court went as still as the air just before a summer storm, a slow-building explosion churning inside. She wanted the kiss never to end. She wanted to feed the hunger with the teasing brush of her lips and the taunting touch of her tongue. She wanted to make Ben as crazy as she had somehow become. She wanted to kiss her until the thunder rolled.

Court realized her palms had somehow found Ben's chest, where the muscles tensed and trembled, and she curled her fists in the soft fabric of her shirt. She could have stepped away, could have broken the kiss so easily. Could have made some light comment or casual invitation, and the night would have become one she recognized, one where she would be safe. And she would have lost more than she'd known she wanted—the yearning as sweet as any pleasure, the ache more piercing than any climax.

Ben dropped one hand away from Court's face and circled her waist, her fingers spreading on the hollow at her lower back, holding her deliberately against the length of her tight body. Ben's lips slipped over hers, escaped for a heartbeat, a bird on the wing, and landed again with a flutter that became a demand.

Court moaned. No, she would not, could not, stop. This kiss, and another and another, was what she craved—where the heat of Ben's mouth stole her breath and the shuddering tension in Ben's thighs made her own weak. Court pressed closer, and then her arms were around Ben's neck and her breasts were against Ben's chest, and her hips lifted to join their centers.

Court flicked at Ben's lower lip with her tongue and nipped, desperate for the taste of her. Ben growled deep in her chest and angled her mouth, joining them more inescapably. The storm in Court's depths rose, furious and wild, pounding against the shores of her reason. She moaned, a need she didn't recognize driving her. Soon, soon, she would be lost. A whimper, foreign and helpless, escaped in a breathless gasp.

Shaken, a stranger to herself, Court buried her face in Ben's throat. "Oh my God. Ben."

Ben lifted her mouth away and whispered against Court's temple, "I'm sorry. I didn't think to ask."

"You did—when you touched me the way you did," Court said, pressing her mouth to the angle of Ben's jaw, nipping lightly, "you asked. You gave me all the room I needed to stop. Believe me, I didn't want to."

Ben's heart pounded against Court's breast, erratic and fierce. The drumbeat of her desire made Court's nipples tense. Ben's hand pressed along her spine, each fingertip a separate point of fire burning the length of her clit. Court bit her lip against another whimper. She couldn't take much more.

Ben's lips brushed her ear. "I think I could keep kissing you all night."

"If you tried," Court said, slowly trailing her thumb down the center of Ben's chest, making Ben twitch, "you would have to do a lot more than I could possibly do in Ida Rivers's house."

Ben rested her forehead against Court's and laughed unsteadily. "You and me both."

"But just so you know," Court said, her voice just as unsteady, "I really, really want you to. Kiss me again."

"Court…" Ben's voice broke, and she muttered a curse.

"All night would be good for starters," Court went on, pressing her palm against Ben's abdomen, reveling in the quick clench of muscle at her touch.

"Court, we—"

Court lifted her fingers to Ben's mouth, lightly tapping her lips. "Whatever you're going to say, don't. All we did was kiss, Ben. Let's just let it be that."

Ben shivered, so unexpected a reaction that the storm Court thought she'd leashed threatened to swamp her. God, she wanted her. And knowing that Ben wanted her aroused her even more.

She slid both hands back to Ben's chest and traced the course of her collarbones lightly before rising up and gently kissing her.

"Good night, Ben," she whispered, stepping away.

Ben's thumb brushed the corner of Court's mouth as her hand fell away.

"Good night, Court."

❖

Ben watched from the window until the red flicker of Court's taillights disappeared around a bend in the road, extinguished between heartbeats with the finality of their broken kiss. The kiss she'd begun without a thought and would never be able to forget. She couldn't claim surprise—not when practically every minute since her arrival had brought some unexpected event. Neither could she pretend to be unaware that almost from the moment she'd opened her eyes, Courtney had been part of those events. First she'd been only the nameless woman standing at the side of the court, watching her play with an intensity that radiated through the quiet morning, who had left her thinking about her long after she was gone. She'd reappeared at the café, meeting Ben's stare and returning that curiosity with a nod of recognition.

Hello, I know who you are.

Of course, she hadn't—not then and not even now, not even after the kiss.

Those encounters might have been forgotten had she not run into Courtney at the hospital, as if she'd been waiting, as if she'd been meant to be there. Ben snorted in pained amusement, remembering that their meeting had been just the opposite, in reality—Court turning abruptly, almost into her arms.

We've met, Courtney had said.

The introductions already seemed superfluous, before Court led her off on a tour to introduce her to the landscape that would become her world. Only hours later, they were thrust together in the midst of a life-threatening emergency, followed by case after case, united across the bodies of the injured they were charged to heal. Just as quickly as the urgency of a day filled with crises threw them into one another's path, a ride through a golden September evening to another world filled with warmth and connection brought another kind of intimacy. One that lingered and grew until it seemed wherever Ben turned, whatever she touched, with her hands, with her mind, with her every sense, she found Courtney.

And when the night had finally drawn to a close, and the quiet echoed with the images of Courtney's smile and the sound of her laughter and the knowing in her eyes, Ben had had no choice. She'd had to relive every one of those moments with a kiss. Once unleashed, every surge of pleasure demanded more. She might never have stopped—she'd never know. Courtney had kissed her, had cleaved to her, heat to heat, and had finally done what she could not. Stopped.

Even now, all she wanted was to touch her again, to rekindle every moment.

We've met, Courtney had said.

So many things she'd wanted to say with that kiss, and she hadn't known it until too late.

When no returning headlights broke the black night, she quietly made her way down the stairs and out through the kitchen to the shed beside the barn where Flann had stored the basketball earlier. She found it and began to play.

❖

Courtney got back to town at a little before eleven. Wide-awake—beyond awake. She couldn't have slept if she'd wanted to, and she didn't. Her skin seemed too tight to contain her body. Her muscles hummed as if electrified. She was a live wire searching for a place to go to ground.

She could run, she could try a cold shower, she could try her own hand to release the tension scraping her nerves raw. None of that appealed. Not when she knew very clearly exactly what she needed and *who* she wanted. Since Ben Anderson was not going to magically appear in her bed tonight—and if she'd read Ben right, very possibly not any night—she was in no hurry to get there. All she'd have to look forward to would be an hour of tossing and turning and wondering how Ben's misplaced sense of responsibility would declare itself. Because Ben was going to worry about that kiss, that amazing, off-the-scale kiss that—oh, by the way—they'd *both* wanted. And which she'd like very much to repeat, and soon, thank you very much. Because when had a kiss ever been more exciting than any other thing she'd ever done with a woman? How was that even possible? But it had been. Ben had kissed her, and every single atom in her body had begun vibrating, while a furnace opened inside her and stoked a hunger so great she ached. Still.

She had to move, go somewhere she wouldn't torture herself wondering what she would do if a kiss was all she would have.

On a weeknight, everything was closed in town with the exception of Bottoms Up. She left her car in front of her house and walked the block and a half to the tavern.

"Hi, Denny," Court said as the ex-biker, now family man turned business owner and bartender, turned her way. "A draft, thanks."

He nodded, handed her a foaming glass, and she sipped as she turned to look for a quiet place to drink. Jane waved her over to a table in the corner.

"I didn't expect to see you tonight," Jane said as she pushed out a chair. She'd traded in her flight suit for black jeans, a wide black leather belt, and a white tank top that showed off her shoulders and the wings tattoo on her right delt.

"You either." Courtney settled back and took another long swallow. The beer was cold and tangy, beads of sweat collecting on the side of the glass and dripping down to her fingers.

"I just got off the second shift," Jane said. "What a day, huh? How's Val?"

"I saw her just before I left around seven. She was stable. The surgery went well."

"I know I said it before, but you did a great job on all of that." Court tipped her glass to Jane. "We all did that."

"That we did." Jane tapped Court's glass with her bottle. "So, how was it working with the new surgeon all day? Looked pretty intense from up in the gallery."

Courtney rubbed at the streaks on her glass with her thumb. "Fine. Great, really. Ben's a terrific surgeon. I'm glad she was the one to take care of Val."

"You went out to the Homestead, didn't you?"

"Yes, great as always."

After a moment, Jane said, "Are you all right?"

"Sure." Court looked at Jane. How often in her life had she said that when she'd been hurt, or afraid, or scared, and she hadn't known who to trust? This was now, and this was Jane. "No. I'm a mess."

Jane said, "Let me guess. The new surgeon."

Court nodded.

"What happened?"

"Not that much," Court said.

"Looks like more than not much."

"Just a kiss."

Jane didn't say anything.

"All right, there was a kiss," Court said. "And it…shook me. I don't know why. I mean, I've kissed women on a lot shorter notice, who I knew a lot less well than Ben, and never worried about it."

Jane laughed. "I think I might've been one of them."

"No, you weren't." Court nudged Jane's calf with her foot. "All right, we didn't waste time, but you were *not* the shortest acquaintance I've ever had before getting into bed."

"So what's the deal this time?"

"A lot of things happened today I didn't expect. A lot of things I never thought I'd feel. Because of her. The kiss kind of brought that all home."

"Some pretty life-changing experiences can happen in a

short time between people," Jane said quietly. "Given the right circumstances. Being open to being seen, or understood, or even vulnerable at just the right moment."

"And you get that's a pretty scary thought, right?" Court drained her glass and pushed it aside.

"I do. That's probably why I'm single."

"Am I being an insensitive ass telling you all this?" Court said.

Jane laughed. "Babe. We had what we both wanted. We were great then, and we still are. It's all good."

Court sighed. "Really glad about that."

"So what's your plan?" Jane said.

"I don't have any idea," Court said. "I'm not sure I even want one, if a simple kiss has me this off my game."

"Maybe it's time for a new game plan."

Court shook her head. She was afraid Jane was right, and she wasn't sure she wanted to play. Losing might hurt more than she was willing to risk.

CHAPTER NINETEEN

"All set for tryouts tomorrow?" Dave Kincaid asked as he pulled out a chair next to Blake in the cafeteria.

"Pretty much." Blake had been eating lunch alone after Margie and Taylor left early to put together some Instagram posts about the last QSA meeting. "Mostly I've been working on free throws. Everybody says that's important."

"Are you over seventy percent?" Dave broke open a package of chocolate chip cookies. He had the build of a quarterback, with strong shoulders and arms, sleek hips and thighs, and a lot more muscle than Blake just about everywhere, without being bulky. Blake admired his form, but he really envied the muscles. No matter how hard he worked out, he couldn't put on the kind of muscle that Dave had. He was destined to be lean, although he *did* have pretty good muscle definition. Not that he minded too much since basketball, not football, was his thing, and being quick and wiry worked for what he wanted to play. Dave had let his hair grow, and it curled a little on his neck. Blake liked it. Liked it and considered letting his own grow out a little bit. He'd kept his pretty high and tight ever since he'd finally been able to cut it short a few years before.

"Yeah, running right around seventy-six."

Dave snorted. "Hey, when most of the guys are practicing dunking like that's, you know, the most important shot and can't hit sixty from the free-throw line, you're gonna be fine."

"I'm hoping Coach will be looking for a shooting point guard," Blake muttered. "'Cause I don't have the size for anything else."

"You're plenty big enough for b-ball. Don't sweat it."

"I'm good." Blake wished all he had to worry about was hitting the layups and not screwing up on the drills, and handling the ball like he knew he could. He knew most of the guys who'd be trying out, but not all that well. If they didn't want him on the team, there were a lot of ways they could foul him up. Not that he could do anything about it—all he could do was show up and give his best. He knew it—sometimes it was just tough for that to seem like enough.

Dave bit into a cookie and leaned back a little in his chair. "So you and Margie have a date, huh?"

"Not exactly a date...we're going to the drive-in." Blake reconsidered. "Yeah, I guess that sort of qualifies."

Dave grinned. "I'd say so. Drive-in, by yourself, in the dark. With *popcorn*."

The way he said *popcorn*, with a little lowering of his voice and wiggle of his dark blond eyebrows, made Blake laugh. "Come on. Stop giving me crap."

Dave lifted a shoulder. "Okay. Maybe the popcorn's not all that necessary."

Blake really liked him. After Margie, Dave was one of the first friends he'd made in town. He was funny and easy to talk to and never seemed to think of Blake as anyone other than who he was. He'd stood up for Blake a time or two, when he'd been new in town and a few of the guys had hassled him. That hadn't stopped, but Dave knew now that Blake could handle himself and let him. Blake liked that about him too. "Are you bothered about the drive-in thing?"

Dave offered him a cookie and Blake took one.

"No," Dave said, finishing off another one. "Margie's cool. So are you. I don't see how it's going to change anything for any of us if you two get serious."

"Well, I don't know that it's going to change anything for me and Margie either," Blake said. "I just kinda"—he ran a hand through his hair, thinking once again he ought to let it grow out some—"just kinda wanted to see, you know."

"Right. Be alone."

Blake knew he was blushing. Damn it. "Well, yeah, that."

"I'm not asking." Dave grinned.

"Oh, come on," Blake said, self-conscious.

Dave laughed. "Yeah, okay. That answers the question."

Blake leaned forward. "I'm not gonna talk about it."

"I didn't think you would," Dave said. "I wouldn't either."

Blake wondered if Margie had told Taylor about the kiss—bet she did. Blake thought about if that bothered him and had just decided it didn't when he saw Donnie Winslow striding toward them with his trademark sneer and swagger. "Oh, for fuck's sake."

Dave glanced over toward Donnie and casually rested his hand on Blake's forearm.

Donnie stopped abruptly next to their table. "I always knew you were queer, Kincaid."

"Really?" Dave said. "I didn't think you were that smart."

Donnie's hands fisted by his sides. "So you and the little fag are a thing now, is that it?"

Dave shook his head. "I wish. I can't get Blake to go out with me."

Donnie's mouth dropped open before he turned his back and stomped away.

Dave squeezed Blake's forearm. "I hope you didn't mind me saying that."

Blake looked down at Dave's hand on his arm. Dave's hand was much bigger than his, and some of his knuckles were bruised, probably from scrimmages. The muscles in his forearm stood out beneath the suntanned skin. The golden brown hairs glimmering on his smooth skin looked soft. When he looked up, Dave was watching him expectantly.

"You know Donnie's going to run with that all over school," Blake said.

Dave's brows flickered. "I don't care."

"Neither do I."

"I was serious."

Blake swallowed. "You never said."

"Been thinking about it awhile," Dave said. "I'm pretty sure I'm bi."

"I'm pretty sure I'm not," Blake murmured.

Dave smiled. "Well, I guess we'll see, huh?"

Blake grinned. "I guess so."

Dave squeezed his arm again and drew back. "I want to come to your tryouts tomorrow."

"Thanks," Blake said. "I'm glad you'll be there."

❖

Court paged her senior resident at a little before five p.m. to sign out. She'd made arrangements the day before to be sure she could leave in time for tryouts. They were expecting a big turnout. When she'd finished giving her report, she changed into the team warm-up pants and T-shirt, maroon and gold with the Blazers lightning bolt prominent on both, grabbed her backpack, and drove over to the high school. She'd driven to work just in case she ended up running late. The general surgery service was always busy with scheduled routine surgeries plus emergencies that often kept everyone in the OR late into the evening, and she'd spent most of the last few days running scut work, filling in when extra hands were needed for a case, and covering the service on night call. Nothing she wasn't used to, but not what she'd been hoping for after the day she'd spent working with Ben—of course, that had been a fluke. In a whole lot of ways, as it turned out. Keeping the disappointment at bay hadn't been all that difficult when she'd been at the hospital and all her focus had been on the next task, the next decision, the next person who needed her attention. Now, in the quiet of her car, the hollow thrum in her midsection surged.

When she'd shown up at the hospital the morning after dinner at the Homestead, she'd reported to the general surgery service she'd been assigned to, but even as she listened to report from the night residents and made notes on the day's work, she'd been waiting to hear that she'd gotten pulled to Ben's service. Word never came. Maybe Flann had nixed it—and she could see why. Ortho was a specialty rotation that she elected to take, but general surgery was her main responsibility and where the staff needed her assistance most. Ben probably wanted a more experienced resident too. That all made sense. Only why hadn't Ben at least given her some word one way or the other, when she'd suggested she would talk to Flann about it? Or at least say she'd changed her mind? Something?

Instead, she heard nothing—about work or anything personal. As in—hey, we had a moment the other night. She'd seen Ben briefly in passing in the halls and the OR lounge in the last few days, but they'd both been working, and there hadn't been any time to do more than nod. At first she'd waited for a call or a page or a text, and that hadn't come either. After twenty-four hours, she told herself if Ben had been any other woman she'd met, shared a brief intimacy with, and then not heard from—an intimacy that hadn't even progressed beyond a kiss—she'd have forgotten her by now. Long before now.

The fact that she was still sitting in her car, staring at the gym and thinking about Ben, not even sure if she *wanted* to hear from her any longer but unable to stop wondering, left her irritated and confused. Neither feeling was welcome or familiar, and when the Volvo pulled into a spot a few rows in front of hers, she jumped out, grabbed her backpack, and strode over to it.

"You weren't even going to call me?" she said before Ben had even stepped out.

Still seated behind the wheel, Ben wordlessly raised a brow, turned and grabbed a duffel from the passenger side, and climbed out of the car. She was wearing plain black sweats, a red polo shirt that stretched nicely across her shoulders and hugged her biceps, and gym shoes. Not a bit of flash or anything else to suggest she'd ever stepped onto a basketball court. She looked good too. Damn her. Why did she have to look that hot?

"Hi, Court," Ben said, in that voice she had that said *I'm totally here with you, and everything you are about to say is more important to me than anything else in the world.*

Damn her. Why did she have to sound so sexy?

Not to be distracted by all that hot and sexy, Court frowned. "That's it? Hi, Court?"

"I should've called," Ben said. "I apologize."

That took all the steam out of her irritation. "Well, I could've too, I guess."

As they started toward the gym, Ben said, "Why didn't you call?"

Court hadn't wanted an apology. She wanted an explanation. Actually, she wanted to know a lot of things, and she was either going to get them or walk. "You first. After all, you kissed me first."

Ben grinned, just a flicker, but Court saw it.

"And don't say I kissed you back—I am aware of that. Still doesn't explain the disappearing act."

Ben's smile disappeared. "I've been trying to figure out if that was a good idea. Not the kiss—that wasn't an idea at all—it was an act of will, and I'm not sorry about it."

"Good. So what's the problem?"

"Things could be complicated. I'm trying to sort it out."

"All by yourself?" Courtney asked sharply. Really, did someone as bright as Ben really think that was going to work?

"Not a good idea?" Ben asked, opening the door for her.

Court liked the way she did that, held the door, even though it was completely unnecessary. Obviously she could open her own door and do pretty much anything else that needed doing—although some things she preferred to make a joint venture. But there was just something nice about this little gesture that showed Ben was thinking about her. Corny, maybe, but secretly quite pleasant.

"Do I need to answer that? To be fair, though, I don't know why I waited myself." Court huffed. "I'm not that sort of woman."

"I'll bet."

Court stopped and faced her. The sound of basketballs thudding off the backboard, whistles blowing, and the general tumult of sports emanated from the open gymnasium doors. They were alone in the hallway, but in a few more steps they'd be swallowed up by the noise, adrenaline, and work they were both there to do—just like they had been every day at the Rivers. And Court could not wait another day, wondering how Ben had walked into her life, turned it upside down, and left her uncertain of what she wanted.

"We should talk," Court said.

"All right."

"Tonight. Are you on call?"

"No," Ben said.

"Neither am I." Court halted at the door of the gym. "Then

when we're done here, you can come over to my place. I'm just across the street."

Ben's eyes darkened a little, and satisfied that she wasn't the only one on shifting ground, Court turned her back and stepped into the gym.

CHAPTER TWENTY

Ben followed Courtney through the gym to the bleachers where a cluster of women and men holding a variety of clipboards, tablets, and gear gathered. The coaching staff and trainers—a fit bunch, looking pretty much exactly like they'd looked when she was playing. Only the uniform styles and logos had changed. Groups of girls in regular gym clothes filled the court—shooting hoops, running layups, and practicing free throws. A short-haired blonde a few years older than her, the Blazers logo on the chest pocket of her white polo shirt and on her red track pants, jogged toward them.

"Court, glad you didn't get held up," she said in a warm, brisk alto, her gaze skirting quickly over Ben. "We got some late sign-ups and even a couple of walk-ins, so we'll need to break into three groups instead of two."

"I'll get with Rich on that," Court said and gestured to Ben. "Anita, this is Dr. Anderson. She's a sports medicine orthopedist. She'll be taking over for Dr. Meriwether."

"I heard you'd be joining us." Anita held out her hand. "I'm Anita Gold—Anita. Did Kurt Meriwether already resign?"

Ben laughed and shook her hand, a warm, firm grip with the faintest hint of calluses along her palm. She had a few herself, even now when her hands were softer from hours in the OR instead of on the court handling a ball every day. "Possibly the instant Flann Rivers asked me to take over the team doctor role for the school."

Anita grinned. "You're going to be busy, Doctor. We've got a lot of teams to cover."

"It's Ben, and that's okay. Sports are pretty much my favorite thing."

"I imagine. I saw you play in the Sweet 16 a while back."

"That was quite a bit longer than a little while ago, I think."

"Still a great game and one I have the kids watch when we're working that particular defense against a bigger, faster team."

Ben knew this conversation, had heard a version a hundred times. A warm sense of familiarity settled over her. One she welcomed, and that was a surprise. "It still works, even though all the players seem to have gotten bigger and faster since my time."

"Well, it's good to have you, Ben." Anita's diamond-blue eyes held hers a moment longer and then shifted to Court. "I think everyone's here. You want to start them on drills?"

"Sure." Court dropped her backpack on the bench and smiled at Ben as she headed for a whippet-thin guy in T-shirt and joggers holding an iPad.

"Hopefully we won't need you tonight." Anita smiled, a nice friendly smile, relaxed and confident. "Let me know what you think of the turnout."

"Looking forward to it," Ben said, and she was. Though it was quite a long way back on the road for her, she could still remember her first tryouts, the nerves and the excitement and the sheer un-self-conscious joy of just playing. Before all the competition, all the hype, all the notoriety created rivalries instead of friendships, and stress and uncertainty rather than enjoyment and confidence. All of that was part of the privilege of getting to play at the highest level of competition with some of the best players in the world, and a price she'd pay again, but she hadn't forgotten there was a price.

Tonight the gym resounded with excitement, and she leaned back against the bench behind her, arms spread along the top on either side, as the shouts and whistles and rhythm of leather on wood pulled her in. She found the spectating side of things pretty enjoyable, especially since she was totally free to watch Court, who had a nice easy command, much the same as she did at the hospital, calling out drills and encouragement, and occasionally redirecting one of the players who hadn't quite gotten the hang of the drill. After a few minutes, Court and Anita took some players to the other half for three-on-two practice. Court looked great demonstrating some technical point or running up and down reffing the practice play.

She moved smoothly, fast and sure, which Ben knew already from playing against her in pickup. Having the benefit of observing with all her attention now, though, she appreciated just how skilled and... attractive she was. The jolt of heat in her midsection had nothing to do with admiring Court's athletic skills—and everything to do with the instantaneous memory of Court's mouth against hers.

Ben snapped upright, shaking off the haze of almost lust, and focused on the spectators who had somehow filled much of the bleachers while she'd been engrossed in Courtney. Blake Remy sat a few rows behind her about halfway down the length of the gym with a tall, dark-haired guy and a girl with shimmering gold hair caught back in a ponytail. Blake pointed, and Ben followed his gaze. Somehow she'd missed Margie Rivers among all the other players out there when she'd been watching Court, but Margie instantly stood out at a brief glance. She played the way she seemed to do everything else, as Ben recalled very well from Margie's direct questions about her past and her competitive drive when they'd played pickup—straightforward, confident, and to the point—or, as the case might be tonight, to the basket. She had a little bit of what made both her older sisters such solid competitors—Flann was the fireball, quick to ignite and fast to flame, while Harper was the slow burn, unflagging and determined. Margie had that spark, offering a word now and then that brought a laugh or a look of surprised satisfaction to the face of one of the other players. She didn't look like she was competing for a place—she looked like she was playing with the team. Court would've noticed and so would Anita Gold. You could teach skills, most of the time, and you needed the flash, but most of all, you needed a solid core to keep the team tight when it was coming apart. Margie'd make a strong small forward. Ben would put money on seeing her on the floor later in the season.

A fortyish guy, his brush cut tinged with gray, in a tight maroon T-shirt and sweats came in with half a dozen boys who spread out on the bleachers. The returning players on the boys' basketball team, at a guess. They had that look of almost senior guys, not quite totally mature but closer to being out of high school than in. They seemed pretty interested in the tryouts and cheered now and then at a well-made hoop. Good to see the camaraderie. She hadn't seen much cross-team activity or interest when she was coming up, but things had changed and for the better, she thought. She hoped that inclusiveness would extend to players like Blake Remy.

At one point, Anita Gold walked over and talked to the boys' coach, who said something that made her laugh. Ben relaxed, enjoying the familiar sounds of players cajoling, encouraging, occasionally good-naturedly taunting. She watched the vocal ones, the ones with the energy, the ones who coaches counted on to lift the team when they were behind or facing a team that everyone else said would beat them. Those were the kind of kids coaches wanted, assuming they had the basic skills.

Ben tensed when she heard a sharp cry from out on the floor. Court trotted over to a girl whose dark hair hung in a braid down her back as she bent over, clutching her knee. Court looked over to signal Ben even as she jogged to join them.

"Kalani, this is Dr. Anderson, our team doc. What happened?"

"Nothing," the girl said quickly, although her grimace as she straightened said otherwise. "I just came down wrong and twisted my knee a little." She forced a smile. "I'm fine."

"How about we take a walk over to the bench," Ben said, "and have a quick look. We don't want to miss anything now that might hold you up during the season, right?"

Kalani glanced from Ben to Courtney. "Does this mean I'll be disqualified from the tryouts?"

"No," Court said. "But we need to make sure you're okay. That's always the most important thing. You don't play hurt, ever."

Kalani took a deep breath. "Okay, all right. But it really does feel fine now. Really."

"Let's be sure." Ben walked her over, watching her as she put weight on her leg. She didn't flinch, even though she appeared to be walking cautiously. Pointing for Kalani to sit on the bench a distance away from the students and staff, Ben squatted in front of her. "Have you ever injured your knee before?"

"No," Kalani said quickly.

"What other sports do you play?"

"Oh. Um, tennis, soccer, and I run."

"Does it bother you during any of those activities?"

Kalani hesitated. "Once in a while, if I do a lot of hill work."

"Okay. Let's take a look. I'm going to move your knee, and if anything I do hurts, tell me." Ben gently ranged the knee through a full range of motion and palpated the patellar tendon. "Tender here?"

Kalani shook her head, but her silence was a different kind of answer.

"This is where it bothers you after you run the hills?"

"Sometimes," Kalani said, "but not for very long. Sometimes I ice it, but most of the time I don't even have to do that."

"Your patella—your kneecap—is pretty mobile. That's not uncommon, especially in women," Ben said, "and the good thing is I don't find any significant instability in your knee. All the same, we need to make sure that this isn't going to get worse or hamper you while you're playing. Some judicious K-Taping will probably take care of it."

"Can you do that now?"

Ben smiled. "As a matter of fact, I can."

As she taped the patella to stabilize the lateral motion, she said, "One of the trainers can go over with you how to do this yourself. If you have pain again, let them know."

"I will. I promise."

"Okay, then. You can head on back out."

"Thanks. Thank you."

She jogged back out, and Ben watched her go, checking her gait. Everything looked fine. Court glanced over as Kalani rejoined her group, and Ben nodded.

Anita Gold joined her a moment later.

"We see a lot of overuse injuries," she said, "and we need to do more to instruct the kids in how to avoid overtraining. Do you think we can set up a series of talks, maybe?"

"Of course, be happy to do that."

"Excellent." She paused, watching a girl on the free-throw line. "You know, once the season gets going, we hold playing clinics with some of the other area schools. I'd love to have you instruct."

"It's been quite a while. I'm not sure how valuable I'd be."

"You don't really think I'm going to buy that, do you?" Anita said. "I doubt you've forgotten too much."

"I'll get back to you on that, then."

Anita nodded. "Good enough."

When the tryouts ended, Ben packed her gear and waited until Courtney was done conferring with the other coaches. The gym emptied of spectators and players, leaving her with nothing to distract herself from Court's question.

You weren't even going to call?

Court was right—she should have called. It wasn't her style to share something like that, to start something personal, and then pretend it hadn't happened. She'd owed Court an explanation on several fronts. When Flann had asked her how Court had done, and if Ben wanted her to continue on the service, all Ben could think about was that she'd kissed her and wasn't even sure what that meant. Or what to do about it.

"She did an excellent job—she's a strong first year," she'd said, "but I think she probably needs to get a little more general surgery under her belt before she rotates on a subspecialty. I can do with an ortho resident when you can get one free, and until then, I'll take whatever general surgery resident is available."

"Good enough," Flann said and had moved on to something else.

Ben would have texted, at least, if she'd known what to say, which she hadn't. If she could just figure out if wanting more… of everything—the easy moments and the wild, lose-her-mind, exhilarating ones—was safe. For either of them.

All by yourself? Court had asked when she'd tried to explain that.

Thinking about it now, not really one of her better ideas.

"Ready?" Court asked as she strode over.

Ben stood. She could make an excuse and walk away. She searched Court's eyes. Deep brown. Unwavering. Offering her a different path than she'd planned. If she dared.

"Yes." Ben held that gaze a moment longer as Court slowly smiled. The smile was enough to make her forget what she'd been worried about, but then, being around Courtney always did that.

"Good," Court murmured. "It's about time."

CHAPTER TWENTY-ONE

D id you eat before you left the hospital?" Ben asked as they walked outside into a cool evening that presaged the coming of fall.

"I had lunch—does that count?" Court shivered, although she wasn't cold. Just like that, in a few short days, the seasons had changed. Sometimes change just came that way, almost overnight.

"Not at seven thirty in the evening. You were on call last night," Ben said, "so technically you shouldn't even have been *at* the hospital this afternoon. So you definitely need to eat now."

Court wasn't sure what shocked her most—that Ben knew she'd been on call or that Ben was always trying to feed her. Both thoughts made her uncomfortably pleased. "How do you know?"

"That you must be hungry?"

Court stopped, forcing Ben to turn and look at her. "No—that I was on call."

"I checked the resident on-call schedule posted in the OR."

"Oh." That sounded like something Ben would do, considering she didn't have a full complement of residents assigned to her yet. Court felt a bit foolish for thinking she'd been the cause, as if she really was special or something equally pathetic.

"Because I wanted to know what you were doing," Ben said, walking off toward the parking lot without looking back.

Court hurried to catch up while trying to ignore the twist of pleasure that was making her uncomfortable in an entirely different way now. Ben wasn't the type to tease, so she had to know what those little remarks did to her, didn't she? Annoyed at herself for being so damn easy, and a little thrilled to think Ben *was* trying to turn her on, she blurted, "Are you trying to make me crazy?"

Ben stopped by the Miata and cocked her head, regarding Court with a bemused expression. "Am I?"

"Yes," Court said through her teeth. Ben was so, so good at turning things around on her. "The question is whether you meant to."

"Does someone caring about you make you crazy?"

Court sucked in a breath. Too close, way, way too close. She wouldn't know, as she rarely let anyone, even Jane, in a position to try. "No."

Ben's mouth twitched as if she wanted to push the point, but she said, "Good, because I don't want to make you crazy." She paused. "At least not over whether you've remembered to eat or not."

Court wasn't ready to ask just how Ben wanted to make her crazy. If she went much farther down that road, she'd be too distracted to say any of the things she needed to say. Deflection always worked well when she needed to lighten the atmosphere. "I've got food at my place. You can leave your car here in the lot until later. No one will bother it."

"Okay," Ben said in a tone that suggested she knew exactly what Court had just done. Ben slid into the passenger seat as Court started the engine. "I have to get the loaner back over to Sam as soon as I get a free day. Actually, I might see if he wants to sell it. It's a good enough car."

"That's most likely why he picked it for you. Helping you decide," Court said as she drove the short distance to her block and pulled up in front of her bungalow.

"Smart businessman." Ben got out and waited while Court grabbed her backpack. "Although I'm not sure he'd know me well enough to think I was a Volvo kind of person."

Court rested her forearms on the top of the Miata and gazed across the car at Ben. "No. I put you more in the Porsche category."

"Really?" Ben grinned wryly. "I'm not sure that's a good thing."

"Oh, I don't mean the dilettante pretend-race-car-driver Porsche people, but I can see you going for a little speed, letting everything out on a dark country road in secret."

"You might be right," Ben murmured, her gaze sweeping Court's face and seeming to fix on her mouth. "Dark country roads at night appeal to me."

Court's heart thudded with strange anticipation as she unlocked her front door and held it for Ben this time, smiling to herself as she did. Ben walked inside in front of her and waited in the middle of her tidy living room. At least she hoped it was tidy. She didn't usually leave the house with the thought that she might be coming home with visitors, but she did on occasion, so she made an effort to make sure nothing too embarrassing was left lying around. She tried to see her home as Ben might see it—modest furnishings chosen for comfort and utility, not the biggest television in the world, and probably too many bookcases crammed with books in no recognizable order. The navy blue sofa, she noticed, had a slight indentation on one end, where she preferred to curl up with a book or a journal when she wasn't too tired to stay awake reading. The lone side table with a stack of *Annals of Surgery* piled precariously on the end. Definitely no dorm room vibes, but clearly the place of a solo occupant who wasn't around much.

"This is nice," Ben said. "How long have you owned it?"

"Just a year. It was my graduation present to myself." Court gestured to the kitchen visible through the doorway on the far side of the living room. "I can offer homemade chili from the café—I just got it yesterday. It's vegetarian."

"Are you a vegetarian?" Ben asked, following Court. "I was too busy eating at Ida's the other night to notice what anyone else was having."

"Would that be a dealbreaker?" Court turned on the under-cabinet lights, giving the room plenty of light without the glare from the overhead. She looked over her shoulder as she opened the fridge.

Ben's grin returned, and a little bit of heat flashed through her eyes. "I suppose that would depend on the deal."

Court refused to get crazy again, and she was almost successful. If she could just get her hormones to cooperate. "Well, I try to eat plant-based whenever I can, but I wouldn't turn down a burger if I was stranded on a desert island. You?"

"I try to eat as healthy as I can, but I suppose I wouldn't turn down a bean burger in dire straits."

Court laughed. "You'll like the chili. We'll do burgers next time. Wine?"

"Yes," Ben said, pulling out a stool at the center island and leaning her elbows on the countertop. "I'd offer to do something, but I have no idea what that might be."

"You can open this." Court passed the bottle to Ben along with a corkscrew and a couple of glasses. "I hope white's okay. It's all I've got at the moment."

"It's great."

Court would've thought she'd feel awkward with Ben in her kitchen. She didn't entertain, not in any sense of the word, but like every other time she'd been alone with Ben, no matter where they were, she was comfortable. If she thought about it, how comfortable she felt, she might've worried. Her spine prickled, and she said abruptly, "I don't chase women."

Ben pulled the cork on the wine and poured it, maddeningly placid as she observed Court across the kitchen island. "No, I don't imagine you ever have to. Or want to."

"What does that mean?"

"I can think of a dozen reasons," Ben said, sipping her wine, "starting with the fact that you're beautiful, outgoing, bright, and accomplished. And you've got an incredibly seductive laugh. Women would be fools not to notice."

Damn her. She was doing it again. Court felt the heat rise to her face. "You know, you don't look like a slick operator, but you really are."

Ben laughed. "I've never been accused of that before."

"Then no one's ever been paying attention." Court passed her the chili she'd heated in the microwave, and for a few moments they ate in silence.

"You're right, that was good." Ben pushed her empty bowl aside. "So. Are you chasing me?"

"Absolutely not," Court said. "That whole thing in the parking lot, about you not calling—I was just pissed. You kissed me and then poof. Nothing."

Ben grimaced. "I know, and I can only apologize again."

"Instead of that, how about an explanation," Court said quietly.

"I don't kiss women ordinarily."

"Then I've been reading you wrong, I guess."

Ben waved a hand. "No, I don't mean that. Yes, I kiss women. But not easily, not without a lot of thought and consideration. At least ninety-nine percent of the time."

"I don't mind being an exception."

Ben laughed, a wry self-deprecating sound. "Oh, believe me, you're an exception. And I'm not explaining this very well. I don't usually have serious relationships, and I'm not into casual intimacy."

"Those two statements, covering most kinds of relationships, begs the question why. Why neither?" Court said.

"I guess because most of my life all my intimate relationships were time-limited," Ben said seriously, working her way through things she'd never really put words to before. "The people I cared about most were my teammates, and that kept changing. I kept losing them. First I graduated from high school and then college and then the Storm—and all of the people that mattered to me disappeared at regular intervals. So I guess I don't form attachments all that easily."

"No serious girlfriends?" Courtney asked quietly.

"Mostly no. First I was too young and all I cared about was basketball. Then I was too tied up keeping my scholarships and playing the game. Even when I started with the Storm, we were still all really young, and those of us who tried to have serious relationships usually couldn't. Too much time on the road, other... temptations."

Court smiled wryly. "Somehow, Ben, you don't strike me as the type who could be tempted."

"Well, you're wrong about that. At least where you're concerned, I was plenty tempted from just about the minute I saw you."

Court made a small humming sound in her throat that shot straight down to Ben's groin. Temptation wasn't the word for what Court did to all her carefully constructed logic and rationales. All the rules she never gave any thought to but that had kept her apart for most of her life. Insanity was more like it. And now she was rattled enough to tell her the rest of it. "There was one sort of serious relationship, at least I thought it might turn into one, about a year ago."

Court grew very still. "Really. Who was she and what happened?"

"Her name isn't important. Let's just say I made an error in judgment. She was—is—an ENT surgeon in Nashville. She was a head and neck surgery fellow when we met. Not anyone I had any direct supervision over or anything like that when we got involved. It turns out she thought I would be a good contact to help her get a staff position."

"I'm sorry. That sucks."

Ben shrugged and drank some wine. "It took me a while to realize how the conversation kept coming around to how much influence I had with various important people in the department, and finally she just outright asked me."

Courtney winced. "You don't think I—"

"No," Ben said instantly. "Not for a second."

"So what happened?"

"When I said no, she was angry enough to suggest to a few people that I had misled her—well, not anything formal or even specific enough for anything to really come of it, other than to cause me discomfort. She got her staff position without any special influence that I was aware of, but I still decided it was time to move on."

"That's terrible. I am so sorry," Court said.

"Like I said, bad judgment on my part."

"There's something you need to know about me," Court said, and then she laughed a little ironically. "There's probably a lot of things you should know about me, but the key thing is that I don't want anything in my life that I haven't earned. I grew up with a father who was angry and nearly paralyzed with jealousy because his younger brother—Val's father—was favored by their parents. That's what he believed. I have no way of knowing if that's true or not. But I've seen what can happen to someone who feels they're owed something that they haven't gotten. His resentment and anger turned him from a loving father into a bitter man who walked away from his family. I will never be that person. I will never want what I haven't earned."

"Court," Ben said gently, reaching across the kitchen island to grab Courtney's hand. She thought for a moment Court might pull away, but at the last second she didn't. Instead her fingers gently intertwined with Ben's. If the island hadn't been between them, she would've pulled Courtney into her arms. She was just as glad that she couldn't. As much as she wanted her, and being around her pretty much meant she always wanted her, they needed to say the things they were saying. "I believe you."

The rigid tension in Court's shoulders eased, and she pressed her lips together, as if holding in all she wanted to say. "Thank you."

Ben took a deep breath. "But you should know that it would hurt you in the surgery program if people thought you were getting special attention for any reason. That would make a relationship between us inadvisable."

"You're going to have to let me be the judge of that," Court said. "How I run my personal life is no one else's business. But I'm not naive, and I know to watch my back."

Ben blew out a breath. "You're determined that no one will ever take care of you, aren't you?"

"I suppose that's true."

Ben should have been happy to hear that. Courtney wasn't looking for anything serious. Uncomplicated was definitely desirable. Ignoring the flare of disappointment, she said, "Have I answered your question, then? About why I'm here and single?"

"Almost." Court asked steadily, "What about the Storm? I don't for a second think it's because you couldn't cut it. If I did think that, I wouldn't have asked."

"That's not related to what we were talking about." Ben caught herself diverting, and Court deserved better. With a deep breath, she said, "I got a message from the ICU in Nashville that my father had been admitted with a massive upper GI bleed. He was in critical condition."

"God," Court said abruptly. "I'm so sorry, that's awful."

"Yes, well, my father and I hadn't been close, or even much in touch, for almost a decade. He was a chronic alcoholic, and when I was fourteen, I went to live with my aunt, my mother's sister, because my home life was a little nonexistent. If it hadn't been for her, I probably would have finished high school in the foster system. She did her best, but she had five kids of her own. Basketball was my only real place."

Court's jaw tightened. "No wonder your teammates were so important to you."

"Yeah." Ben swallowed hard. "When I got the message, I flew home to see him. He survived the episode and swore he'd stop drinking, but he didn't have any support system, and it was clear to me there was no way he'd stay sober without one. I'd always known my pro basketball career would be shorter than most because of my medical school obligations. It seemed that fate had made the decision for me when I had to decide to turn my back on him or help him save his own life. I left the Storm, moved back to go to school, and saw that he got an apartment. I did what else I could to get him into a situation where he could help himself."

"That's a lot to take on and a lot to give up," Court said.

"It seemed like the right thing to do. He lasted five months before he started drinking again, and a year later he died. By then I was halfway through med school. That's the road I was going to end up on anyway."

"I'm sorry for you and him," Court said.

"I wasn't ready at the time to change direction," Ben said, "and I was angry for quite a while, but that's the past. I'm glad for where I am now." She lifted Court's hand and brushed a kiss over her knuckles. "I can't think of anywhere else I'd rather be tonight. Or anyone else I'd want to be with."

"No one has ever done that before," Court whispered. "Or said that."

"I'm glad," Ben murmured against her skin.

Without letting go of Ben's hand, Court slipped around the end of the small island and stepped in between Ben's legs, her free arm going around Ben's neck. Court kissed her. The kiss was everything Ben remembered and so much more. Court's mouth was gentle on hers at first, and then heat flared in the scrape of teeth over her lower lip, urging her to open, and when she did, Court took control. Want, a dark, deep and demanding force, flooded her as Court's kiss devoured her. She groaned and tugged Court's T-shirt loose until she could get a hand on skin.

Court surged tightly between her thighs and nipped at her tongue. "I want…no…I need your hands on me."

Ben gasped. "Courtney."

"Don't talk," Court whispered and kissed her again.

When Ben could find breath, she gasped, "About what I said before…about kissing all night? I don't think that will be enough."

"Neither do I." Court grabbed both Ben's hands and tugged her to her feet. "Come upstairs."

CHAPTER TWENTY-TWO

Court liked to lose herself in sex. Fast, hot, hard sex with women who were in it for the pleasure and not afraid to say so. Sex was a remarkable panacea. When she let her body take control and her mind go quiet, when she felt the heat flare and the flames roar until every thought incinerated and all that remained was sensation, she was free. Free of uncertainty, free of loss, free of loneliness. All the ghosts of past failures that haunted the hidden recesses of her mind faded, and the voices that whispered she was still finding excuses to be alone grew silent. Sex was a safe road to travel as long as she directed the route.

Tonight, standing in the middle of her bedroom with the sun just down and twilight holding back the dark, Ben's face, stark and beautiful, held her motionless. Drinking in the sight of Ben, *here,* where she'd barely dared dream she might be, Court registered sensations she'd never experienced with any other woman—her heart fluttering in her chest, the muscles along her inner thighs trembling, her too-fast breath that never seemed to bring her enough air. She didn't know what to do with her hands. Confused, something she never was where sex was concerned, she covered her anxiety the same way she handled every other challenge. She hit it head-on.

Grasping the bottom of her T-shirt in both hands, she stripped it over her head and seconds later followed it with her support tank. She watched Ben watching her, and want curled through her. Ben's eyes blazed, her jaw tensed, and the set of her mouth looked hungry. Court's hands shook as she hooked her thumbs in the waistband of her sweats and pushed them down, taking everything else with them. Naked and somehow more comfortable now that she had some bit of control, she stepped within arm's length of Ben, who hadn't moved the whole time she undressed.

"I can undress you next," Court said, barely recognizing her own voice through the rough veil of desire.

"I think I can handle it," Ben said and pulled off her polo shirt.

"Wait," Court said before Ben could lift the tight tee underneath it. She lightly palmed the curve of Ben's delts, traced the swell of muscle to the delicate hollow of her collarbone, and rested her fingertips on the hard columns of her traps. Leaning forward, keeping her body away from Ben's, she kissed the swell of her pec above the top of her tee. "You have a gorgeous body."

"Says the naked woman torturing me when I want to touch her so badly," Ben murmured, still not moving. Her body quivered as if it took all her will not to move.

Court loved that she could do that to her—make Ben want the way she wanted. So desperately she'd rather stop breathing than stop what they were doing. "Why don't you, then."

Ben cursed so quietly Court almost didn't hear it and ripped the tee over her head. When she unzipped her pants, the sound of metal snicking down filled the room like a gunshot. Court caught her lip between her teeth. How could she be so excited when they still hadn't touched? Kissed, yes, and the barest of caresses, but she was wet and hot and so ready. Why wasn't she doing something? Not like her to wait.

"Tell me what you like," Ben said, clasping Court's waist the way she did everything else. Confidently, powerfully, with absolute certainty. Ben kissed her, the other hand splayed across her back as if to be sure she didn't escape. Or fall. The kiss drove through her, a hot spike piercing every bit of armor she'd ever had.

"Fast, I like it fast," Court moaned against Ben's throat. She licked the little bit of salty sweetness and nipped the spot a second later, wanting more of everything. She nipped again, this time the edge of Ben's jaw, and Ben gasped. Blood rushed to Court's clit, and a pulse beat wildly inside. "I want you to make me come hard."

"I can do that," Ben said against Court's mouth, her teeth rasping over Court's lower lip.

"Only…" Court arched her neck, and Ben, following her cue,

kissed along her jaw and down the column of her throat. "*Usually* I like fast...I...tonight—I...I don't know."

"Good," Ben murmured against the hollow of her throat, and Ben's fingers skittered over her ribs, and her palm closed over her breast. Court jerked in her arms.

"Every time you touch me," she murmured, "I think I can't take any more, but that's what I want. More."

"Lie down with me," Ben said and tugged Court toward the bed.

Court pushed the covers quickly aside, and then they were face-to-face, a wild tangle of arms and legs and hot, hot skin. She gasped when Ben's thigh, strong and smooth and so hot, rose between her legs and pressed against her center. Her body, always so quick to climb, her hands, always so fast to demand, stilled. Breath trapped in her chest, she struggled to absorb every ecstatic pulse of pleasure.

"All right?" Ben stroked the length of Court's back and cradled her backside, pulling Court more tightly against her.

Court gasped. "I feel so good. I want you to make me come. But...it feels too good to end."

Ben shivered. Cradling Court's nape in her palm, she kissed her.

Court moaned. The swift demand of Ben's tongue and almost painful press of teeth against her lower lip nearly undid her. She rocked on Ben's thigh and her hips surged. The pressure between her thighs grew unbearable. "I need to come soon."

"Not yet," Ben said. "Not fast tonight."

"I don't know if I can," Court whispered, her voice cracking.

"Sure you can." Ben brushed her lips over Court's nipple, and she cried out.

Court arched and climbed higher. "I want you inside me when I come. I need you now. Please."

"Hold on, baby," Ben whispered and, supporting herself on one arm, feathered her fingers down Court's quivering abdomen and between her legs.

Court pulled in a breath, unable to catch enough air to talk. Her every fiber focused on the pulsing drive deep in her core, pounding and pressing and pushing. Then Ben was inside her and she was tightening, bracing her thighs and rocking to the beat of desire beyond her control.

"Now," Ben's gravelly voice commanded, "now we'll go fast."

But she didn't, she went deep, one confident stroke, and before she could stroke again, Court exploded, stars blazing across her consciousness. When the exquisite pulsations ended, Ben was still there, unmoving, filling her.

"Do not ever move," Court said very, very deliberately.

Ben laughed. "With pleasure."

Court brushed her mouth over Ben's bicep, and Ben's arm trembled. Had she done that? Awestruck, she whispered, "You're shaking."

"I can't help it," Ben said. "You destroy me."

Ben's eyes were so dark, her desire so very beautiful, Court's heart threatened to weep. She had to close her eyes or she might.

"I haven't quite destroyed you yet," she said when she'd gathered her will and regained some of her control. With a slow, purposeful tilt of her hips she separated them and, with one swift surge, turned Ben onto her back. "But now I might."

When she slid down the length of Ben's body, Ben groaned. Court liked that sound. She liked it very much, and she intended to hear it again as many times as she possibly could. She took her time bringing Ben to the edge, teasing with her hands and her mouth and her tongue. The third time she almost brought her over, Ben groaned and twisted a fist, not ungently, in her hair.

"Damn it, Courtney. *Do it.*"

Court laughed and gently kissed the inside of her thigh. "*I* like to come fast. I like to take my time with you, though."

"Take much more, and I'll come if you breathe on me."

"Mm," Court said. "Let's see."

But she wanted what Ben wanted. She wanted Ben to come apart for her, and when she found the spot that made Ben tense and the hand in her hair tighten, she stayed there until Ben jerked with a harsh shout.

When she was sure Ben was sated, she rested her cheek on Ben's thigh and caressed the taut planes of her abdomen. "I love your body."

"It's all yours."

Court smiled. "Good. As soon as I catch my breath, I plan to explore."

Ben pushed herself up on her elbows and looked down at Court. "You think you could come up here so I could hold you first?"

Court liked sex. Loved sex. Intimacy, vulnerability? That wasn't part of the deal. Ben watched her, giving her the choice, letting her see the need reflected in her eyes.

"I can do that," she said softly and settled into Ben's arms. As her body relaxed and her mind drifted, she told herself she'd be careful. She knew how to protect herself, after all.

❖

Ben brushed a strand of hair away from Courtney's temple and kissed her. The last thing she wanted to do was get out of bed. What she wanted to do was touch her again, everywhere. She couldn't seem to get enough of her scent, her taste, the sounds of her pleasure, and her laughing demands to *get on with it already*. She'd not had a lot of lovers, but enough to know none had ever delighted her, or surprised her, or satisfied her the way Courtney had. If she thought about it even a little, she'd know that none ever would. She didn't want to think about it. She didn't want to think at all. What Courtney had shown her, demanded of her, was the incredible freedom that came with pleasure, pleasure at the hands of a woman she trusted. A woman who wanted her. A woman she wanted more than she'd ever wanted anything or anyone in her life.

"I know you're awake," Court muttered. "And I know you're thinking. You should probably stop that."

Smiling, Ben nuzzled her neck. "So you're an expert at reading my mind as well as my body now?"

"Am I?" Court asked, face still turned to the pillow.

"Are you what?" Ben stroked her naked back and kissed the vulnerable spot just behind her ear.

"An expert at reading your body?"

"Oh, I'd say so. Three or four times ought to have proven that."

"Your mind isn't so very hard to read." Court turned onto her back and wrapped an arm around Ben's neck, pulling her in for a kiss. A breathless moment later, she sighed softly. "You think loudly. Thinking after sex is not always recommended."

"If you must know," Ben said, unable to resist kissing the soft skin at the angle of her jaw, "I was thinking about how much I liked...loved...being with you last night."

Court's eyes widened. "Oh." She smiled a little crookedly. "I guess that's okay, then."

"Good." Ben tamped down the sudden arrow of pure, unmitigated want that struck low in her belly. "My car is still in the lot, and I need a change of clothes before I go to work. I should go."

Court gave no sign of letting her go, and Ben didn't resist. "Do you have ten minutes?"

Ben laughed. "Why do I think that might be more than enough time?"

Court grasped Ben's wrist and pulled her hand down between them, pressing Ben's fingers into her heat. "That might be an answer."

Fifteen minutes later, still a little dazed from Courtney's orgasm and her own, Ben pulled on clothes and trotted the block and a half through the quiet early dawn to her car. Her body and mind still lazily content, she pulled quietly down the drive to the Homestead a few minutes later. Unusually, Edward's station wagon was still under the portico. Hoping not to rouse the household, she eased open the kitchen door and stepped inside.

Ida sat at the kitchen table with a steaming cup of coffee in front of her. The kitchen smelled like heaven. "Good morning."

"Uh. Hi." Ben considered backing out through the door and running away. She'd actually done that, when she was thirteen and came home to find her father only semi-stuporous in the kitchen and in a vicious mood. But that was then and this was now, and she hadn't been safe then and now she was. Embarrassed now, a little, but she was an adult, and Ida was clearly not one to judge or be easily shocked.

"Coffee is fresh," Ida said.

"Thank God," Ben muttered and poured herself one. She lifted the pot in Ida's direction. "Do you need a refill?"

"Not quite yet. We'll have biscuits in about five minutes."

"Is there anything I can do to help before I go shower?"

"Just come down and enjoy them."

Ben showered and changed quickly. Ida hadn't asked if she'd worked all night, and she suspected that was intentional. There could only be two answers. Yes, she had, or no, she'd spent the night somewhere else and almost certainly *with* someone. Ida Rivers was a very smart woman who knew the value of silence.

When she got back down to the kitchen, Margie sat at the table with her own cup of coffee and a biscuit steaming from the oven and running with melted creamery butter.

"Did you make that butter?" Ben asked Ida.

Ida laughed. "As a matter of fact, no. I have made my own butter, and it's wonderful, but it's also time-consuming, and I don't actually spend all my time in the kitchen."

Ben helped herself to a biscuit and a slice of ham from a second platter. "I already know you're a wizard and can probably be doing five things at once."

"Thank you. How are things going at the hospital?" Ida asked.

"Good," Ben said. "Busy."

"I'm asking as a friend, as family, because Brody is one of mine, but you don't need to say anything that might be inappropriate. Is Val all right?"

"Val is fine, although she's getting a little impatient with me. She wants to be up and moving, and we're not quite there yet." Ben smiled. "She reminds me of Flann that way."

Margie laughed. "Ooh, I don't think you should mention that to her."

"Good advice. But everything looks good." Ben rose, washed her cup, and grabbed her go bag. Pausing at the door, she said, "By the way, Margie—I don't have any insider knowledge, but I thought you did a great job at tryouts. When will you find out?"

"Early next week," Margie said.

"Well, good luck."

"Thanks. Did you happen to see the boys' tryouts too?"

"I did," Ben said. "They've got some strong contenders there. Blake showed well."

Margie blushed and looked down at her biscuit. "That's good. I thought so too."

"You can tell him I said so."

"I will," Margie called as Ben headed out.

She hadn't been kidding that both of them had looked very good, and she couldn't see how either one of them wouldn't make their respective teams, but sometimes in sports being the best wasn't the only criterion. Players had to fit well with the team too, have the kind of attitude a coach wanted. She'd seen good players passed over because a coach or even a star player hadn't thought they would mesh well.

When she got to the OR lounge to wait for her first case to be prepped, she grabbed a second cup of coffee despite knowing it would be a tremendous disappointment after Ida's.

Flann came in a few minutes later, poured a cup of coffee, and said, "Talk to you a minute?"

"Sure." Ben followed Flann out into the hall for a little privacy.

"Nothing urgent," Flann said, "but I need you to come by and talk to me about your contract. You're only signed on for a year, and I need to know if we're extending it. Obviously we want you to."

"It's a little soon, isn't it," Ben said noncommittally.

"We're having a bit of trouble contracting interested residents, especially more senior people who want to track into sports medicine, because we can't tell them that you're going to be here next year. No one wants to join a program in flux. You are not the problem. In fact, *you're* the draw, but if a resident thinks you're going somewhere else next year, they don't want to come here."

"I get it," Ben said.

Initially, she'd planned on giving herself some time to decide her future, concerned she wouldn't like living without a lot of the conveniences and interests of city life or that the hierarchy of a small rural hospital wouldn't suit. Neither of those concerns seemed an issue now—in fact they seemed pretty trivial. Other considerations seemed a lot more important than whether she could get Thai takeout—like her just having spent the night with Court. That changed everything. If she stayed, and they didn't last—and she couldn't pretend she didn't want more with Court than just a night now and then—she'd have to see her every day and somehow stop wanting her. Contemplating *that* left her with a hollow sensation she didn't want to have to live with. If she planned on leaving at the end of a year, she'd have to stop seeing her now—that was the only fair course, and the last thing she wanted to do.

"Can you give me a few weeks?" Ben asked.

Flann nodded. "Sure. And if there's anything you want to talk about, you know I'm available."

"Sure, thanks," Ben said, quite sure the last thing she'd be doing was talking to Flann about Courtney Valentine.

❖

"Bye, Mom," Margie called. "I'm going to Taylor's later tonight. Be back by midnight unless I stay there."

"Doing something fun first?" Ida asked.

"Oh." Margie halted in the doorway. "I'm going to the drive-in with Blake."

"Isn't that the *Avengers* movie?"

"Yeah, that's second. The first one is some dumb comedy."

Ida smiled. "That's different, isn't it, just you and Blake."

"Yeah, I guess."

"I hope you have a good time," Ida said.

"You don't think it's weird?"

"That you're going on a date…Is it still called that, these days?"

Margie rolled her eyes. "Mom. It's not like you're from some ancient time or anything."

Ida snorted. "I won't even talk about how things used to be—"

"Good. So anyway, yes, we're hanging out."

"How is that for you and your friends?"

"It's good. We've all talked about it. Well, Dave and Taylor. And Tim doesn't talk about a lot of things, usually, but he and Taylor are close, and if he needed to say something, he would."

"Have fun and be careful, then."

"Thanks, Mom," Margie said, "I will."

She jogged out to her truck and, on the short drive to Blake's, wondered why she felt a little nervous. That was weird. She'd picked up Blake for a night out about a million times before. And okay, yeah, tonight was different, but not *that* different. So it would just be the two of them. It was still Blake. Still the person she shared just about everything with—not exclusively, not all the time, because there was Taylor, and Taylor was special. And she talked to Dave and Tim almost as much as Blake. Blake was a friend. The jittery sensation in her middle persisted, but she didn't have time to worry about it any longer as she pulled up in front of Blake's new house.

He came down the drive right away and climbed into the passenger seat. His hair was damp, as if he'd just showered, and he had on a short-sleeved button-up shirt and jeans. And loafers. She'd put on a new top she'd been saving for something, she wasn't sure exactly what, but this seemed like the thing. And capri pants she'd bought one day shopping with Taylor because she liked the light green color, even though she couldn't possibly wear them around the farm.

"You're all dressed up," she said as Blake buckled in.

"So are you."

"Are we being weird?" Margie said.

"I don't think so." Blake paused. "Maybe. You look really nice."

"So do you."

The drive-in was a half an hour out of town, and on the way, Margie said, "Ben said you looked good at tryouts. I thought so too."

"I felt pretty good about it. I keep telling myself, no matter what, at least I didn't screw it up."

"No matter what," Margie said, "you ought to be on the team."

"Thanks," Blake said softly.

When they arrived, they got a place in the third row center, and while Margie fiddled to get the sound right, Blake went to the concession stand. He climbed back into the truck and put a couple of sodas in the cup holders on the dash and juggled a cardboard tray of eats before sliding over to the middle of the bench seat.

"I'm glad you wanted to come with me," Blake said.

"Me too." Margie went on in a rush, "But I am not ready yet to think about something serious...like being a couple thing."

Blake actually looked relieved as he nodded quickly. "I know. Me neither, but sometimes…you know, just us is okay, right?"

Margie nodded, stifling the urge to laugh out loud. That was weird, but it felt good. "Sure. Just us."

Blake moved a little closer until their thighs touched and rested a big cardboard bucket on their legs. "Popcorn?"

CHAPTER TWENTY-THREE

At just after six in the morning, Court paused at the open door of Val's private hospital room and peered inside. Only the safety lights above the bed and by the bathroom door illuminated the room. The whole floor was still quiet—the night staff hadn't yet started morning rounds. Val's upcoming surgery wasn't scheduled until seven thirty, and if Val had managed to sleep, Court didn't want to wake her.

"I'm awake," Val said.

"Hey, I just wanted to check if you were all set for this morning," Court said, walking to Val's bedside.

"I've been all set for a week."

Val sounded cranky at the moment, but Court couldn't blame her. If she'd been at nearly absolute bed rest for almost a month, she'd be pretty damn cranky too. Val propped herself up on her pillows. She'd long since traded the white cotton hospital gowns with the little blue boats for her own pale blue pj's with yellow piping, had washed her hair with Court's help just two days before, and generally looked more like herself than she had in the month since her injury. "I hope you're not here to tell me something else has gone FUBAR."

"Nope." Court smiled. "The chest X-ray Ben wanted last night is crystal clear. So anesthesia will be very happy."

"I could've told them it was going to be fine," Val said. "A little pneumonia isn't such a big deal."

"Um, Val, we kinda think it is."

Val blew out a breath and pushed her hair back from her face. "I know, I know. But damn it, Court, this sucks, and it's getting

suckier every day. I want out, and I want up on my feet. Ben said—"
She sighed and dropped her head back, staring at the ceiling. "I am
being a whiny pain in the ass. Sorry."

"Hey." Court edged a hip onto the side of the bed and rested her
hand on Val's forearm. "You're not—well, maybe a little."

Val laughed.

"But you're right," Court went on. "The whole thing has been
lousy. No one should have to go through this."

"I shouldn't be complaining," Val said. "I'm alive, I have my
leg, and when this is over, I'll have my life back."

"It doesn't make the surgeries or the pain any easier," Court
said, "but you're right. After the bone graft today, your PT will go
into overdrive, and before you know it, you'll be mobile again."

"I just want to get home. Back to Brody, back to work, back to
the things that make me feel like me."

"Yeah, I know what you mean."

"It helps I can complain to you. I hate to dump it all on Brody
every time I see her. She's a worrier as it is."

"I'm happy to listen," Court said. "Dump away."

"Thanks." Val smiled. "So, how are you?"

"Me?" Court didn't get the question.

Val rolled her eyes. "Yes, you. As in, how's life. How are things
going—the residency, is it what you expected?"

How's life?

Not what she'd been expecting. Oh sure, she'd been as
prepared for the residency as she could have been—the hours, the
stress and strain, the situations she'd have to face that she might
not be prepared for, like seeing her cousin pinned under a wrecked
car. What she hadn't been prepared for was Ben. A woman who
mattered in her life in an entirely new way. How quickly her life had
changed because of Ben. On most nights when she wasn't on call
or they weren't at a game, they met for dinner, relaxing at her place
afterward, making love until one of them insisted they go to sleep
because they both had to work in the morning. More often than not
that was Ben, who always seemed to be thinking about her. About
what she needed or wanted. That was new, different, unsettlingly
special. She'd never felt that way with anyone before. She'd never
felt *about* anyone that way before. Ben turned her on the way no

one ever had, but more than that, she brought excitement to sharing everyday things and wonder to the quiet moments when they woke together. Ben rocked her world, and she couldn't be happier. Except when she thought about all of that ending—of waking one morning and finding Ben gone.

"Something wrong?" Val asked.

"No," Court said quickly. Whatever happened to her motto of living in the moment? Ben had happened—Ben had made her want to think about tomorrow. "No, not at all. The residency's fine. I wouldn't say it's exactly fun all the time, but it's what I expected, and definitely what I want."

"And ortho? You mentioned before it was a possibility. You still leaning that way?"

Faced with the question, she didn't hesitate. "Yeah, I am. I haven't scrubbed on that many cases, but it's got everything I like— emergencies, reconstruction, even the rehab. And sports medicine."

"Are you going to switch?"

"Ah, I don't know. That might be complicated."

"Why?"

"Well, I…" How to explain *she* wouldn't have a problem being an ortho resident and seeing one of the ortho staff—Ben wouldn't be signing off on her residency certificate, after all—but that Ben would see it as a problem.

Val pursed her lips and narrowed her eyes. "Something personal? Is someone making life difficult for you? One of the more senior residents?"

"No, no. I'm fine." Court's throat tightened. No one in her adult life had ever sounded as if they were about to go to battle for her. No one, except Ben, who cared about everything she did—when she ate, when she slept, how she felt about an upcoming case. What she wanted in bed. But this, Val's concern, this was different. This was like family. "I'm kind of involved with someone."

"Define kind of."

Court grinned. "Seriously gone for her."

Val smiled. "You sound happy about it."

"I really am."

"Is she serious?"

"Yes, I think so." Court paused. "I don't think she does anything she isn't serious about. And she makes me feel…well…like I really matter."

"One of the other residents?"

"No. Not a resident."

"Oh boy. My radar is still working, it seems. I wondered. Is it Ben?"

Court nodded.

"She's pretty amazing."

Court smiled. "Yeah, she really is."

"And really attractive." Val smirked.

"Yeah, that too."

Val laughed. "Have you told her about it?"

"Not yet," Court said. "We're still kind of new, and we haven't talked about anything long-term." She snorted. "Listen to me—I've never even *thought* about long-term with anyone before. I do know a relationship with her is as important as surgery, and that's…scary."

"So take the time to think about what you want—with her, for yourself," Val said. "Residencies don't last forever, but your career and a relationship you really want hopefully will."

Court let out a long breath. "I know. I will."

Val grasped Court's hand and squeezed. "Hey, I'm here, so I want to know what's going on."

Court kept hold of Val's hand. "I don't think I've ever said out loud that I'm sorry about all the family stuff. I never took the time to find out who you were—I just listened to my father and believed everything was the way he saw it."

"Hey," Val said forcefully, "that's not on you. You had every reason to believe what your dad told you. And neither one of us handled things all that well. We're smarter now than we were then. I know who you are, Court. You're family."

The tears that came to Court's eyes shocked her, and she quickly blinked them away. Family. Family had created the rift between them and now helped to heal it. "Thank you. I feel the same way."

"Good. You *are* scrubbing with Ben today, right? Because I told her I wanted you to."

"Yes, just like all your other surgeries. I'm your special resident."

Val laughed again. "You certainly are."

Court rose. "They'll be coming to pre-medicate you in another twenty minutes. You should just relax until then."

"I'm waiting for Brody," Val said. "She should be here soon."

"Then I'll see you when we're done."

As Court wrote the pre-op notes, she thought about long-term. What she wanted—what she needed. What Ben might need. Ben had left Nashville because of a relationship like theirs—sure, she wasn't using Ben, and she had to believe Ben knew that, but Ben'd also said more than once she didn't want their relationship to compromise Court's standing in the program. What would Ben do if the chance of that seemed even more likely? Court grew cold inside. She couldn't answer for Ben, but she knew what her first step needed to be.

❖

Courtney hadn't seen Ben since they'd finished with Val's surgery midmorning. After she'd gotten Val settled back in her room, she'd been called to scrub with Flann on Mike Wells's pancreatic resection. She'd never seen a case like that before, and she wasn't the only resident interested. She *was* one of only three who got to scrub, though, because she'd taken care of him in the ER, and Flann remembered. They didn't do the kind of resection they were doing that day very often, an aggressive surgical procedure to try to eradicate all his tumor. Most patients weren't candidates for that kind of radical surgery, the diagnosis having been made far too late in the course, but Mike Wells's exhaustive workup hadn't shown any sign that the tumor had spread. She couldn't exactly think of him as lucky, but the word had been used more than once when discussing him. He had a chance at a cure. She had a chance at being part of that, and the feeling was almost more satisfying than anything she'd ever experienced.

The case had been long and at times tense, and as the most junior member of the team, she'd been responsible for helping to transport him to the intensive care unit and writing his post-op orders. By the time she was done, it was almost eight p.m. She texted Ben when she was finally ready to leave.

Are you done at the hospital?

Ben texted back right away. *Waiting on you. How did it go?*
Really well. Awesome.
Interest you in pizza?
YES
Meet you at your place in 20

Court hustled out to her car before someone could grab her and ask her to find an X-ray or check a lab result or do a post-op check. She wasn't on call even though at any other time she wouldn't have minded. Tonight she wanted to see Ben. Needed to see her.

She made it home in under ten minutes and raced into the shower. She'd just wrapped a towel around herself when Ben let herself in with the key she'd given her. That had been strange too, even though when she'd given it to Ben, she'd told her it just made sense. With their schedules, they were always on different clocks, and one was invariably waiting for the other to show up. Ben couldn't very well sit on the steps at midnight. But Court'd never given a key to anyone else. And she'd never imagined liking the idea of a woman having her key. But she liked it now.

"I'm upstairs," she called.

A few seconds later, Ben stood in the doorway to her bedroom, a slow smile spreading over her face. "Just in time."

And just like that, Court was ready. She let the towel fall even though her hair wasn't completely dry, and beads of water still stood on her shoulders. Ben was beside her in an instant, brushing her palms over her damp skin.

Court shivered.

"Cold?" Ben murmured, lowering her head to kiss a droplet of water pooling in the base of her throat.

Court moaned softly, dropped her head back, and pressed her wet nakedness against Ben's warmth. "Not cold. Hot."

"Can you wait for pizza?" Ben whispered, her voice husky. She wrapped both arms around Court's waist, palms cradling her backside, and kissed her way down the center of Court's body. Eventually kneeling in front of her, Ben looked up, her eyes hot.

Court tensed everywhere, a tight knot of need thrumming between her thighs.

"It won't get that cold," she gasped. Threading her fingers through Ben's hair, she steadied herself against her, and when the heat of Ben's mouth enclosed her, she bit her lower lip to hold in a cry. She couldn't hold back when the orgasm thrashed through her, her thighs trembling against Ben's shoulders. Ben held her tightly, refusing to let her pull away until her sensitive flesh could take no more.

She pushed Ben's head away and laughed. "We're done."

Ben looked up and grinned. "Sure?"

Court was naked, Ben was completely clothed, and Court wanted her with a force that hurt. She grabbed Ben's shirt and jerked. "Get up."

Ben was on her feet in a second, both of them working to pull off her clothes. A minute later they tumbled onto the bed, and Court straddled her, pressing Ben down with one hand between her breasts. "I'm awfully hungry, so you better brace yourself."

Ben gripped Court's hips and pushed up against her. "Fast is just fine."

Court watched Ben's face as she reached behind her, delved into the intoxicating heat she knew she would find, and stroked. She knew Ben's rhythm now, knew the places that made her arch and grit her teeth, knew when to circle, when to slide, when to press just so. Ben wanted fast. She took her without pause, savoring each second.

Ben came hard, the tendons and muscles in her neck and chest straining as she broke. The sight never failed to pierce Court to her very soul.

When Ben tensed one last time and slowly relaxed, Court dropped down and kissed her.

"I love you," Court said.

She'd planned all day to tell her but hadn't known exactly when or how. But the words simply came. The beauty of her, the power, the vulnerability she let Court see. The way Ben made love to her, giving her endless pleasure and, with it, tenderness and joy.

"God, Ben. I do."

Ben framed her face, kissed her gently. "We're never going to get to the pizza."

"It's good for breakfast."

Ben rolled her over, sliding one thigh between hers. "Courtney."

Court smiled, loving it when Ben called her that. So serious, as if the word itself was some kind of prayer. She trembled. "You don't have to say anything. I—"

Ben kissed her again. "You don't get to decide this one. I love you, Courtney." Another kiss, longer, deeper. "I've known for a while, but I worried you might not want to hear it yet."

"You think too much."

Ben laughed. "I love you for a lot of reasons, and that's one of them. You seem to think you can stop me from overthinking."

Court brushed the hair off Ben's forehead and trailed her fingertips over Ben's cheek. "I probably can, given enough time. I want enough time, Ben."

Ben sucked in a breath. "So do I. More than anything."

"Don't forget," Court murmured, and kissed her. "No matter what."

A small frown formed between Ben's brows. "Are you all right?"

Court smiled. "I'm great. And right at this moment, I'd really like you to make me come again."

Ben got that look she got when she was contemplating exactly *how* she was going to make Court come. She nipped at Court's lower lip. "I can do that. As many times as you want."

Court pressed her face to Ben's throat and whispered, "Always. Always, Ben."

Chapter Twenty-four

Y ou've got your first appointment for full PT scheduled for ten this morning downstairs," Ben said as she finished checking Val's cast.

"Thanks," Val said. "I know I haven't been the ideal patient. More like a right pain."

Ben smiled. "Considering the circumstances, not at all. Those of us in medicine always know too much and, sometimes, never enough."

"It's meant a lot to me, anyhow, because I know you've been doing a lot of the routine care yourself when you didn't have to," Val said softly.

"It's a privilege."

"So," Val said, briskly, "how soon will I be walking?"

"That's more like it," Ben said and Val laughed. "With or without the cast?"

"Right now, I don't really care."

"Don't hold me to it, but here are the estimates," Ben said and went on to explain the hoped-for timetable. "I'll get a report from PT after every visit, and I'll try to get down as often as I can to review your progress."

"Isn't that above and beyond your responsibility at this point?" Val asked.

"No, not in my opinion. The surgery isn't successful until you're back to where you want to be or as close as I can possibly get you. PT is part of the post-op care, and that's my deal too."

"I can see why Flann wanted you here. From what Brody tells

me about the patients they're bringing in, you're going to be very busy."

Ben nodded. "Unfortunately, that's probably true."

"If it's going to happen, the patients will be lucky if they end up here. I know I am."

"Thanks—but it's a team effort, and that includes you. Don't try to get back everything in one day in PT."

"Um. Right. I'll take it easy."

Ben snorted. "*Try*. I'll talk to you tomorrow."

Val grinned as Ben left. She'd just finished writing up her notes and filling out some instructions for PT when Flann rounded the corner.

"Hey," Flann said. "Just the person I wanted to talk to."

"Same here," Ben said.

"You first," Flann said.

"I just wanted to let you know that I'll be by to sign the contract." The last few nights with Courtney had been more than she'd ever expected to share with another person, emotionally or physically. She'd never told another woman she'd loved her. She'd wondered, when she was younger and in the throes of lustful infatuation, if maybe that's what was happening, but she'd never even come close to really understanding the connection that went deeper than blood and bone. Blood and bone she understood, but the feelings that had taken up residence deep inside, in a place she couldn't touch but that felt as vital as any part of a body she'd ever help to heal, were beyond what she had imagined. Making love with Courtney was exciting and satisfying and, sometimes, so intense she had no words for it. Love wasn't something to be understood, she finally realized, but simply and inexplicably something to be felt.

A grin spread across Flann's face. "You're staying. Excellent. I've got a few people who will be very happy to hear that. Several ought to be showing up very soon."

"That's good to hear. I've been fine with the residents you've assigned me," Ben said, "but I'm happy we'll have some more. I think covering mine is thinning out some of the other services a little too much."

"That's because you're already so damn busy. That's not a

problem—it's good for the training program and for the hospital. Half the physical therapists are in love with you, by the way."

Ben smiled. "That might be an exaggeration."

"Well, maybe just a little, but I can give you names if you're looking for company."

Laughing, Ben held up a hand. "No, actually I think I'm okay in that regard."

Flann gave her a long look. "Really. Someone back in Nashville?"

"Ah," Ben said, wondering exactly how to go public about her and Court when they hadn't actually talked about it yet. Courtney managed to avoid the actual question or distract Ben whenever she wanted to talk about their relationship and the potential professional repercussions. Ben almost smiled again, thinking how pleasant those distractions always were and how little she ever protested, but a small kernel of worry formed all the same. She had very little to actually worry about in terms of their involvement. There were no regulations against a staff person and a resident seeing each other. For the resident, though, even when they were in different departments, a little question of favoritism always came up. Residents were dependent upon one another for survival, despite being competitors. At her stage especially, Court couldn't afford to be ostracized.

"Well, I'm glad to see life is working out here," Flann said and questioned her no further. "I did want to catch you up about something else. I know we talked about Courtney not rotating on your service, but something's come up."

Ben stiffened. "I'm sorry? What do you mean?"

Flann winced and shook her head. "Court came by to see me the other day, just to get a little career advice. She's interested in switching to ortho and was asking me about how difficult it might be to transfer to another program."

Ben went cold. "Another program. When was this?"

"Yesterday sometime."

"I see."

"I tried to subtly tell her, hell, no, she can't transfer, but anyhow," Flann went on, "if she *is* going to transfer, I think it would be appropriate for her to rotate through ortho to give her a decent recommendation. Plus, you can use another resident until we get more on board."

"Can you hold off on telling her that for just a little bit," Ben said.

"Something wrong?" Flann asked.

"No," Ben said, surprised that she sounded as if she was telling the truth. "Nothing at all. I just want to look at our upcoming surgery schedule and see when might be the best time to bring on more residents."

"Sure—good idea. Let me know."

"I'll do that," Ben said as Flann strode away. Just as soon as she knew what she was going to do. She ought to be used to life changing in a heartbeat by now—it had happened enough for her to expect it. Somehow, she'd forgotten that—in the hours and days and nights with Courtney. In her own unguarded dreams.

She didn't see Court before surgery kept her occupied the rest of the day. Shortly after five she finished post-op rounds, discussed a couple of patients with the on-call resident, and left the hospital. Her phone signaled a text as she turned into the drive at the Homestead. She parked and checked the message.

Hey. I'm off call. You want dinner? I'm cooking

Ben stared at the message. She still hadn't found an answer to her question—at least not one she was ready to let herself consider. After another minute, she replied.

Thanks—sorry, can't make it tonight.

She slid the phone in her pocket, got out of the car, and after a few steps, pulled her phone out again and silenced the notifications. She'd have to decide if she would go or stay, and she wasn't going to be able to do that with Court anywhere around.

❖

Thanks—sorry, can't make it tonight.

Court stared at the message three times in an hour, and it still said the same thing. She'd never gotten a reply like that from Ben before. Oh, she'd gotten similar replies—though, usually from a woman she'd been seeing who had decided that whatever they'd been sharing was over. None of those women had been Ben. None of them had ever touched her the way Ben had. None of them were women she loved.

She put her phone down on the counter and ignored it. She was totally overreacting. Ben was busy. They were *both* incredibly busy—that was the nature of things. Their relationship was always going to be one of stolen moments. Maybe when her residency was over, the almost-controlled chaos would settle down a little bit, but even then, if she allowed herself to imagine it, she could see them both, surgeons, taking call on different nights. That would cut down considerably on the evenings they would be alone together when one or the other wasn't tired, worried about a case, or just thinking about the next one. There were a lot of reasons that residents who got involved usually ended up with relationships that didn't last. Even when they did make it through the training years, long-term was always a challenge. She couldn't freak out every time Ben wasn't around and start imagining disaster scenarios.

Fifteen minutes after she'd convinced herself of that, she grabbed the phone and checked her messages again. Nothing. There were a million things Ben could've texted and hadn't—like, why, exactly, she couldn't make it *sometime* that evening, when there'd been plenty of nights they hadn't been able to connect until well toward morning. That had never stopped either of them from showing up.

Something wasn't right. She knew Ben. Ben would not brush her off with a single line of text or anything else.

This was Ben, trying to work something out.

Without her.

Again.

With a shake of her head, Court changed out of her hanging-around-the-house clothes into a sleeveless V-neck T-shirt, shorts, and sneakers and walked over to the high school. Margie, Blake, and a handful of their teammates from the Blazers and the Comets played pickup ball like they did most nights when they didn't have a game scheduled. No Ben, who could often be found here while she waited for Court to get finished for the night, sometimes shooting alone and other times giving in to the kids' pleas to shoot with them.

Her other choices were few—Ben might still be at the hospital, but if she'd had an emergency or a late case, she would have said so in her text. No—Ben was alone somewhere, and when she was working something out, she did it with a basketball in her hands.

Ten minutes later she turned into the drive to the Homestead. After pulling in behind Ben's Volvo, purchased exactly as Sam had predicted after Ben'd driven it for a few days, Court climbed out of the Mazda and stood listening in the cool October twilight. The leaves had turned, but not yet fallen. The nights were brisk but not yet cold. First frost was coming soon, and then full fall would be upon them. She heard it in the distance, the rhythmic thumping followed by the faint clang of a metal basketball hoop vibrating as a ball soared through it. A few seconds of silence passed before the sequence began again. She started down the path toward the barn, and Ben.

Lights shone in the kitchen and a couple of rooms upstairs. Edward's car sat under the porte cochere. When she reached the barn, she stopped at the edge of the hard-packed dirt court and watched Ben dribble and shoot, catch the ball as it came through the hoop, and dribble back out for another shot. Still just as beautiful to watch as that first morning.

After a minute or two, Court intercepted the ball as it came through the hoop and dribbled around Ben, turned, and launched a shot from the corner.

"Hi, Court," Ben said, catching the ball on the bounce.

"Ben." Court rebounded the ball again, dribbled, and shot. She hit the barn backstop and banked it in. They traded shots for a while, neither of them forcing a play, until Court finally propped the ball on her hip and called, "When were you planning on talking to me about whatever you're thinking about?"

"When were you planning on telling me you wanted to leave the program?" Ben responded.

"What? Who told you that?"

"Courtney," Ben said, an edge to her voice that was almost never there. "Flann told me. What do you think you're doing?"

Crap. She'd only talked to Flann to see what the possibilities were—so when she talked to Ben about switching to ortho she'd have a plan ready in case Ben objected. That was fair, right? Not a reason for Ben to get all twisty. She passed the ball perhaps a little harder than she should have. "Is that what this is about?"

Ben's eyebrows rose in surprise as she caught it. She set it on the ground between them. "Don't deflect, Court."

Court huffed. She wasn't—she was. "How about thinking about the future. About us. You know, the thing you've been trying to get me to talk about for the last couple of weeks?"

"So you decide that you're leaving?" Ben shook her head. "You could've told me. I could've saved you the time and energy of talking to Flann about changing programs."

Court's chest tightened. "What are *you* talking about?"

"I could've told you that I'd only signed on for a year."

Something sharp twisted inside her chest. The pain was so swift she caught her breath. "When were you planning on telling me that?"

Ben blew out a breath and strode toward her. The barn lights came on at that moment, chasing away the encroaching dusk and highlighting her face. Damn it, she couldn't be beautiful tonight. That would be too unfair.

Court took a step back, and Ben's eyes widened. "Courtney. Come on. It's not what you think."

Court laughed, shocked that the sound was broken. No. She would not break. She'd never broken, not even when she'd finally understood that her father was never coming back. But, God, this was so much harder. "I'm sorry, you didn't really just say that."

Ben visibly gritted her teeth. "Damn it. Let me explain."

"That might've been a good idea a month or so ago, don't you think?" Court was one step away from backing out of the light and disappearing into the dark. Ben would find her, of course. She wasn't about to run out on her life—her training, her future—just the part she thought she'd share with Ben. She just wanted to erase the image of *that*. Then she could cope. Court held her ground—she wouldn't run. Not from Ben. She…couldn't. She just wasn't sure if she had the strength to hear Ben say good-bye.

"I didn't say anything before, because a month or so ago, I wasn't in love with you," Ben said.

"Oh, and now you are?"

"You know that I am. God, Court, tell me you don't know that."

Court bit her lower lip. "I thought I knew."

"Then how could you leave? How could you just—" Ben turned her back, her shoulders stiff.

"Is that what you think? That I wanted to leave you?"

Ben spun around. "Well, explain to me what else changing programs would mean. Why would you want to leave, Court? *Why?*"

"I don't want to go anywhere, you idiot," Court said. "I want to be with you. If you didn't make it so damn difficult."

"How am I making it difficult?"

"By deciding what's best for me," Court snapped.

Ben stared. "I…" Her chest rose as she took in a long, slow breath. "Fuck. I'm sorry."

Court smiled just a little. "I love you for worrying and caring about me. I love it a lot. But I have to be responsible for what I do. Especially where this is concerned."

"Do you want to leave the Rivers program?"

"No," Court said. "It's a very good program, and it's even better now that you're here. One of the medical residents is engaged to an attending cardiologist. No one has a problem with that. If Flann doesn't have a problem with us—and I'll bet my house she won't— then you shouldn't either."

"Yes, but—" Ben caught herself. Heard herself. She loved a hundred things about Courtney, but none came higher than her strength, her certainty, and her ability to handle anything that came along. Court had proven a dozen times over that she knew what she wanted, and what she could handle. "You're right. I've fucked up. I can't believe I'm lucky enough to have you fall in love with me."

Court skirted around the basketball that sat on the ground between them and put her hands on Ben's shoulders. "You didn't fuck up…much. But if we're going to be an us, we still have to be who we are. You have to trust me."

"Then how could you think about leaving?" Ben whispered.

Court framed Ben's face and kissed her. "I wasn't leaving you. I was trying to make us work. The plan was I would finish my residency somewhere else, and then I'd come back here, and Flann would be so impressed with my skills that I would get a staff position. And we would live happily ever after."

Ben laughed. "I like the last part of that but not the part where you have to go somewhere that I'm not."

"Well, they do make cars and airplanes. It's not like we wouldn't see each other." Court sighed. "It was the backup plan, after all. I don't want to do it. And I should have told you my idea before I talked to Flann."

"Yeah, you should have—so next time we'll both do better. It's not a *bad* plan. I know plenty of people do it, but"—Ben pulled Courtney closer and kissed her—"I don't want that. I want to be with you. I want to share as much of every day for the rest of our lives as I can."

"Well, what about your one-year contract?"

"I'd already told Flann I was planning to stay when she told me you were thinking of going."

"You might have led with that, Ben," Court said. "Although if you wanted to go elsewhere, there's still the car and airplane option. I'm not letting you leave me."

"Not a chance," Ben murmured, pulling her tighter.

"Okay," Court said on a long breath. "So we have some details to work out."

"Whatever path we take, we decide together," Ben said.

"That's exactly what I want."

Ben threaded an arm around Court's waist. "We'll talk to Flann, and if necessary, you can do your sports medicine rotation somewhere else to avoid any speculation about favoritism. Rochester is excellent, so's Mass General. It won't hurt you to get some experience with a sports medicine surgeon other than me, anyhow. You'll just be better rounded when you join the staff."

Court's eyes lit up. "You're okay with me switching to ortho, then?"

"I think it's great," Ben said. "You've got all the qualifications for it. You're a natural."

"A natural, huh?" Court murmured, running a hand down the center of Ben's tank top.

"If you're thinking about sex—" Ben half choked, breaking off when Court's fingertips skimmed the front of her shorts. "Ida and Edward are home. We can't go inside."

"I'm definitely thinking about sex." Court sneaked a hand under Ben's tank, laughing softly when Ben groaned.

"Come on, Court," Ben pleaded. "Have a heart."

"Ben," Court said with exaggerated patience, "we're standing in front of a barn. Have you ever made love in a hayloft?"

Ben smiled. "No, but I think I'd like to."

Court grabbed her hand. "Follow me."

About the Author

Radclyffe has written over sixty romance and romantic intrigue novels as well as a paranormal romance series, The Midnight Hunters, as L.L. Raand.

She is a three-time Lambda Literary Award winner in romance and erotica and received the Dr. James Duggins Outstanding Mid-Career Novelist Award by the Lambda Literary Foundation. A member of the Saints and Sinners Literary Hall of Fame, she is also an RWA/FF&P Prism Award winner for *Secrets in the Stone*, an RWA FTHRW Lories and RWA HODRW winner for *Firestorm*, an RWA Bean Pot winner for *Crossroads*, an RWA Laurel Wreath winner for *Blood Hunt*, and a Book Buyers Best award winner for *Price of Honor* and *Secret Hearts*. She is also a featured author in the 2015 documentary film *Love Between the Covers*, from Blueberry Hill Productions. In 2019 she was recognized as a "Trailblazer of Romance" by the Romance Writers of America.

In 2004 she founded Bold Strokes Books, one of the world's largest independent LGBTQ publishing companies, and is the current president and publisher.

Find her at facebook.com/Radclyffe.BSB, follow her on Twitter @RadclyffeBSB, and visit her website at Radfic.com.

Books Available From Bold Strokes Books

A Convenient Arrangement by Aurora Rey and Jaime Clevenger. Cuffing season has come for lesbians, and for Jess Archer and Cody Dawson, their convenient arrangement becomes anything but. (978-1-63555-818-0)

An Alaskan Wedding by Nance Sparks. The last thing either Andrea or Riley expects is to bump into the one who broke her heart fifteen years ago, but when they meet at the welcome party, their feelings come rushing back. (978-1-63679-053-4)

Beulah Lodge by Cathy Dunnell. It's 1874, and newly betrothed Ruth Mallowes is set on marriage and life as a missionary...until she falls in love with the housemaid at Beulah Lodge. (978-1-63679-007-7)

Gia's Gems by Toni Logan. When Lindsey Speyer discovers that popular travel columnist Gia Williams is a complete fake and threatens to expose her, blackmail has never been so sexy. (978-1-63555-917-0)

Holiday Wishes & Mistletoe Kisses by M. Ullrich. Four holidays, four couples, four chances to make their wishes come true. (978-1-63555-760-2)

Love By Proxy by Dena Blake. Tess has a secret crush on her best friend, Sophie, so the last thing she wants is to help Sophie fall in love with someone else, but how can she stand in the way of her happiness? (978-1-63555-973-6)

Marry Me by Melissa Brayden. Allison Hale attempts to plan the wedding of the century to a man who could save her family's business, if only she wasn't falling for her wedding planner, Megan Kinkaid. (978-1-63555-932-3)

Pathway to Love by Radclyffe. Courtney Valentine is looking for a woman exactly like Ben—smart, sexy, and not in the market for anything serious. All she has to do is convince Ben that sex-without-strings is the perfect pathway to pleasure. (978-1-63679-110-4)

Sweet Surprise by Jenny Frame. Flora and Mac never thought they'd ever see each other again, but when Mac opens up her barber shop right next to Flora's sweet shop, their connection comes roaring back. (978-1-63679-001-5)

The Edge of Yesterday by CJ Birch. Easton Gray is sent from the future to save humanity from technological disaster. When she's forced to target the woman she's falling in love with, can Easton do what's needed to save humanity? (978-1-63679-025-1)

The Scout and the Scoundrel by Barbara Ann Wright. With unexpected danger surrounding them, Zara and Roni are stuck between duty and survival, with little room for exploring their feelings, especially love. (978-1-63555-978-1)

Can't Leave Love by Kimberly Cooper Griffin. Sophia and Pru have no intention of falling in love, but sometimes love happens when and where you least expect it. (978-1-636790041-1)

Free Fall at Angel Creek by Julie Tizard. Detective Dee Rawlings and aircraft accident investigator Dr. River Dawson use conflicting methods to find answers when a plane goes missing, while overcoming surprising threats and discovering an unlikely chance at love. (978-1-63555-884-5)

Love's Compromise by Cass Sellars. For Piper Holthaus and Brook Myers, will professional dreams and past baggage stop two hearts from realizing they are meant for each other? (978-1-63555-942-2)

Not All a Dream by Sophia Kell Hagin. Hester has lost the woman she loved, and the world has descended into relentless dark and cold. But giving up will have to wait when she stumbles upon people who help her survive. (978-1-63679-067-1)

The Secrets of Willowra by Kadyan. A family saga of three women, their homestead called Willowra in the Australian outback, and the secrets that link them all. (978-1-63679-064-0)

Turbulent Waves by Ali Vali. Kai Merlin and Vivien Palmer plan their future together as hostile forces make their own plans to destroy what they have, as well as all those they love. (978-1-63679-011-4)

Protecting the Lady by Amanda Radley. If Eve Webb had known she'd be protecting royalty, she'd never have taken the job as bodyguard, but as the threat to Lady Katherine's life draws closer, she'll do whatever it takes to save her, and may just lose her heart in the process. (978-1-63679-003-9)

Trial by Fire by Carsen Taite. When prosecutor Lennox Roy and public defender Wren Bishop become fierce adversaries in a headline-grabbing arson case, their attraction ignites a passion that leads them both to question their assumptions about the law, the truth, and each other. (978-1-63555-860-9)

Unbreakable by Cari Hunter. When Dr. Grace Kendal is forced at gunpoint to help an injured woman, she is dragged into a nightmare where nothing is quite as it seems, and their lives aren't the only ones on the line. (978-1-63555-961-3)

Veterinary Surgeon by Nancy Wheelton. When dangerous drugs are stolen from the veterinary clinic, Mitch investigates and Kay becomes a suspect. As pride and professions clash, love seems impossible. (978-1-63679-043-5)(978-1-63679-051-0)

All That Remains by Sheri Lewis Wohl. Johnnie and Shantel might have to risk their lives—and their love—to stop a werewolf intent on killing. (978-1-63555-949-1)

Beginner's Bet by Fiona Riley. Phenom luxury Realtor Ellison Gamble has everything, except a family to share it with, so when a mix-up brings youthful Katie Crawford into her life, she bets the house on love. (978-1-63555-733-6)

Dangerous Without You by Lexus Grey. Throughout their senior year in high school, Aspen, Remington, Denna, and Raleigh face challenges in life and romance that they never expect. (978-1-63555-947-7)

Desiring More by Raven Sky. In this collection of steamy stories, a rich variety of lovers find themselves desiring more: more from a lover, more from themselves, and more from life. (978-1-63679-037-4)